Hope is Built

The
CAÑON CITY
CHRONICLES
5

DAVALYNN SPENCER

~

My hope is built on nothing less
than Jesus' blood and righteousness.

~

~

Now the God of hope fill you with all joy and peace in believing.
Romans 15:13

~

CHAPTER ONE

Cumberland County, Pennsylvania

Early Spring, 1912

"You're going to end up an old maid unless you accept one of the eligible dairymen. And you might try to be cordial when they come calling."

Mary McCrae ground her teeth and glared at her brother whose eyes bugged out in his anger. He thought of one thing and one thing only, and it was not her welfare. She crushed her response between her teeth rather than spew what she wanted to say across his arrogant face.

Just because he was a man and she wasn't.

Just because he was the first-born and their parents were in their graves, he had no right to order her around like a hired hand. Or tell her how to behave toward the bow-legged, toothless Mr. Bourgher and others like him because they too had Aryshire cows. It was the twentieth century—or hadn't Lewis noticed?

She turned and stomped from the milking parlor, reaching into her skirt pocket for the letter from Aunt Bertie. Since last fall, when Papa's heart finally gave out, Mary had read the letter over and over until she could recite it from memory—an invitation to come to Colorado to visit her aunt and uncle and see their farm.

Mama's sister and her husband, Ernest, had filled the hole

left when Mama passed suddenly a decade ago. But not long after, they'd left Pennsylvania with their sights set on the wide-open land of the West.

Mary had wanted to go with them, but Lewis insisted he needed her help. What he needed was a cook and housekeeper, and someone to draw another dairyman to the farm.

Mary had kept all of Aunt Bertie's letters. Colorado was good for cattle, and good for growing peaches and apples, potatoes and berries of every kind, her aunt had said. Mary's mouth watered at the thought, and her emotions tugged along with the door to the kitchen, where she pushed the coffee pot to the back plate and stoked the fire. This most recent letter drew her more than all the others.

The kitchen's warmth wrapped a tender longing around her, chasing away the morning chill and stirring memories of Aunt Bertie and Uncle Ernest. Oh, how she missed them. Nearly as much as she missed Papa.

Truth was, Lewis did have the right to tell her what she could do with her breeding stock. She had no rights as an unmarried woman, despite the fact that Papa had bequeathed prime Ayrshires specifically to her in his last days. It stuck in Lewis's craw as the surviving male heir. He had rights to everything Papa had left behind, and he repeatedly reminded her of that fact.

Mary took a teacup from the cupboard and slammed it onto the counter in frustration, breaking off the handle and leaving a large V-shaped gap in the rim. Her temper had gotten her in trouble more than once—repeatedly, if she were honest with herself—but it simply wasn't fair. She knew as much about the dairy as Lewis and could run one of her own. If she were out from under his surly *lordship,* she could do as she pleased.

As she scooped up the ruined china, a sudden and rebellious thought struck with a force equal to her cup-smashing. What was there to keep her from acting on Aunt Bertie's invitation? It wasn't like Mary was a child. At twenty-four, she had done every interesting thing there was to do in Pennsylvania. But she'd not traveled out of the state.

The idea stirred her, and she hurried to Papa's study and his prize globe near the window, stopping to peek through the heavy curtains. No sign of Lewis heading to the house, so she gave the globe a twirl until it brought the Western Hemisphere into view. Leaning in, she traced her finger from the East Coast of the United States to the Rocky Mountains' ragged spine. She knew Colorado sat roughly mid-way, top to bottom, of those mountains.

Massive mountains, Aunt Bertie had said, much grander than anything in the Appalachians. And abrupt. No rolling hills. She recalled her aunt's first description of the lofty peaks lifting their shoulders like giants guarding the plains.

Mary's heart lifted as well, guarding her fledgling idea.

A distinct sizzle from the kitchen and the smell of burned coffee snatched her from the study. With a folded towel, she pulled the pot forward. Lewis would grumble when he came in for supper.

But she wouldn't be there to hear him.

She uncovered the ham they'd been eating, cut several thick pieces, then sliced bread from a fresh loaf. A butter crock and Mama's silver sugar bowl crowned the kitchen table, and Mary laid a place setting at the head. Plate, napkin, knife, fork.

After a quick look around, she added water to the charred coffee, hoping it would suffice. Lewis could add cream. They certainly had plenty. Some of the best this side of the Appalachians.

What might people think of such cream and butter in Colorado? Surely, they had dairy animals, but no other breed could hold a candle to an Aryshire.

Her thoughts ran ahead as she hurried up the stairs to her room for her coat and scarf. Snow still draped the hills around the farm, and if she didn't hurry it would soon be dark. She'd best leave Lewis a note that she was staying at Celia's tonight. Celia's husband had gone to the livestock sale in Shippensburg, so the timing was perfect. He always stayed two days.

The buggy and horse barn were on the opposite side of the main barn from the milking parlor, and Mary took the long way around the dormant garden plot and rose bushes. No reason to alert Lewis to her plan. This evening's outing to Celia's was merely a precursor to her escape of Lewis's domineering ways and all the Mr. Bourghers he could find. The thought was nearly intoxicating.

Lettie whinnied a soft greeting from her stall and was ever so aggreeable at being hitched to the buggy. Mary tightened her scarf around her neck and ears and set Lettie to a gentle walk as they left the barn. At the juncture of the farm lane and the main road, she snapped the reins on the mare's rump and set her into a high trot.

Celia Griffith had been Mary's dearest friend since grade school. Tight as two fleas they were, still to this day, though Celia had married and borne three beautiful children.

In no time, Mary turned into Celia's lane, two farms over from the McCrae dairy. The sun kissed the tops of the oak trees and winked through the white pines that lined the path to the Griffith home.

Hopefully, Mary's friend would share her excitement.

~

"But you can't leave!" Celia's hushed cry pushed tears into her pale blue eyes, and she covered her mouth with a hand and glanced toward the nursery.

Mary pulled off her scarf and hat and laid them on the settee in Celia's bedroom. "I'm not leaving *you,* Celia. I'm leaving Lewis. At least for a while. I need a break from his overbearing ways. And his last attempt at finding me a husband brought Mr. Bourgher to the door."

Celia gasped into a coughing fit, and they laughed like schoolgirls, squashing their giggles into silent fits lest they wake the children.

Celia pushed the scarf aside and sat close, reaching for

Mary's hand. "Oh, but I will miss you desperately. I don't even remember not knowing you."

"I'm only going for a visit, not forever." But the idea of a longer stay snagged a corner of Mary's thoughts and she didn't free it.

"It's more than halfway across the country. How can you go so far—and alone at that? People with consumption go to Colorado. And ruffians and miners. I'll be worried sick about you."

"You can't believe everything you read in those novels of yours, Celia."

"It wasn't a novel. It was the *Pittsburgh Post Gazette.*"

Why should she care what people in Pittsburgh thought? "You can't believe everything you read in the newspaper, either."

"Are you telling me you don't read the paper?"

"No, I'm telling you I need prayer more than I need to know what people in a big city have to say. And I need you to do the praying. I'll count on it, Celia. It will get me across the miles and make me feel as if you are traveling with me."

Another tear slid down Celia's cheek.

"Please don't do that, or you'll have me doing the same." Mary pressed a hankie from her sleeve into Celia's hand. "And Peter will be thinking you pined away for him while he was gone."

Her friend snickered at the idea.

"And speaking of Peter, do you think he'll keep my yearling bull and heifers while I'm away? I don't trust Lewis not to sell them off just to spite me, claiming possession is nine-tenths of the law and it's his right as the male heir."

"But that is how things are. You know that." Celia blew her nose. "Peter will keep them for you, though. If not, he can sleep in the barn. But I know he will. And don't be surprised if their ears are tagged when you return. You know how modern and up to date he tries to be. He's tagged all of our cows."

Mary considered the notion for a moment and realized what

a blessing it would be. "That's fabulous, Celia. Lewis can't worm his way into ownership of a gifted, identified animal and claim he got them mixed up. There is nothing he would not do to *improve* the herd, including selling *my* bull and heifers."

"But you're a woman, Mary. You don't own them outright."

Mary clenched her jaw until it ached. "Can Peter register them in my name?"

"I don't know—He takes care of all that. But what does Lewis think about you going off on your own to the Wild West?"

Mary picked up her woolen scarf and busily pinched off the pills.

Her friend leaned over and looked at her, the same way she had when they were children and she wanted to weasel a secret out of Mary.

"You haven't told him, have you?"

Mary frowned. "I'll tell him, but he's not going to stop me. I'm going."

"When are you leaving?"

Mary hadn't thought things through that far, but it seemed sooner would be better than later. "It will take a day to secure a train ticket, pack, and get my stock and their papers to you. And an extra day in case things don't go well—which I don't anticipate—but Mama always said to plan for the worst and pray for the best."

"Two days? Why, that's Wednesday." Tears threatened again.

"Yes. Spring is trying to break through, and I don't think Lewis would expect me to leave with snow clinging to the shady spots. But it's still cold enough that the road to town won't be a sloppy mess. I'll leave the buggy at the station. Can you and Peter pick it up for me and drive it home?"

"Of course." Celia pressed the hankie to her nose.

Mary offered another. "Here, take a fresh one. You've soaked that one. And please thank Peter for me after I'm gone. I'll write to you, I promise."

"You'd better." Celia glanced around the settee. "Did you

bring a night gown to sleep in?"

"No. My slip will do. It'll be like old times."

~

By Tuesday, Mary had her ticket, a carpet bag packed with the barest necessities, and money from her savings to purchase anything else she'd need in Colorado. She'd moved her yearling bull and heifers to an outside pen for washing and checking, and Lewis never questioned her.

Up and dressed before he left to milk Wednesday morning, she went out the front door in the fading dark. Peter and his two oldest boys met her at a pre-arranged site, and she gave him papers proving her so-called ownership of the stock.

He folded them into his coat pocket.

Not to draw attention to her scheme, Mary stood near a clump of silky dogwoods watching the Griffiths lead her future through the woods as the sun peeked over the barn. Melancholy inched its way into her thoughts, coloring her mood about leaving.

Would she return? Would Lewis come after her, or send someone? Would he figure out that six animals were missing and discover them at the Griffiths'?

Was she acting like a foolish child?

By habit she reached into her pocket and felt the edges of Aunt Bertie's folded letter, envisioning her aunt's fine script in her mind's eye.

Come for a visit, sweet Mary Agan. You're sure to fall in love with these majestic mountains and the clear dry air. It's breathing air, it is. And the sunshine makes roses blush and lilacs bloom like heather.

Faint and far away, Mary heard the screen door slap its frame.

Lewis.

She dashed across the field next to the house, shed her muddy boots at the foot of the steps, and eased through the front door.

All through breakfast she questioned her motives and cast furtive glances at her brother. Should she tell him she was leaving? Yesterday she'd posted a letter to Aunt Bertie that would arrive in Cañon City before she did.

Guilt peppered her fried eggs and stuck in her throat. She must tell him.

"What's got you in a twit?" Lewis threw a glance across the table, still chewing. "Having second thoughts about turning Bart Bourgher away?"

Apparently, her nerves had tipped him off, but his full-mouth remark emboldened her.

"I'm going to see Aunt Bertie and Uncle Ernest."

Lewis looked up with a tolerant expression, as if discussing the matter with a child. "And when are you planning to leave?"

"This morning."

His fork clanked against Mama's china when it fell. He stared at her, his mouth open like a Pennsylvania brook trout's.

Building steam, Mary continued. "I've already made arrangements so you needn't worry about a thing. My departure will not interfere in any way with the milking schedule. I'll have dinner in the oven for you, so you shouldn't have to cook for a few days. I've also made fresh bread."

His face reddened and he pushed his plate away. "Is Celia Griffith in on this?"

"No, she is not, so calm down. I made this decision on my own."

He reclaimed his plate and went after his ham and eggs as if they were to blame. "I advise against this harebrained notion."

"I knew you would." Mary felt oddly at ease once the news was out. She sipped her coffee and then buttered her toast.

"Give me one good reason why you think this is a good idea."

She had many, but she offered the first that came to mind. "I need a change of scenery."

He snorted.

Perhaps he loved her as a brother ought, but he was hard-pressed to show it, even now. He'd never gotten over their father's untimely death—neither had she. But she didn't take it out on him a bite at a time.

Without finishing his breakfast, he took his plate to the sink and downed the last of the coffee. "I'm going to the Overholts'. Tom wants to talk about ear tags, of all things. Crazy notion if you ask me."

He spoke with his back to her, so she couldn't read his expression, but his voice was cold as winter, and she shivered involuntarily.

At the door he paused but did not look at her. "Don't know when I'll be back."

Mary clapped a hand over her mouth as the door closed. She could say the same thing.

Did Lewis hate her? Did he blame her for their father's weak heart? He offered no goodbye, no well-wishes. Nothing. But with him off the farm, leaving would be easier. And the Overholts lived two miles in the opposite direction from town.

Heartsore, she offered silent thanks while clearing away breakfast. Then she set one place at the table for dinner, a fresh napkin, knife, and fork, and a hopeful wish that things between them could be as they were when they were children.

Such a foolish hope, she scolded, setting a roaster on the counter. Her brother had hardened when Papa died. With no wife to soften his rough ways, he'd grown bitter over the past several months. Mary had prayed he'd find a good woman to share his life, but he seemed intent on finding her a husband instead.

With a heavy hand, she seasoned a beef roast, taking her frustration out on the slab of meat. She added potatoes and carrots to the pot, set the lid on, and slid it in the oven. Then she hurried upstairs to change into her green wool coatdress. The suit was a bit outdated, for she hadn't gone anywhere in ages, but Mama used to say green set off her eyes in a lovely way. The memory pricked, but she did not have time to be pathetic. Not if she was to be at the train station on time. She tucked her black spool-heel shoes into the bag and went downstairs in her stocking feet.

Mornings were still chilly, and she fastened every button on her overcoat. At the bottom of the front steps, she pulled on her Wellingtons, then went to the barn, where she'd left her bag beneath the buggy seat, and harnessed Lettie.

"Another drive to town, you sweet thing. Are you up for it?" She combed the mare's forelock as if were important that she look her very best. "I'll be right back, ol' girl."

Mary held her skirt high as she climbed the small rise, stepping carefully lest she slip and muddy her suit and overcoat. But as always, the view from the family plot was worth the effort with farmland rolling green and fresh around her. A premonition settled within her that this would be her last time for a long time, and she stood between her parent's headstones, as straight as her father's. Her mother's had tilted and grayed over the years and collected moss.

Of course Mama's and Papa's loving spirits were not entombed in the cold earth, yet she felt a closeness with them as she whispered her goodbyes. Kissing the palms of her hands, she laid one atop each stone. A familiar tune hummed through her— Mama's favorite hymn—and she sang in hushed tones.

"On Christ, the Solid Rock, I stand … All other ground is sinking sand."

Atop the hill she felt as if she were on that solid rock, the foundation of her parents' faith.

"I love you both so much, and I'm grateful for what you've given me." Her throat tightened, thick with tears. "Not only in land and livestock, but in faith and honor." She closed her eyes against the sting of sadness and drew a stuttered breath. "I'm on my way to Aunt Bertie's farm. Wish me well."

A silly thing to say, but she knew they would do so if they were there.

In the barn she changed into her black shoes, then climbed

to the seat. "We're on our way, Lettie. At least I am. Off to freedom and adventure."

CHAPTER TWO

Cañon City, Colorado

Early Spring 1912

Curiosity was a powerful poison.

It drew Hugh Hutton to the Dodson place in the late afternoon when he should have been mending a cracked corral pole and haying the horses.

The farm was deserted. Had been since the old couple passed last fall. Hugh had a mind to buy it, run-down and neglected as it was. The land bordered the Rafter-H and offered good grazing. It wasn't much—a section, he figured—but another six hundred and forty acres of virgin grass would help. He drew rein in front of the barn and peered into its shadowy innards.

An abandoned buggy hunkered toward the back, the shafts lying empty and still. And a farm wagon stood next to it, harness on the near wall.

The double doors faced south, but good light reached only so far. He stepped off Shorty and dropped the reins. Fresh straw covered the floor—an uncommon site for an abandoned barn. The hair on the back of his neck rose as he eased forward, looking up at the loft—

The snap of a thin board dropped him like a rock in a dry well, jamming his legs to his collar bone. He rolled over and swore. Little good it did.

By the sounds of it, Shorty was having a wild horse fit.

He focused on a jagged hole eight feet up, straw fluttering off broken boards. Feeling around on the dirt, he connected with the busted edge of a thin plank and stood it on end. He pushed up to his knees and sucked air. Might as well breathe through a flour sack.

Light-headed, he waited a bit, then with a hand on the dirt wall, got his boots under him. He closed his eyes, let them adjust to the dark, then looked again to make out the shadowy sides of a man pit—or bear pit. Dug straight and smooth with no lip of nothin' for a foothold and walls far enough apart that he couldn't brace two opposite sides and shimmy out.

He jumped and reached for the edge but it set his head to spinning when he hit bottom. Leaning against the wall, he rubbed his face and swore again.

Helen was right. Swearing didn't do him a lick o' good.

He whistled for Shorty.

The gelding answered but didn't show. If his horse returned to the ranch with an empty saddle, Cale would come looking for him tonight. Maybe.

"Shorty!"

The gelding nickered.

Hugh trusted his horse. Had for ten years, and Shorty'd never let him down. He whistled through his teeth and waited for the clop of hooves.

"Come on, fella."

The gelding blew and pawed the dirt.

Hugh swore under his breath.

Maybe he needed to ask Somebody for help rather than foul the air, as Helen would say. That woman had kept his son's mouths clean and full of good cooking, and Hugh was grateful, though he didn't say so often enough. If it weren't for Helen helping him and Cale all these years, there'd be no Rafter-H Shorty could light out for.

He whistled again, low and calm. "Come here, boy."

A whicker and a step.

If the gelding came close enough, the reins might drag over the edge. Not that they'd hold Hugh's weight, but they'd be better than nothing.

Disgusted, he kicked at the dirt. "Have it Your way, Lord, I'm listenin'. You got me in a hole I can't get out of."

Silence.

"All right. *I* got me in a hole I can't get out of."

An old story came to mind, one his ma had told him and Cale and Grace when they were kids, something about a talking donkey and a man who didn't pay attention.

Hugh could relate.

Dig a step.

He jerked a look behind him, though he knew no one was there. The words weren't spoken—more like a thought landing in his gut. Heck of a thought since he didn't have a shovel.

He bent over for his hat, shoved it on, and stepped onto another broken plank.

One with a sharp end.

~

Mary ached from being cooped up like a chicken for so long and welcomed the change of trains in Denver. Carpet bag in hand, she stepped off the passenger car and into Denver's Union Station, relishing the opportunity to stretch her legs and back and neck—everything that had tightened into knots on her trip across the country.

Hunger took a bite, and she pressed a hand to her growling stomach. She'd not thought of packing food for the journey, a foolish oversight, and she'd paid dearly for fare on the train. But she was hungry enough to pay the exorbitant dollar and a half for a cheese sandwich and a bottle of Hire's root beer at the terminal. Amazing that Mr. Hire's drink had made it all the way from Philadelphia to the Rocky Mountains. The world was indeed shrinking.

Glad she had the sweet drink to wash down the dreadful *cheese* sandwich, she at least felt a bit refreshed and got in line at the ticket counter for a transfer to Pueblo, where she would change trains, yet again, for Cañon City.

"I tell you, sir, a motorcar will cost you little more than a ticket and save you time. No switching trains. No coal smoke staining your clothes. It's just the thing."

At the earnest argument, she turned casually to her left and glanced behind her to find a bowlered man encouraging a traveler to follow him.

"Let me show you the models I have parked outside. I'm sure you'll want to take this once-in-a-lifetime opportunity to drive yourself to your next destination."

As the salesman urged the man in line behind her to "come this way," Mary found her own feet following suit. Imagine, driving a motorcar herself. And why not? Oh the stories she'd have for Celia, not to mention Aunt Bertie and Uncle Ernest.

Clutching her bag tightly, she followed the two men through the heavy front doors of Union Station, staying close enough to hear each and every detail, but not so close as to intrude upon the transaction. When the traveler finally agreed and paid the required sum, which was far greater than the *little* first promised, she approached the salesman as he counted the bills in his hand.

He glanced up at her, disinterested, and continued counting. She waited.

Looking somewhat puzzled as he pocketed the money, he asked, "May I help you with something, ma'am?"

She despised being called *ma'am*. It made her feel like an old maid. But *miss* was nearly as bad. "I'd like to ask you a few questions about your motorcar rentals."

The man looked her up and down as if confirming the fact that she was indeed a woman. "I am sorry, ma'am, but is your husband at hand? It would be better if I spoke with him."

That quickly, she determined to drive to her aunt's farm if she had to buy the automobile outright. Which she could not, but still. The man was as arrogant as Lewis.

"I am the person making the arrangements." She paused and looked around. "Unless there is someone else offering motorcars—"

"No—no, that won't be likely. It's just that, well, I've never done business with a woman. Ma'am."

She gave his pinstriped suit and shiny shoes her own once-over, then stopped at his doubtful expression. "Are these the only motorcars you have?"

"Uh, yes—yes." He backed toward the nearest one. "This one is a new Ford Roadster, complete with windscreen, tool kit, tire pump, and oil can."

The amenities raised unwanted doubts in her mind.

"The Roadster is easier to handle than a larger touring car—not that you couldn't manage that."

His nerves were getting the better of him.

"How much?"

By proportion, nearly as bad as the sandwich. But oh so worth the experience. "Throw in a duster, cap, and goggles and you've got yourself a deal." She might be only a milk maid who lived on a farm, but she'd seen pictures of horseless carriages, and most drivers wore such things.

He stuttered, doffed his bowler, and rubbed his head before resetting it. "I usually charge for those items."

She turned slowly and looked up the street where automobiles outnumbered horse-drawn carriages. A few yards away, another man was gesturing to motorcars parked at the edge of the road and doing a fine job of persuading a man and his wife, it appeared, that a drive would be grand. She took a step their way.

"But I'll make an exception for you, ma'am."

A smile pulled and she quelled it before turning to the bowler. "Very well. I'll take it. And the clothing. And information on where I can find fuel."

"Very good. The Roadster runs on either gasoline or kerosene and must be returned here one week from today."

She frowned. The drive back to Denver meant she'd have to purchase a train ticket regardless. "Are there automobiles for rent in Pueblo?"

His smirk said, "I knew it," raising her hackles for a good argument. However, adventure was one thing—common sense another.

"Never mind. Thank you, sir, for your helpful information. Perhaps another day." Before he could smirk any further, she turned for the depot. She had just enough time to buy a connecting ticket.

Mary chose a seat on the right side of the car, where she sat staring out the window all the way to Pueblo. Aunt Bertie had not exaggerated in the least—the mountains were magnificent, much grander than Mary had imagined. She'd read harrowing accounts of explorers and pioneers who crossed them at great personal and emotional peril. But she wasn't going to California, nor was she traveling in the dead of winter. And Cañon City marked the apex of a triangular valley where the Arkansas River spilled from its great canyon onto the plains.

The canyon was called "The Royal Gorge," a postcard from her aunt had declared. It pictured an open-air touring car carrying people along the river via an extremely narrow railway passage. Another adventure to recount for Celia should Mary get the opportunity.

Alighting at the Pueblo depot, she immediately looked for men renting motorcars and found two. Only one offered the Roadster, a gray-haired fellow with an impressive mustache. She handed over her money, grateful that she'd brought as much as she had, but confident that she could wire her bank for additional funds if needed.

"I will be here to pick up the automobile one week from

today," the man said.

"I understand." No doubt her uncle would follow along in a buggy or wagon and escort her back to their farm.

"If the vehicle is not returned on time, the local authorities will be notified." The man's dark brows drew down as if to intimidate her.

They did not.

Admiring the tuck-and-roll leather seats, retractable top, and spoked wheels, she tucked her excitement in as tight as the upholstery. The man instructed her on using the three floor pedals and steering wheel, as well as the hand-crank to start the engine, and insisted she do so herself.

She did.

"Ma'am." the fellow cupped her elbow as she stepped up to the seat, and his hand trembled slightly. Either that or the car's noisy engine gave her that sensation.

He raised his voice. "Ma'am, please. Do not drive overly fast. There is no way to tell how fast you are going, but if you feel you are traveling as speedily as the train, *please* slow down."

Condescension or guilt at renting her a motorcar, she wasn't sure. But she gave him a curt nod and stepped on the accelerator. Luckily, there were no other vehicles—horse-drawn or otherwise—in front of her.

Darkness had descended by the time Mary drove into Cañon City, quite adept at handling the vehicle, even to the point of having found how to light the headlamps. The streetlight at the corner of Main and Seventh Street washed the Denton Hotel's welcoming profile, and she parked in front as other motorcar drivers had. Weariness overrode satisfaction, and she carried her bag through the ornate door and dropped it at the front counter.

The clerk raised his brows at her dust-covered attire, but she didn't care. With no duster, cap, or goggles available in Pueblo, she desperately needed a bath. And a bed, preferably in that order.

She gestured toward a sign in the lobby. "Hot and cold

running water?"

"Yes, ma'am." The clerk slid her room key across the countertop.

"Excellent."

"And the dining room is to the right of the stairs or left of the elevator across the way."

Indeed. She'd had quite enough motorized transport for one day.

"Your room is on the second floor, third door on the left," he offered. "The bathing room is at the end of the hall. Enjoy your stay."

His eyes didn't quite match his words, but that was the least of her concerns.

After a deliciously hot bath, she donned her wrapper and returned to her room, her wet hair wrapped in a towel from a folded stack near the copper tub. A surprisingly genteel amenity for a far-west hotel.

A meaty aroma wafted up the stairs, but dining required dressing and she didn't have the energy. Without combing her hair, she crawled beneath the bed covers and surrendered to blessed sleep at her final thought.

Cañon City, at last.

CHAPTER THREE

Mary's arms and shoulders woke first, burning is if she'd been struggling with ornery calves all night—until she opened her eyes to an unfamiliar ceiling. Discomfort quickly gave way to anticipation, and she rose, though slowly.

After dusting her suit as best she could, she dressed and coiled her hair into a presentable knot at her neck, securing it with her tortoise-shell combs. She had cleaned her teeth the night before, but they still felt gritty and she cleaned them again.

Bag in hand, she double-checked the room for any stray item, satisfied herself that the bed clothes were in order, and followed her nose to the dining room downstairs.

Biscuits, gravy, and eggs filled her empty insides, followed by two cups of the best coffee she'd ever tasted. Even Lewis would approve.

Odd, she hadn't thought of him the entire trip until now.

At the lobby counter, she returned her key to a different clerk, a young lady perhaps in her late teens.

"The bath was lovely, especially the towels."

The girl smiled shyly as she picked up the key.

A collection of postcards on a counter rack caught Mary's attention, and she chose one of The Royal Gorge. "Do you have stamps for these, and can you post it for me?"

"Yes, ma'am."

As Mary jotted a quick note to Celia, the girl retrieved a stamp and laid it on the counter. "That will be one cent, please."

"Thank you." Mary signed and addressed the card and slid it toward the girl with a penny. "Can you also direct me to where I might find fuel for my motorcar?"

At that, the young woman's jaw dropped, but she quickly regained her composure.

"*Your* motorcar?"

"Not exactly." Mary smiled at the obvious reason for the girl's gape. "I rented it in Pueblo, and I want to make sure I have enough fuel to make it to my aunt's farm and back."

"Did you drive it yourself?"

Pride threatened to smear Mary's face with a wide grin, and she reached for her own composure before answering. "Yes, I did."

The girl leaned across the counter. "How wonderful! My father warns me all the time about doing such a thing, but I know it would be dreadfully fun and I'm certain I could do it. I can drive a team of four. How much more difficult could it be?"

Mary leaned in an equal distance, familiar herself with driving a team on the farm. "It *is* different, and takes a little getting used to, but I'm certain you could do it. Try the smaller model first. The Roadster."

She could not have thrilled the young lady any more than she had with those words and she wished her the best as she left the lobby.

After buying gasoline at the eastern edge of town, she turned north. The man who had fueled her Roadster gave her directions to "the Dodson place," as well as a quizzical look. He seemed about to say more, but she put the motorcar into gear and lurched ahead as his mouth moved. She really needed to perfect her starts.

Spring had not yet arrived in Cañon City, nor had it shown up along the mountains on her way from Denver. Aching for a touch of green, she soon relented to the wonder of layered buttes, red stone formations, and hills covered with dull bushes, more like short trees and grayer rather than green.

The scrubby trees eventually gave way to farmland, and Mary marveled at the cultivated fields and tidy orchards. The area seemed a veritable garden, but several turns took her to higher country, where miles of grassland spread around her. A different sort of grass, nothing like the fields where her family's herd grazed.

As the peaks of a barn and house rose in the distance, memories of Pennsylvania faded, and she accelerated on the rough road, her body bouncing as much as her thoughts.

It had to be her aunt and uncle's farm.

Mary's hands tightened on the steering wheel. How surprised they would be when she arrived, in a motorcar no less! She'd not asked them to meet her at the train station in Cañon City, and she doubted they had telephone service. It was all part of the adventure, figuring out how she would get to the farm. But their steadfast love over the years assured her that she would be as welcome as Aunt Bertie had promised, regardless of how she arrived.

At a narrow track, a faded board on the fence corner said "Dodson," and she turned toward the buildings. Excitement tingled through her arms—and quickly dwindled to dismay.

The outlying orchard was not as neat or trim as others she had passed, and no livestock grazed in the open areas. She rolled to a stop in front of a house that stood dreary and neglected, one shutter hanging askew on a front window.

Did she have the wrong farm?

She turned off the engine and sat in deafening silence. No chickens scratched in the yard. No dogs barked. No horses looked curiously from the corral.

Grasping one last lingering thread of hope, she got out and brushed dust from her sleeves and skirt. She patted her hair and put on a cheerful face, though she felt anything but. The front door yawned, and she poked her head inside.

"Aunt Bertie? Uncle Ernest?"

A chill crawled her neck with spidery speed, and rather than enter, she walked around to the back, where a large kitchen garden lay bare other than for a corner patch of rhubarb. Nibbled to the ground by what—deer? Her throat tightened and her mouth went dry.

A back screen door also stood ajar, its spring unhooked from the frame. As she mounted the steps, scurrying noises came from beyond the wooden door, also open.

"Aunt Bertie?" Her pulse quickened. "Uncle Ernest?"

A dreadful mix of fear and curiosity drew her into the kitchen, through a dining room and parlor, and upstairs to a large bedroom. Again she called her aunt and uncle's names, but the forsaken furniture and sagging curtains pushed her down the stairs and through the front door, heart racing.

"Lord—where are they? What happened?" She pressed her hands against her cheeks, sticky with road dust, tears, and unanswered questions.

Perhaps the barn held a clue. A horse. A carriage. Anything that offered a hint of what happened to her family. Swiping at her eyes, she crossed the wide yard and stepped through the open barn doors, hoping to find proof that her aunt and uncle were well and safe.

The air smelled of dust, not livestock. She stepped farther into the shadowed interior and too late saw the gaping hole beneath her extended foot.

Too late to stop her downward plunge and frantic scream.

~

At least Hugh's brother hadn't been around when he rode in with his head split open and the reins wrapped around Shorty's neck. Sore as blazes from the fall, he'd given Helen the barest details of what happened while she doctored him and stitched the crease closed. The pain dang near knocked him out, but for the whiskey she insisted he take.

Spring branding had claimed the following day, as well it should. He owed his labor to the Rafter-H. But the idea of a pit dug on a deserted farm kept eating at him.

A farm he wanted.

Were there other traps laying wait? And why? Surely old man Dodson hadn't dug that hole last summer when the grizzly was on the prowl. Had he hired it done?

Or was there somebody else out there who wanted the farm and figured to discourage any lookers? Somebody who had spread fresh straw over thin finish boards. It might be worth a ride into town to see the sheriff.

But he couldn't let some hapless person or animal fall in that pit, so he loaded a wagon with timber and tools and set out early the next morning, calculating how many head could graze the fine grassland. It was exactly what he and Cale needed to increase the herd. With his brother married now, there was an extra mouth to feed and another one soon to come. And there'd likely be more children. His insides twisted thinking about his own boys with no mother.

The Dodson place opened up east of the Rafter-H with good flat land as well as prime mountain grass. The couple had been mostly farmers with potatoes, berries, and a small apple orchard north of the barn and outbuildings.

He approached off-road from the west, and a chorus of red-winged blackbirds cut loose from new-leaf cottonwood trees. But as he neared the house, an eerie feeling climbed his shoulders like the first time he'd ridden over. The place must have been in decline for years with the older couple unable to keep it up. He and Cale would have helped if they'd known, but the Dodsons kept to themselves, even the few times he'd seen them in town.

Didn't matter. Neighbors were supposed to help neighbors. It's how things were.

Rather than start right off on the barn, he stopped behind the house and went inside through the open back door. The place was run-down and dirty with the wind blowing through. It must have been a nice home at one time. He reminded himself he was no trespasser, for if he had his way, he'd soon be the owner.

Word was, the place was up for taxes and overdue mortgage payments, but there would be an auction. Just like the government to milk every penny they could get. So be it—he'd play their game. A fat worm if there ever was one, and he planned on being the early bird.

A rolltop desk drew him to the parlor like deer to a creek, but so did something he hadn't expected to see through the front window.

A black and green Ford hunkered in the yard. A smaller outfit than what Thorson and his flicker crew had rented last year. The hair on Hugh's neck stood up again and his right hand reached for his Colt—the sidearm he'd left at the ranch in exchange for a rifle under the wagon seat.

He slipped out the back door, grabbed his Winchester, and came around the south end of the house. Who was there and what did they want?

He waited, listened, watched. Nothing moved. But that rattle trap hadn't driven itself.

He circled back the way he'd come, crept inside the house, and checked upstairs, where small footprints dotted the dust-covered floor. Looked to be a woman's shoe. He doubted Ella had been out here in her condition, nearly ready to calve. His lip pulled up at the corner thinking of what she'd have to say about his comparison.

Outside, he cut around behind the barn, senses heightened. He saw no sign of anyone there or in the outbuildings. Didn't make sense.

He lifted the rifle, aimed gut-level. "Come on out!"

His breath hooked on his ribs as the thought hit him.

He slid through the corral poles and entered the barn

through an open side door. Checked every corner and shadow, nerves tight, expecting to be jumped. Heat waves rippled off the hood of the car just beyond the broad open doors, and the odor of gasoline rose with it.

Morning light angled into the barn, hitting a corner of the hole. But he knew where to look for it. Would someone else?

Still gripping the rifle, he stretched out on his belly and inched up to the hole. A body lay crumpled at the bottom. Based on the skirt and loose hair, a woman's body. Had someone left her down there and run off when they heard him coming? A swear word hit the back of his teeth, but he swallowed it.

Exactly what he needed—a dead body to explain.

He went for the wagon, drove it around to the barn, and gathered a coil of rope. After tying it off to a stout timber, he lowered himself and his Winchester into the pit.

With the rope looped around his waist, he knelt next to the body. A chill shimmied up his back. It could have been his sister, Grace. She'd do something all-fired hare-brained like drive a bucket of bolts out here. Maybe this gal had too. But why here of all places? The Dodson's had passed one right after the other, Doc Miller had said. He'd found the old man a few weeks after his wife died from a fever.

For the second time, Hugh churned up a prayer in that blasted pit, then he turned the body over. The woman's left arm flopped—dislocated. Hair splayed across her face and spooled out around her neck.

He touched her opposite shoulder and leaned in. "You awake?" Fool question, but what was he supposed to say to someone he hoped wasn't dead but looked it?

As gentle as possible, he pushed her hair back. Beneath the dirt on her face, she was white as death. Leaning closer, he turned his cheek to her mouth, and his skin prickled at a slight breath. A thready pulse met his fingers at her neck, and his hands started to shake. She was alive, all right, but there was no telling for how long or if she'd survive him hauling her up and over the side. All he knew for certain was he couldn't leave her there.

The lesser of two evils. Pa's advice from years ago bounced off the close dirt walls. It wouldn't hurt to pray again.

"Lord, help me get her out of this hole without killing her."

He tugged on the rope to confirm its hold, then picked up the woman and laid her over his shoulder, surprised she weighed as little as she did. Bracing himself with the rope around his hips and the rifle tucked in the rope, he toed up the steps he'd dug earlier, closest to where he'd tied off, stumbled over the edge, but kept her from falling.

At the wagon, he off-loaded his tools with one hand and slid the timbers out one at a time, then laid her in the back. A deep gash in her forehead bled from where it had scabbed over. His air squeezed off. Had he been too rough with her?

Clammy to the touch, she scared the fire out of him.

He set the mare to an easy walk, well aware of how rough the ride was. But town was more than twice as far. This way, Helen could tend to her while he rode Shorty in for Doc Miller. He prayed the gal wouldn't be dead by the time he and Doc got to the Rafter-H.

CHAPTER FOUR

A sharp note brought Mary to wakefulness. She turned her head toward the melodic call and flinched with pain.

Again the song, unrecognizable. Resisting the light not far from where she lay, she attempted to lift her hand as a shield, but her right arm was bound to her chest. More pain—in her shoulder. No, in her arm.

Wrong again. She hurt everywhere, from her ankles to her forehead, but the worst was her right shoulder. She squeezed her eyes tightly, then forced them open.

Another strange ceiling. Dull plaster met her gaze and she blinked, trying to focus. Slowly, she turned her head toward the light—a window without shade or curtain. Double hung with glass that rippled. Old.

Her pulse beat like a lone drum, quickening with realization. She most certainly was not at home. But where was she? An infirmary? A neighbor's house?

Her attempt to sit up met with crushing opposition from every part of her body. She surrendered to the pillow at her head and trudged through her cloudy memory. What had she been doing last? Suddenly aware of something tangled about her legs, she raised her left arm and noted fine lace edging the ruffled sleeve of a nightgown similar to what her mother had worn but several times larger.

Had she dressed herself? If not, then who?

Such questions made her head hurt, and she closed her eyes.

Tried to think. To remember.

Lewis. Lewis had been doing what Lewis did—milking cows, feeding cows. Feeding himself. The last time she had seen her brother was at the kitchen table for breakfast. And he was going to a neighboring farm and she was—

"Leaving." Her voice creaked like the opening of a long-closed door.

"Oh, I hope not, dear. You're not in any shape for leaving, if you ask me. And I dare say Dr. Miller agrees."

A buxom gray-haired woman set a tray on the table next to the bed and drew up a chair. She rested her hands in her shallow lap and smiled as if consoling a child.

"You took quite a tumble, according to Hugh." The woman reached for Mary's left hand and patted it gently. "When he carried you in the house yesterday morning, you gave me a fright. So pale and hardly breathing. I prayed you'd survive your injuries."

Gray eyes swept Mary's forehead, and Mary did the same with her hand, connecting with a bandage and tenderness. No wonder her head hurt. "What happened?"

A work-worn hand lifted the woman's apron hem to her mouth. "Thank the Lord, you can speak." She leaned forward. "Do you remember anything, dear?"

Mary closed her eyes again and let out a long breath.

"Oh, I don't want to weary you. You need your rest. But I brought some broth for you and some powders the doctor left. If you'd rather wait to eat, I can come back."

Mary lifted her hand. "Don't go. I'm thirsty. May I have some water?"

"Heavens, yes. Right here." The woman slid her arm beneath the pillow, lifting Mary enough to sip from a china cup.

The water was cold and ever so good to Mary's dry lips. She laid back, sensing the liquid running through her body as if giving her life. "Where am I?"

"You're at the Rafter-H Ranch not far from Cañon City.

Hugh found you yesterday—he's one of the Hutton brothers who own the ranch. And I'm Helen. I cooked for those two cowboys until Cale married Ella Canaday last year and moved to his own place, but I'm still here helping Hugh and his sons."

She flashed Mary a guilty look. "I'm sorry. Get me talking and I'll gab your ears off. What is *your* name? If you don't mind me asking."

"Mary. Mary McCrae."

"Mary. What a lovely name. It fits you, dear."

"Yes, my mother thought so too." Her tongue hadn't been injured. "I apologize—"

The woman chuckled. "Oh, don't you bother. You've been through more than most young ladies your age and style. Your suit is lovely. Badly soiled, but lovely."

"Why am I here, in bed in this strange gown and with all these trappings?"

Helen leaned in with a near whisper. "You don't remember?"

Mary retained enough of her wits to know she was being tested. Tested to see if she had a working mind. Something horrible must have happened.

"I've tried to remember, but my head is foggy. Maybe if you give me a clue, it will help. You said someone carried me here. Where did he find me?"

Helen seamed her lips and looked over her shoulder as if robbers hid listening beyond the door. She bunched her apron in both hands, then faced Mary. "He found you at the Dodson place yesterday morning. At the bottom of a man pit, out cold with a dislocated arm."

And that quickly, it all came back—the train, the automobile, the abandoned farm.

Her head throbbed, and she sank further into the pillow. The latch of a closing door clicked in the distance. The strange bird called again, and Mary drifted.

~

Shorty sidestepped a badger hole and jerked Hugh out of his dark mood. He'd gotten little sleep worrying over that other hole in Dodsons' barn floor. Covering it would be a lot easier than hauling dirt to fill it, and the sooner it was done, the better. He didn't need some other witless outsider falling into it.

Like you did.

Doggone it, he couldn't get away from that fact and had the scar to remind himself every time he shaved. He palmed his jaw. Maybe he'd grow a beard.

The gal he'd hauled out of that pit had hair the color of a blood-bay he once owned, but she wasn't from around here. He knew everyone there was to know, and there weren't that many new people moving to town. Even fewer who might know about the Dodsons' virgin grazing land.

He and Cale needed that grass for their growing herd and family. Cale's family, anyway.

It was too late for Hugh. What woman in her right mind would want to take on three young'uns and a husband? And a ranch.

He pulled up in front of the Dodson house and laid Shorty's reins over the hitch rail. Curiosity had gotten him in a fix before, but the old rolltop desk still drew him. And he hadn't seen any holes or trap doors in the house.

Again he felt like an intruder, but he pushed through the door, reminding himself that he'd soon be the owner. The desk looked the same—dusty and neglected. He opened all the small drawers on top, finding ink wells and nibs, pencils and a fountain pen. A few coins, keys, and postage stamps. One small drawer was locked. He tried the keys, but none worked.

The drawers in the desk itself held loose paper and ledgers, envelopes and a rolled parchment tied with ribbon. He looked over his shoulder as if the Dodsons themselves would find him snooping. But they were gone and he wasn't. He pulled the ribbon and read the document. His stomach dropped.

In fancy bold script, *Last Will & Testament* scrolled across the top. It named the Dodsons' niece, Mary Agan McCrae, as the heir to all the worldly possessions of Ernest Edward Dodson and Bertha Agan Dodson, including the homestead and its increased acreage—a second section. The Dodsons had added to their holdings with no one the wiser.

At the bottom, a third signature followed the Dodsons': *T. F. Beckman,* Attorney at Law.

"This changes everything." The words cut harsh through the room. Who and where was Mary Agan McCrae? No one he'd ever heard of in Fremont County had a name like that. Where were these people from?

Like a black snake, an idea slithered through his mind. He could destroy the will and no one would know.

The parchment grew warm in his hands, and everything good and pure that his ma had ever been came flooding back.

He dropped the will, rubbed his hands on his denims, then rolled it, retied the ribbon, and tucked it inside his shirt. He'd not leave it there to be found by whoever had dug the pit. He doubted old man Dodson had dug it to catch that rogue bear Cale brought down last year. But Hugh didn't doubt that someone else who also wanted the Dodson's place would stoop to such a lily-livered tactic.

The sheriff could handle that news *and* the will.

An hour later, Hugh laid the last board across the hole in Dodsons' barn floor, pushed it forward, and dug a two-inch trench eight inches wide that reached to the edge of the hole. Then he walked around the boards already in place, cut a corresponding trench at the opposite end of the last board, and set the board in both trenches. It laid smooth and even with the floor, which was his intent, exactly like the other ten boards he'd set.

Someone had gone to a lot of trouble to dig that pit, and he'd raked his brain over who would do such a thing. Did they check on it? Had they been out snooping around, waiting to see what they caught? He had a mind to set a snare of his own and see what he came up with.

He gathered his tools and stuffed them in his saddle bags. Shorty stood at the hitching rail, turned at right angles to the motorcar, ears cocked like it was a coiled rattler.

Hugh felt the same. He reset his hat and walked over to the confounded contraption. Surely that gal hadn't driven it out here herself, but he'd found no sign that told him another person had been there.

The carpet bag on the passenger side grabbed his interest more than anything else. Looked a little flowery to his way of thinking. Could be that gal's. He slapped the dust off and opened it. A folded paper lay on top of what looked like a woman's sleeping gown that stirred an image of Jane—the way she braided her long hair at night and slipped into bed beside him.

Would he never stop gouging himself with her memory?

He started to close the bag but hesitated. Might as well read the paper. He'd snooped into everything else on the place. One more thing wouldn't make it any better or worse.

"Lease Agreement" headed the top, naming one Mary McCrae as the lessee of a 1912 Ford Roadster to be returned to Union Depot in Pueblo one week from two days ago.

Same name as on the Dodsons' will. Confound it all. He folded the paper, stuck it in the bag, and tied the flowery thing to Shorty's saddle. Helen could go through it. She'd already done plenty helping the gal, but he'd not go through a woman's unmentionables. No telling what he'd find in there.

When Doc had looked Mary McCrae over, he'd set her arm in place, stitched her head, and told Helen to keep her in bed until he returned in a couple of days. Likely she had a concussion but would hopefully come to, he'd said.

Doc's *hopefully* hadn't sounded real hope-filled. If that gal died, whoever dug the hole could be held responsible for her death. Hugh had told Doc where he found her, and he hoped the man's professional oath would keep the news from spreading.

But he doubted it. A town the size of Cañon City had a way of spawning news right off the wind.

Disgust churned up a few unacceptable phrases as Hugh turned from his horse to the Roadster. He knew how to start the blasted thing. He'd seen Thorson's movie crew start their rattletraps often enough last year. And if that featherweight of a woman could do it, so would he. Tying Shorty to the door handle would be the hard part.

He proved right on both counts. Winning one proposition out of two wasn't his preference, but he'd have to settle. He rattled off down the farm road, Shorty trotting through the field fifty yards away, reins looped around the saddle horn. The carpet bag bounced as bad as Hugh did in the driver's seat.

When they crested the rise that looked down on the backside of the Rafter-H, Shorty took off in an easy lope, straight shot for the barn. Hugh rattled around the long way, following the wagon path. By the time he pulled up at the ranch house, his boys were picking things up off the ground, waving them in the air and laughing. When Ty pulled a lacy piece over his head and sashayed around like that actress, Mabel Steinway, Hugh couldn't jump out of the Roadster fast enough.

"Take that off! And bring it over here right now. All of you—get all those things over here!"

Shorty stood at the corral watching him. The carpet bag dangled by one handle with a woman's skirt spilling out. The gelding blew and shook his head as Hugh approached.

"All right, all right." He unlashed the bag and stuffed the skirt inside. He could speak horse as well as the next cowboy.

"What is all this stuff?" Kip walked up with an armful of unmentionables, followed by the dog and Jay, who waved a long, thin stocking in each hand as if they were streamers. Tug jumped for them, and Jay jerked them higher.

"Put those down!"

The stockings dropped. Tug snatched one up.

"Not there!" Hugh was losing what was left of his mind. "Bring them over here, just don't wave 'em around like some kind of flag."

Jay pulled the stocking from the dog's mouth, tearing it in the process.

Ty, crowned with a silky undergarment, snorted and elbowed his younger brother.

"Get that off your head right now." Hugh held the bag opened for each boy to add his findings. "Where did all this start flying around?"

Kip pointed past the house.

Hugh saw a couple of white spots out in the pasture, but he wasn't about to send his boys after them.

"Jay, unsaddle Shorty, brush him down, and turn him out." He addressed the younger two. "Ty, take the carpet bag inside to Helen—without digging through it. Kip, you tell Helen what happened."

Kip leaned sideways and looked past Hugh with a question wrinkling his face. "Did you buy a devil wagon?"

"No, I did not buy a devil— And don't call 'em that."

"You do."

Hugh ran his hand over his face, wiping away what he wanted to say at being dressed down, first by his horse and then by his youngest son. "Don't talk back. Just do what I told you."

Ty and Kip skedaddled inside, too fast for him to call them back and warn them to be quiet about it. Like that would help.

He set out for the east pasture, following a thin trail of women's clothing. Found a hair brush. Toothbrush. A near-empty tin of face powder next to a small sage brush with flesh-colored leaves. It could have been Jane's possessions scattered across the grassland.

Helen had looked after her things seven years ago, and at first, he resented the purging. But he soon realized it was for the best. Finding reminders of his wife in unexpected places only dug the wound deeper.

Until now, all that had reminded him of his dead wife were two dark eyes looking up at him from the face of his youngest son.

CHAPTER FIVE

Propped against several pillows, Mary endured the doctor checking her pulse, redressing the wound on her head, and squeezing every inch of her legs and arms, as well as both shoulders.

When he pushed on the right shoulder, she flinched.

"Is it as tender as it was three days ago?"

He was a kind-eyed man. Gentle in his prodding. But that didn't keep her from feeling like an Ayrshire heifer at the sale barn. "Not quite."

He closed his black bag and stepped away from the bed. "Your legs appear to be uninjured. With help, you can walk around the house once a day"—he dipped his chin and looked over the top of his spectacles—"but not without someone assisting you. Do you understand? Not alone and not outdoors. I expect you'll be dizzy and weak at first, and you don't need another fall."

"I understand."

He left the door to her room ajar, and she strained to hear what he said to Helen, but loud whispers and scuffling in the hallway prevented her from doing so. She knew from Helen's meal-time chatter that there were three little boys living in the house, and judging by the number of times they prodded and shushed each other outside her bedroom door, they were dying to come inside and look at the strange lady who had shown up at their ranch.

She pulled her hair over her shoulder, finger-combed and

braided it. Helen had refused to give her a mirror, so there was no telling how bruised and battered she looked.

She tugged the covers under her arms and loudly cleared her throat. "You may come in."

Sudden and complete silence. For several beats. Then the door squeaked farther open and one small face peaked around it, followed by two more below in stair-step fashion.

"Can we really?" asked the shortest of her visitors.

"Yes, you may. But no roughhousing."

Scuffling ensued and one astonished voice said, "She uses the same word as Helen!"

Mary swallowed a laugh and folded her hands atop the quilt.

By the count of ten, the shortest boy stepped into the room, followed by the other two in order of height.

"Hello, boys." She smiled slightly and found the activity a bit painful. She must look frightful. "It is nice to put faces to the whispers I hear so often."

"Told you," badgered the middle boy as he elbowed the taller one.

"Wasn't me." A return poke.

"Boys?" Frowning hurt as much as smiling.

They stilled, stalk straight and hands at their sides. Helen must be a domestic taskmaster.

"My name is Mary. What are yours?"

They all started talking, and she held up her left hand. "One at a time please, beginning with you." She pointed to the shortest, all too familiar herself with being the ousted youngest.

"I'm Kip and these are my brothers, Jay and Ty."

"Don't talk for us," the middle one jabbed, elbowing his point.

"How old are you, Kip?"

The boy stretched as tall as possible. "I'm seven. Ty here—"

The elbow found its mark again.

Mary skipped the elbow master and addressed the tallest.

"And you might be …"

"I'm Jay and I'm eight goin' on nine."

The middle boy sneered up at his bother. "I'm all the way nine and I'll be ten before you're nine." His finger found the taller boy's belly.

"Excuse me." Mary interrupted the rivalry. "And what is your name?"

"I'm Ty. I'm the oldest."

"I see." Indeed, that explained a great deal. Not simply rivalry, but jealousy over position by height—a very important thing to boys, as Mary had learned from her older and, at one time, shorter brother.

Kip stepped in a little closer and tipped his head to the side. "Does your face hurt? It looks like it does somethin' awful."

Clipped steps outside the door turned him and his brothers. "What did I tell you three?"

In unison, the boys ducked at Helen's harsh question, squirreling through the door as if in flight for safety.

"I'm sure you've got barn chores, so you best be after it." Her increased volume followed their frantic pace through the kitchen. "Or I'll have you darning socks and washing long johns."

A screen door slapped against the house three times as the brothers ran outside and then slapped again as it closed.

Helen shook her head and chuckled. "Those three will see me in my grave sooner rather than later, but oh, how I love them." She dropped herself into the chair by Mary's bed and wiped her brow with her apron hem before scrutinizing her invalid visitor.

Mary detested immobility as much as she disliked being called *ma'am*. However, some things were beyond her control. Most things, lately.

"I'm glad to see you lively enough to tolerate those hooligans." Helen leaned in with a worried look. "They didn't jump on the bed, did they?"

"No—*oh*." Mary laughed and frowned and flinched all at the

same time. She cradled her left cheekbone. "I must look a fright, for I feel as if I fell on my face."

Helen studied her apron a moment, then glanced up with a grieved expression. "I'm sorry, dear, but I think you may have." She added quickly, "But it will heal in no time. Merely bruises, you know. Lovely shades of purple fading into softer yellows and blue."

Mary felt her jaw gape and covered her mouth.

"Is there anything I can bring you? Dinner's about ready. I have a roast today, with potatoes and carrots and onions. I'll be bringing you a plate."

"That is exactly the same meal I prepared before leaving—"

Helen's rapt attention stopped Mary midsentence. It wouldn't do to ramble on to this kind and caring woman. Mary was already indebted to her for the room. Hopefully, it wasn't hers, though Mary doubted it, considering the massive desk shoved into one corner and an outside entrance. It looked more to be a man's study, a familiar detail it shared with the home she'd left.

"I do hope I have not put anyone out of their room. You have been so very kind to help me after my—whatever it was."

"It was a nasty fall, dear. You probably don't remember me telling you that. But don't be alarmed. Hugh fell in that pit a day or so before you. And a good thing too. That's how he found you at the Dodson place. Went back to cover that hole in the barn floor and there you were, down in the bottom of that man pit or bear pit or who-knows-what."

She shook her head again. "And no, you have not put me out of my room, so don't you worry. This is Cale's old room. Hugh's twin brother. As I mentioned, this is their ranch, them and their sister, Grace, who we haven't seen in more than three years. Cale and Hugh were mirror images as children, I tell you. Played havoc with their schoolteacher when they were kids. And with the moving picture folks who were here last year." Another swipe of her brow. "They're looking less alike these days, what with Cale married, happy, and about to be a father, and Hugh still carrying around the death of the boys' mother seven years ago. Poor man, I hate to see him suffer. He can't seem to let it go."

Seven years. The age of Kip, the youngest boy. Another telling detail.

A distant sound of gushing water raised Helen's head, and she looked toward the window. "That will be Hugh washing up out back. I best be gettin' dinner on the table. I'll bring you a plate. Do you drink coffee? It's about all we have around here."

"I do, thank you."

~

"Has she asked for her carpet bag?" Hugh forked in a hunk of beef after the question, stalling in case Helen said yes. Or no.

"Not yet, thank goodness. I want all her things washed and ironed before I give them to her, and any tears mended. I could certainly use Ella's skills on that. Some of the finer things snagged on cholla cactus and ..."

Ty looked about to choke to death, and Kip and Jay weren't much better. Hugh cut them a sharp glare and the snickering stopped immediately.

Helen cut a tender carrot in two. "This one's on me, Hugh. I shouldn't have mentioned such things at the dinner table."

She probably expected him to take full blame for bringing up the carpet bag in the first place. He stuffed in a mouthful to keep that from happening.

Not waiting on another question, Helen launched right into the latest on their *guest*, for lack of a better word.

"Mary was much better today. Doc Miller said she could get up and walk around in the house, but she has to be accompanied by someone when she does."

The boys looked up like three ground squirrels, expectation smeared across their faces.

Hugh shook his head.

They dropped their shoulders and went back to shoveling in their food.

"Slow down, boys, or you'll all end up with the colic." Helen looked at Hugh and switched leads without warning, something she was mighty good at. "I don't have time enough in the day as it is, so I expect you to help her walk through the house once a day until she can walk by herself."

Hugh stared at the woman he owed so much to. But not that much.

"I am not asking." She set her jaw and glared him down as if he were a youngster like his boys. Blast it all, she had him cornered with an audience and she knew it. "Yes, ma'am. Soon as I finish with chores."

His sons stared open-mouthed, forks dangling from their hands.

"And you three," Helen added. "I need three chickens rung and plucked before dark. I'm making a kettle of chicken stew, and I know how much you like it."

Jay rolled his eyes and Ty kicked him under the table.

"Yes, ma'am," Kip offered, earning himself a kick for being a traitor.

Hugh swallowed a laugh. Something he hadn't done in a long time. The boys were him and Cale twenty years ago.

"The first two who bring Helen a clean chicken can take Barlow up to Cale's house and ask Ella if she'll come down and give us a hand tomorrow." He looked at Helen. "A slow ride in the wagon won't hurt her, will it?"

"May I be excused?"

Three scraped plates perched in three pairs of hands, and Hugh would have sworn they were church choir boys all singin' the same note.

Helen jumped in. "You be careful setting those plates in the sink and do not run out the door. Walk."

"Yes, ma'am," they chorused.

She waited until the door closed, then loosed a heavy sigh. "No, a wagon ride won't hurt Ella. Probably do her good to get out of the house and talk to another woman. I've been wanting to talk too, but to you about Mary."

Not exactly Hugh's choice of topics.

"When the boys brought the carpet bag in, I found a piece of paper that says she leased that car in Pueblo. Did you see that? She's in no condition to return it, and it's due in a couple of days."

Hugh wiped his mouth and dropped his napkin on the plate. "I saw it. It was right on top before my horse went buggy and scattered everything to kingdom come. I figure Cale can follow me to Pueblo on horseback, leading Shorty, and we can ride back together. If that gelding wasn't so all-fired spooked by that bucket o' tin, I'd tie him to the back."

Helen chuckled. "Frankly, I don't blame him. And if Ella comes tomorrow, then you and Cale can take the car back the next day."

Hugh grabbed his plate.

"I've made a tray for Mary. If you'll take it to her, I'll get the kitchen cleaned up and ready for those naked birds." Helen laughed at her own joke and didn't give him a second glance.

Looked like he'd been commissioned.

He'd rather pick feathers.

~

Hands full with a loaded tray, Hugh toed the bedroom door farther open with his boot. He hadn't seen Mary McCrae since he'd carried her in the house half dead and left her in Helen's care, and the sight of her on the bed spooked him nearly as bad as the motorcar spooked Shorty.

Her long braid hung over her shoulder, and if not for that and the mean bruises on her face, she'd blend right in with the sheets.

Her left arm lay over the quilt, pale and fragile looking, and the large gown she wore sagged open at her white neck and shoulder.

Something fierce rose up inside him—an urge to protect her. Fight for her in her defenseless condition. Work over the scoundrel who had beaten her black and purple—'cept there wasn't one.

He made it to the bed table without spilling the coffee or dropping the whole thing, but he bumped the lamp when he set the tray down and startled her awake.

"Oh!"

"Par—" Both spoke at the same time.

He cleared his throat. "Pardon me, ma'am. I didn't mean to wake you. Helen insisted I bring your dinner. Said you might be hungry. Or thirsty. There's some coffee here. She makes the best. And her roasted beef—"

He clamped his mouth shut. He was blathering like a fool.

She watched him with eyes the color of summer aspen.

After his explanation, she relaxed a little. "Thank you."

Even her voice sounded fragile. If she was so breakable, it was a wonder the fall in that pit hadn't killed her outright. What was a woman like her doing out in the high country anyway?

Well, he knew what, dadgum it. Probably came for the will. He'd mention it when she was gettin' around and feeling better.

She pushed up on her left elbow and tried to look at the tray. "It smells wonderful. Helen was right. I am hungry."

She wasn't doing a very good job of sitting up, so he reached for the pillow behind her before he got his brain started, then stepped back. "Excuse me, ma'am. Can I help you with that since you've got only one arm to work with?"

Her eyes narrowed and he wondered what he'd said wrong. Maybe he should leave and get Helen to help her.

"You may. If you don't call me *ma'am*."

Judging by the squint-eye, she meant it.

All righty then. He punched the pillow and shoved another one behind it so she sat up straighter. It took everything he had not to pull the gown over her bare shoulder. He really should have volunteered to pluck chickens.

"Will you hand me the tray, please?"

"Of course." He was an idiot.

He set the tray on her lap and stood beside the bed watching her taste the coffee.

She picked up the fork, stopped, and looked at him. "I can feed myself."

"Um, yes, ma'— I mean, yes, you can. I see Helen cut the meat for you, so you'll do fine."

He was dying and couldn't seem to get himself together. "I'll be leaving, then, if there's nothin' else you need help with."

He backed into the chair that hit the table and jostled the oil lamp. "Pardon me again. I'll be going now."

"Thank you for the tray. It was most kind of you."

She didn't exactly smile, but the set of her mouth changed. Like she was laughing at him. Which was exactly what he didn't want.

Somehow, he made it to the hall, through the dining room, and into the kitchen. But rather than stop at Helen's inquisitive look, he kept going—out the door and straight to the barn.

He hadn't been so discombobulated since he was sixteen and asked Jane to the church social.

~

If Mary were a betting woman, she'd put money on that strapping man being Hugh, the one who had rescued her from a hole in the ground, brought her to the Hutton ranch, and carried her into the house.

He left Mr. Bourgher's image in tatters.

Gingerly, she touched the bandage on her head and wondered if she was merely addled by the fall. A distinct possibility. She didn't even remember falling, but these kind people seemed to be truthful. Maybe they could tell her news of her aunt and uncle.

Famished from not having eaten since the cheese sandwich in Denver—no, since breakfast at the hotel—Mary cleaned her plate and drank every drop of coffee. Helen was an amazing cook. Hugh had not overstated that bit of information—if that's who he was. And he had a twin who looked just like him? Could two men both have such captivating blue eyes? At least their names weren't similar. She'd attended grammar school with Tom and Ted Marsh and was forever getting them confused.

The older two of the three boys shared their father's dark hair, if that was indeed who she'd met and not his double and previous occupant of the room in which she found herself. Cale, was it?

But the youngest boy—Kip—he must look like his mother, for his eyes were deep brown, not blue, and his hair was lighter.

A knock at the door interrupted her musings.

"Was dinner to your liking?" Helen accompanied her question into the room and eased herself into the bedside chair, evaluating Mary's plate. "Well, I see that it was." A genuine smile warmed her face as she reached for the tray. "Goodness, child, how long has it been since you had a good meal?"

"A good meal? Not a deplorable sandwich at the Denver terminal or pitiful fare on the train? Oh, it must be at least a week. But I cannot discount breakfast at the Denton Hotel. The fluffiest biscuits with sausage gravy, and coffee nearly as good as yours." It didn't hurt to appreciate the skills of the one feeding her.

"That's Clara's doing, their cook. Best thing that ever happened to the Denton, that woman."

"I'd like to ask you a question." Mary smoothed the quilt covering her legs, and the movement slid the gown off her shoulder. Embarrassed, she quickly drew it up closer to her neck. Thank goodness that hadn't happened when the cowboy came in.

"Two questions, actually. You said a man named Hugh found me in a pit and brought me here. Was he also the one who brought me dinner earlier?"

Helen's eyebrows shot nearly to her hairline. "Didn't he introduce himself? Land's sake, he's as bad as his boys. No—I take that back. He's worse. He knows better."

Startled by Helen's fervor at berating the man, Mary felt obligated to take up for him. "Well, he was quite nervous, as though he'd never tended to someone ill before."

That smoothed Helen's brows and her chin slowly rose. She took on a thoughtful expression, as though she was contemplating new information about a matter. "Is that so?"

The woman's eyes gathered a twinkle at the corners.

"Do you know if he found a carpet bag in an automobile parked at my aunt and uncle's? At least I think it was their farm. A sign on the fence where I turned said *Dodson*, but they weren't there. Things looked as if they hadn't been there in quite some time. Do you happen to know them?"

Helen gathered her apron corners and studied the stitching, running her thumb nail along the fine, straight line. She paused for such a long time Mary feared there was dreadful news.

"Helen?"

The kind woman's lips seamed, and she pressed the apron flat on her lap before looking up. "So the Dodsons were kin. They were from Pennsylvania, weren't they? Is that where you came from on the train? That's a mighty long way."

Helen had not answered her question but danced around it as if the answer was anything but welcome. Grief rose like mercury.

"Please, Helen. I must know the truth. I posted a letter to them before I left home, certain it would arrive before me."

"Oh, child." The apron lifted to Helen's face, stopping short of her perspiring forehead. "I'm so sorry, but your aunt took sick with a fever and passed early last fall, from what I heard. They stayed to themselves, you know. Your uncle died not long after. From a broken heart, I'd say."

Mary clutched her throat, unable to find breath, so great was the shock. Tears fell unbidden, unbridled, beyond her control.

Determined to speak, she took a shaky breath, then another. "Where are they buried?"

"Since they didn't have a family plot in town, they were buried on their property. I don't know exactly where."

"So you didn't attend their funeral." Not a question. She didn't have to ask—regret was etched on Helen's face.

Mary let her head fall back on the pillow. Her carpet bag mattered little now, in spite of it holding everything she had in the world of any value, other than her livestock.

CHAPTER SIX

"**W**hy didn't you tell her who you were? Poor girl had no idea what to make of you."

Helen scowled as she scolded, and confound it, Hugh was too old at thirty to have his ears twisted, verbally or otherwise. But the way she was cuttin' up chickens, he kept a safe distance on the other side of the kitchen table rather than risk warming his coffee from the pot on the stove.

Cold coffee and apple pie was better than no coffee and apple pie.

Too much had changed in the last year. Even Helen was off her feed, but he wasn't about to mention it.

When Cale married Ella and moved out, things shifted. His boys dragged around like they'd lost their best friend, and even their old dog, Tug, drooped. Hugh didn't blame Cale for building his own place and takin' his bride over the ridge, but it seemed like everybody had to find their footing all over again.

His boys missed that city gal something fierce, and he'd seen the spark of life, especially in Kip, when Mary McCrae showed up. But dadgummit, she'd driven a blasted buzz wagon out here that he had to return to Pueblo. Beat all he'd ever heard.

He must have slammed his coffee cup on the table because Helen sliced him a look. "Get hold of yourself before you help Mary with her walking. I've got her cinched up in one of my dresses. Looks like she's wearing a tent, but don't you ride her about it. She's got enough to worry over, what with coming all the way out here and not knowing her kin had passed. What do you think will happen to their place now?"

As usual, Helen threw more than one iron in the fire and had him trying to figure out which one to pick up first.

"Where'd she come from?"

"Pennsylvania."

"She didn't drive all that way, switchin' cars, did she?"

"How should I know? But I doubt it, she's not daft." Helen cut him another look. "Now's a good time to help her get around a little with the boys gone to Cale and Ella's."

He was dismissed. Too bad he hadn't saddled Shorty and ridden off with the boys. He'd sent all three of 'em—Barlow was good for it. She wouldn't take out from under them even if they lit her tail afire.

He shoveled in his pie, and rather than raise Helen's ire any further, went out to the porch pump and washed up. Not that he wanted to look any different than he did, but his hands were sticky, and the bit of mirror above the basin showed crumbs on his chin. A splash of cold water cleared his head, and he dried down good. Combed his hair back. Straightened his shirt collar. Argued with himself over tellin' Mary McCrae he had the will.

If he did, he'd be admitting that he poked around in the desk. He'd thought that was why she came out here, to claim her inheritance. But if she didn't know they'd passed until Helen told her, what did she come for? Blast it, no matter which way he turned he found a knot.

Slipping inside, he made it through the kitchen without Helen's scrutiny.

The door to Cale—Mary's—room was closed all the way, so he knocked. Twice. Hearing no answer, he turned, thinkin' he'd lucked out, when the door opened. There she stood, tented and cinched like Helen had said, and white as goose down but for the bruises.

"Should you be up by yourself?"

Her chin rose. "You knocked."

"Yeah, but—" *Shut up, Hutton. Just do what you came to do.* He offered his arm, and she slipped her left hand in at his elbow, knowing why he was there.

"Where would you like to go?"

She looked up at him with a remark ridin' drag that she kept to herself.

All righty then. "Let's start in the parlor. It's back this way." He stepped aside, turning her to her left in the process, and her fingers tightened. *Slow down, Hutton. She's a newborn foal on fresh legs.* "It's dark in here, so we'll open the curtains first."

They walked across the room in slow motion, and at the window, he tucked the curtain behind a knob on the wall for that purpose. "No one uses this room anymore. Our ma used to do her handwork in here when we were growing up. I think she came in here to get away from Cale and me." He chuckled at the memory.

Mary stood at the window, looking through it as if it held a secret to another world. Must look a mite different than Pennsylvania from what he'd learned in school. He'd heard it was always green there, even when it snowed.

"It doesn't start greening up here in this high country until well into spring. But it's sure pretty in the summer. And fall breaks out with a gold wash of aspen on the mountains and in the gullies. Even by the barn. See that big ol' cottonwood there with the swing?"

He tapped on the glass. "Turns bright yellow. A pretty sight to see."

He hadn't used so many words in he didn't know how long. At least not since Jane had been with him. He'd hung the swing in that cottonwood on account of her wanting one.

"You make it sound lovely."

"You'd probably like the columbines too. They bunch up in the aspen-grove shade. Purple and white, most of 'em. Some blue or pink."

She looked at him as if he had one growing out of his head. Again—words. Where'd they been all these years?

He took a slow step and she turned from the window, following his lead into the dining room, where she pulled her hand free and ran it over the dark cherrywood dining table. He watched her close. Couldn't have her falling and hitting her head on, well, anything.

"This is a beautiful table. Solid. Like the house. Like—" She glanced at him, then turned toward the portraits on the back wall. "Are those your parents?"

No surprise that she saw the resemblance. "Whit and Livvy Hutton. Our sister, Grace, got ma's yellow hair."

Mary moved toward the parlor.

If she fell on his watch, he'd never hear the end of it.

"Hold on there." He offered his arm and she took hold, but not as tightly as before. Had he done something to offend her?

"I'd like to sit here for a while by the window." She let go again and reached for an old rocker with a cane seat that should have been repaired a decade ago.

"Wouldn't you like something more sturdy? Like the settee here?"

"No, this is perfect. My mother had one very much like this, and she sat in it when she did her mending of an evening."

She eased down as if into a memory, and the dry cane cracked and complained. Eyes closed, she leaned back and set the rocker in motion. Just like *his* ma had.

Should he stay with her? If he left, she might take a notion to go to her room. And if she fell asleep, she could fall right out of that armless chair.

He sat on the edge of the settee—the one he and Cale always got cuffed for climbing over. It was for company, their ma had said. What would she think of him sitting in the parlor on the settee and company taking her old sewing rocker?

"You don't have to stay."

Her words were soft as lamb skin, and he nearly missed them. "I don't mind, ma'am." A complete lie.

Green eyes nailed him right where he sat.

"Uh—I mean miss."

"Mary."

"Of course. Mary." He could use that pit in the Dodsons' barn right about now.

~

A rancher like Hugh Hutton across the parlor from her, and all Mary could do was doze in a long unused sewing rocker, wearing a dress four times too big and her hair hanging in a lose braid. Mama would be horrified.

Lewis would be outraged. Her mouth pulled toward a smile.

The old chair carried her to her mother's knee, where she'd learned to thread a needle and tie off a knot with one hand by rolling the thread between her thumb and forefinger. Aunt Bertie knew the same trick.

Heart pain spread to Mary's face as her brows knotted. Again she wondered how she must look. Appearances had not been so important when she could see them for herself. She longed to ask her guard if he'd found her carpet bag and what had happened to the motorcar she'd rented. But propriety insisted she not mention the bag.

"Did you happen to see a green automobile at my aunt and uncle's farm?"

"Yes ma'—. Yes. It's here now, in the pasture across from the house where the flicker crew parked their rattle—their cars last year. I'll drive it to Pueblo tomorrow."

So he *had* found her bag. And looked inside. Gratitude warred with embarrassment but won the duel. "Thank you."

He nodded once from his unlikely perch on the settee, hands dangling between his bent knees. Discomfort marred his features, including his sky-blue regard. Perhaps it was the contrast against his sun-warmed skin that so intrigued her.

"You really do not have to sit with me. I'm sure you have chores or something you'd rather be doing. I promise not to jump up and run outside."

He slid a look her way that said he wasn't sure how to handle her humor, but the slap of a screen door shot him to his feet.

"That'll be the boys. And Ella. My brother's wife."

"Pa!" A small herd stampeded through the dining room and into the parlor, slamming into each other as they stalled at Mary in the rocker.

"Miss Mary," the little one said. Kip, was it? "Aunt Ella is here to help—"

"Outside, right this minute." Helen intervened, waving a dish towel over the boys' heads. "All of you. Go unhitch the mare from the wagon. Your father will be out to help with the collar."

Their father looked at Mary as if he was responsible for her well-being. A foreign commodity in her twenty-four years, but it felt good.

"Thank you, Hugh, for your help. I'm sure I will be fine."

He glanced at Helen and back, then with another curt nod, crossed the parlor in three long steps and went out through a door in the dining room. At least it sounded that way.

Mary looked through the window to see him long-legging it toward a farm wagon in time to help a woman down from the seat. A very expectant woman.

Helen claimed the settee in Hugh's absence and mopped her brow. Apparently, she was always too warm.

"Ella came down to help mend a few of the things from your bag." A smile played tag with good manners, and mischief to rival that of her three charges threatened to break out on her like the pox. "From what I could get out of Hugh, he tied your bag to his horse when he drove the motorcar here, and it came loose. Tossed most of your things hither and yon."

Mary stared at her hostess, trying to assess truth from

tomfoolery. A short laugh escaped and she covered her mouth.

Helen's girth shook as she choked back her own laughter. "Ella was a seamstress for the Selig Polyscope Moving Picture Company that filmed here last summer, so she is quite good with a needle and thread, not to mention my old treadle sewing machine."

Mary wanted to know who had gathered her strewn clothing, but the door she couldn't see opened, and the woman from the wagon made her way from the dining room into the parlor. Hugh came up behind her with a pained look on his face.

Helen rose and escorted the younger woman to the settee. "Ella, this is Mary McCrae from Pennsylvania. She's staying with us for a while. Mary, this is Ella, Cale's wife."

With an extended grunt, Ella dropped to the settee, both hands on her abdomen, legs spread inappropriately wide. Quite like Celia had been with her babies.

"Hello, Ella. I'm pleased to meet you." Mary didn't try to stand for fear that Hugh would rush to her side. Under different circumstances, that would not be an unpleasant thing.

Ella's hair brushed her shoulders, dark and sleek, and a fringe framed her round face—round like the rest of her.

"The pleasure is mutual, Miss McCrae. I apologize for being so out of breath, but lately I've had little of it."

"Please, call me Mary."

Hugh lingered in the doorway, watching Ella as if she would pop any minute.

Helen shooed him away. "Off with you, Hugh. And thank you, but we have things to do and discuss, and you'll just be in our way."

But for his deeply tanned skin, Mary would say a blush colored his face long enough for him to hurry out the near door again.

Helen went down the hall and returned with a carpet bag that she set in Mary's lap. Nearly crying out, Mary sucked in a hard breath at the visual connection to home and family.

"I've gone through everything in there—hope you don't

mind—but seeing as how the boys and Hugh were privy to most of it, I thought a womanly touch and gentle washing was what it needed. Some of your undergarments were snagged on cactus and brush, so Ella's here to do the finer needle work."

Heat climbed Mary's throat and into her face at the thought of Hugh Hutton picking her most intimate apparel from the prairie. She kept her head down as she dug through her belongings, grateful to find the seam in the bottom lining secure and unopened. A smooth lump assured her that the money she'd brought with her was safe, but she would check more closely this evening when she retired.

Her coin purse, however, was missing, as well as her tooth powder, a bar of soap she used on her hair, and her side combs. Tortoise shell with sterling silver scroll work. They had been her mother's.

"What's wrong, dear?" Helen's concern was clear. "Is something missing?"

Mary blinked away her foolishness and forced a weak smile. The effort still hurt, but sympathy from strangers—however kind they had been—was intolerable.

"Only a few things that I'm sure can be replaced."

Other than the combs.

CHAPTER SEVEN

Hugh bounced into Cañon City swearing he'd never own a rattletrap himself, and completely mystified by people who dropped good money into them. Sure, they clipped along faster than a walking horse, but why be in such an all-fired hurry to begin with?

He stopped in front of the sheriff's office and let the contraption cough itself to death. The Dodsons' hand-written will lay in his bureau at the house. It was Mary's after all, and he'd figure out when to give it to her. But he had other business to take care of before Cale met him here in an hour.

The sheriff was filing papers in a cabinet and glanced up as Hugh walked in. "Mornin', Hutton. Any more bears out your way?"

Last year's incident with the grizzly had been the biggest local news in a decade. The recent sinking of the *RMS Titanic* had finally pushed it from newsprint commentaries.

"Nope, and I'm glad of it. But you're not far off the mark in asking."

The cabinet drawer slid closed as Hugh took the chair in front of the big oak desk.

Sheriff Payton filled his seat behind it and leaned back. "What can I do you for?"

Hugh hadn't had that many dealings with the sheriff, but the lawman's habit of talking backwards still jarred Hugh. "You familiar with the Dodson place out our way, six hundred and forty acres of grass and farmland?" He didn't mention the second section.

Payton linked his hands behind his head. "Up for auction, I hear. Shame too. Those were nice folks." He dropped his hands and leaned forward on his desk. "If you're interested in that place, I'm not the fella you want to talk to. Try the bank. I hear there's a few folks wantin' to bid on it. Hopin' to turn a profit, I suppose."

Hugh stiffened. Suspects, to his way of thinking. "I was out there a week ago and found a bear pit."

The sheriff's eyes took on a glint. "No bears in it?" He chuckled, picked up his coffee mug, and took a swig.

"A woman."

Payton choked and aimed for an old spittoon.

Small blessings.

"What was she doing down there?" The sheriff wiped his mouth on his sleeve, giving Hugh time to think of a respectful answer to a stupid question.

"Dying."

The man's face paled.

"I took her to the Rafter-H for Helen to tend, then had Doc Miller come out. She was shaken up pretty bad."

"Thank God she survived."

"I covered the pit so no one else falls through. But I don't think old man Dodson dug it for a bear last year or dug it at all, for that matter. It's too deep, too wide."

The sheriff's dark brows bumped into each other. "You suspect foul play?"

"I do. And your mention of other people wanting the farm increases my suspicion."

Payton rubbed his clean-shaven jaw. "That's a serious accusation, Hutton. Attempted murder."

"Dang right."

Hugh left the lawman scratching notes on a pad and walked a couple blocks to the bank. He'd conveniently left out the part about falling in the hole himself. No sense giving up irrelevant information. Whether he fell in it or not, it was still there to catch something or someone. And it had. Twice.

No happier than when he'd walked into the bank, Hugh returned to the rented motorcar ten minutes later as a lone rider approached leading a saddled horse.

"You checkin' on the property?" Cale drew rein behind the Roadster and tipped his hat back.

It didn't help Hugh's disposition any to see his twin looking five years younger than him and happier than a tom turkey in a hen house.

"We're not the only ones interested in it."

Cale straightened. "Who else?"

"Local ranchers."

"The auction still on?"

"Yup." He wanted to tell his brother about the will but figured he should tell Mary first since it was hers. "Let's get this over with."

He cranked the tin can a couple times and climbed to the seat. Forty miles to the Pueblo depot. They should be there by noon and back home in time to do chores. An entire day lost for nothing.

Nothing other than a busted-up gal from out of town who was entitled to the same land he wanted for his cows.

~

Spending the day with Ella Hutton and Helen had done Mary more good than she thought possible. Celia was the only friend she had at home, and Mary hadn't realized how her mother's absence had affected her over the years. Hearing other women's laughter and opinions somehow reawakened her emotionally as well as physically, and she'd insisted on helping Helen set the supper table that evening after proving to the mother hen that she could walk the hallway without teetering.

Helen's short *humph* pronounced a grudging approval.

Thin slabs from yesterday's roast and sliced bread made up the fare, with a dried apple pie Helen had secreted away.

"If I'd let those hollow legs know I made an extra pie, they'd have scampered off with it like a herd of mice as soon as my back was turned." Helen bunched her apron, took the warmed pie from the oven, and set it on the kitchen table.

Mary set six places, one at each end and two on either side. Heavy steps on the porch announced a man's approach. The trample of smaller feet followed as did the rush of water from the outside hand pump.

Certain of who had arrived, she straightened, determined not to appear fatigued. Between Hugh's and Helen's scrutiny, they'd try to force her to the bed and insist she eat from there. She wasn't having it.

He stepped through the door and stopped, staring at her, she knew, judging her constitution from behind. Discomforting to say the least.

"What are you doing in here?"

Refusing to let his gruffness intimidate her, she placed six napkins under six forks. "Good evening to you too, sir. I trust you had a pleasant day."

Helen snorted, endearing herself to Mary even more.

"Did you have any trouble with the motorcar?" By then she was on the opposite side of the table, and she looked him square in the face.

The muscle in his jaw flexed, and from experience with her brother's ill temper, she guessed what it meant.

So be it. She'd not be cowered by a cowboy. Tickled by her unintentional turn of phrase, she smiled as much as she could, hoping to hide her laughter.

He did not return the favor.

Which made the situation even funnier.

The bread and meat were close by on the counter, and she busied herself setting them on the table.

Three littler Huttons blew through the door and lined up

like soldiers with their hands out for inspection.

Hugh ignored them and took the chair at the table's head.

Helen gave a tilted look to the boys' upheld hands, but Mary caught the wink that sent them to their places. The two taller boys scuffled over who would sit on the far side of the table, and the littlest, Kip, plopped down at his father's left.

Uncertain of where she was expected to sit, Mary feigned checking on the coffee until everyone was seated. The only available place was to Hugh's immediate right.

Of course it was. Maybe eating in the bedroom wasn't such a bad idea after all.

Anticipating a blessing from this family, she folded her hands and bowed her head, surprised that it was Helen who offered thanks. Mary stole a quick peek at Hugh, who sat staring out the window.

Telling.

"Amen." The chorus set the boys to their plates like horses to a race.

"Slow down," Helen cautioned with a repetitious tone, as if she gave the warning at every meal. Based on the boys' enthusiasm, she probably did.

Mary deliberately slowed her movements, and Kip mimicked her from across the table. The other two boys snickered but fell silent at a killing scowl from their father.

Did he not know what he had at his table? Three young blessings and a kind woman who did her best to keep them all fed and in line? Her opinion of the rancher fell dangerously close to that of her brother, but she kept her opinion to herself.

Sudden realization settled in, as brutal as a northeastern winter. Without transportation of her own, she was at the mercy of her host if she wanted to go to her aunt and uncle's farm or even into town where she could rent a buggy. Her movements slowed further, garnering a concerned look from Helen.

Mary cleared her throat. "If I may impose upon your

considerable kindness, I will need a ride to town tomorrow in order to rent a buggy. Is anyone going in?"

Helen dropped her gaze, and Hugh took an oversized bite of his sandwich. The boys looked at each other and shrugged.

She would not beg. She'd walk to town if need be. It couldn't be that far.

"What do you do in Pennsylvania?" Hugh took another bite.

How rude that he dismiss her sincere question with his own unrelated query. Tempted to point out his discourtesy, she drew herself up as much as possible with one arm strapped to her body and addressed the boys rather than their father. "My family owns a dairy farm. We have prize-winning Ayrshire cows that produce the richest cream and sweet butter this side of the Appalachians."

"What's an apple-a-chin?" Kip asked. "Sounds like an Injun name."

"*Indian,*" Helen corrected. "Say it right."

"Well, actually it is. From the Creek tribe. We don't pronounce it exactly the way they do, but it's close. However, those mountains look entirely different from your mountains here. They are more like rolling hills in comparison to your lofty peaks."

Silence hung like wet laundry. Perhaps she had over spoken.

"So you know your way around horses?"

Hugh watched as if he'd asked if she could shoot and skin a rabbit. Which she had as a young girl on her brother's dare.

"Yes. I ride and can hitch up a wagon or buggy horse. There is much more to a dairy farm than milking cows."

"You could help us milk our cow." The middle-sized boy— Ty?—laid it out like a challenge.

"I could—"

"But won't." Hugh scowled at his son.

Mary bit her lip to keep from speaking her mind.

"I'm sure you can use our farm wagon if you need to go to town or want to check on your aunt and uncle's farm." Helen understood, possibly from today's easy conversation among the women.

"I do appreciate that. You've been most generous already in your hospitality. I hate to impose."

Hugh huffed.

Helen visibly stiffened and sent him an arrowed look from her end of the table.

What had soured him so? He'd been halfway cordial as her escort through the house yesterday.

"I'll drive you over to the Dodson pl— your kin's farm— tomorrow. I imagine you'd like to look around some before you go back home."

Ha—a bait! She'd not fall for that sibling prank. It was none of his business whether she returned to Pennsylvania or not. And why should she? Now was the perfect time to ship her bull and heifers west. She could start her own herd right here in Colorado on her aunt's farm.

The idea sprouted into hope.

"The place is up for auction," Hugh said. "A lien against mortgage payments due and unpaid taxes."

Mary's fork clattered as it hit the plate.

CHAPTER EIGHT

Hugh spurred himself over last night. Between Helen shooting daggers at him and the Lord chapping his hide, he knew Mary McCrae hadn't earned his ire. But he was too set in his ways to change now.

The scar at his hairline twinged, a pointed reminder of a donkey and a pit.

He bit off a swear word and double-checked the harness, rubbing Barlow on the shoulder. From nursemaid for his boys to wagon mare, she might be the best horse he had on the place aside from Shorty.

Mary came out of the house in a brown skirt and white blouse, looking fresh as spring with her hair all bunched up at her neck. She walked steadily toward the wagon. No sway to her. The black sling was the only dire-looking thing about her.

With a tight jaw, he handed her up to the bench seat and went around to the right side. A couple miles to the Dodsons' house. Surely he could tolerate her that long without being unneighborly.

Her bruises were fading. Or she'd put on some of her face powder this morning—what was left of it. That whole carpet-bag business with Shorty made him hot around the collar and quick to imagine what else she was wearing. Why hadn't he left the blasted bag in the motorcar rather than tie it to his horse?

He flicked the reins on Barlow, and they took the ranch road to the wagon path that cut east across the range toward the Dodson farm. He hadn't thought straight since he found the will.

It blew all his plans off on a stiff wind—the best land for miles, aside from the Rafter-H, and right next door at that. It couldn't have been a more perfect set up, buying the Dodson place and increasing the herd.

He rubbed the front of his vest. The will was chafing his brain. The sooner he handed it over to Mary, the better. Maybe she'd sell the place to him and go back to her Appalachians.

And maybe he'd take up pig farming.

"I appreciate this, Mr. Hutton." Straight as a board she sat, with no glance his way. Might as well be in church on a hard pew. "I know you have plenty of things to keep you busy on a cattle ranch."

He managed to catch his tongue before it rattled off about her using his last name. Didn't set with him, calling him *Mr.* like that. Plain Hutton was all right, but *Mr.* was his pa.

They'd left early, before the sun was too high, and he cocked his head low, his hat brim blocking the sharp light.

Mary watched the ground beside the path.

As they crested a low rise, she jabbed her arm out, pointing off to her left. "There! Did you see that glint? Something is out there. Stop." She gathered up her skirt before he even slowed the mare.

Fearing she'd jump, he grabbed her arm and held her put.

She cried out.

He'd grabbed her *right* arm. "I'm sorry. I didn't mean to hurt you."

Barlow stopped, jerking the wagon.

"What were you thinking?" A higher pitch than he'd heard before. She wrapped her left hand around her injured shoulder and scooted as far from him as possible.

"I thought you were gonna jump."

Her face turned all blotchy red, and she pinned him with a green glare. "Do you also think I am a complete dolt?"

He bit his tongue. Drew blood. Better that than give an

honest answer to some gal who'd driven a bucket of bolts out to an abandoned farm she'd never laid eyes on.

Again she gathered her skirt, but this time stood and made to climb down.

He bailed off the right side and ran around before she lit. He couldn't catch her by the shoulders or waist, so he scooped her into his arms.

"Put ... me ... down."

He didn't know a woman's voice could chill ice in the summer. Careful-like, he set her feet on the ground and stepped back, hands in the air.

"Theatrics are not necessary, Mr. Hutton." She turned with a snap of her head and marched straight into the sagebrush and cactus in her dandified shoes.

He wasn't about to follow her, so he leaned against the wagon, cocked a boot on a wheel spoke, and crossed his arms.

A few yards out, she picked up something, turned it over a couple times, and stuck it in her skirt pocket. She looked around, walked in a widening circle until she gathered something else.

Come to think of it, that was about how far Shorty was from the Roadster on their way to the ranch that morning.

She found a couple more things for her pocket before returning to the wagon, where she hitched her skirt and gave him the dead-eye.

He offered his hand and she had to drop her skirt to take it, but she managed to climb up with only one stumble.

He'd met softer branding irons.

Until they breached the yard of her aunt's farm, desolate as ever, lonesome too. Then Mary McCrae sagged beside him.

He pulled up in front of the house and set the brake before helping her down. He let her have her head, lead out whichever way she wanted.

She just stood there, staring off toward the barn, maybe

thinking about the last time she saw it. He sure enough did. But the sight of it seemed to take the starch out of her. She wasn't so frosty.

Hugh nearly felt sorry for her.

She turned toward the house and stumbled at the first step, but he reached behind her for her left arm, creating a brace across her back. She didn't resist him and leaned into him a little. The earlier desire to defend her tangled his spurs. What a woman could do to a man when he had no say in the matter.

She tried the door knob and it wouldn't open.

The hair on his neck raised, and he laid a hand on his Colt. Hadn't been fool enough to go off without it this trip. "Let me try," he said.

She stepped aside, but not far.

The knob gave way, and the door opened. "Only needed a hard twist. A little oil will loosen things." *Shut up, Hutton, before you loosen your tongue.*

He held the door open, and she stepped inside as if she were sleep-walking. But it couldn't be memories affecting her so. Helen said she'd never seen the place until recently.

He followed her through the rooms.

In the parlor, she too was drawn to the desk. She opened each drawer—tried the locked one—and fingered the things inside. They appeared the same as they had when he'd searched through them.

Her hands returned to the small, locked drawer, and she tugged on it. "I wonder what's in here." Hushed, tentative. "Why do you suppose it's locked?"

Unsure if she was talking to herself or to him, he said nothing until she looked at him, reminding him of what he'd found earlier. "I've got something to show you."

Dang, if that didn't fall out of his mouth on its own accord.

She blinked. Like a child. Helpless and alone.

Lord, help him.

~

Mary moved toward the kitchen at Hugh's touch to her elbow. She felt hazy, as if she were in the wrong place at the wrong time. The house was familiar only because of her first visit days ago, but she sensed her Aunt Bertie in the quilted pot holders on the counter, the china sugar bowl in the center of the small kitchen table, and last year's calendar tacked to the wall. The picture at the top showed a man and woman in a plowed field with a verse about contentment being found in togetherness.

Her eyes stung and she had no energy to keep them from tearing. *Together* certainly described her aunt and uncle. At her age, she would likely never know such contentment, such a sense of belonging.

Hugh pulled out a chair for her and she sank into it as if it were a place to hide and escape the pain. She brushed at her cheeks with the back of her hand.

He claimed the other chair and set his hat crown-down on the table.

It didn't matter—there was no food. They weren't eating. The table top was dusty, and she wiped a place in front of her, then rubbed her hand on her skirt. If only the sense of abandonment rubbed away as easily.

Hugh took a flattened roll of ribboned paper from his vest and laid it on the clean spot before her.

"I found this one day when I was here looking around." His hands folded together, then unfolded, and he dropped them to his lap. He cleared his throat and looked everywhere but at her. "I had a mind to try to get this farm at the auction. There's good grass here for cattle, and since the place was empty, I was— well—looking around, like I said."

Guilt worried his brows where his skin was three shades darker than his forehead. His conscience was showing.

She, of all people, appreciated the value of land and feed for livestock. And she appreciated his candor. If her aunt and uncle had unpaid taxes and land payments due, of course the farm would go to auction. But that didn't lessen the pain or blunt the needle of knowing he wanted the farm for himself. Did the Huttons have that kind of money? Or had he already taken out a loan?

Perhaps the amount was negligible, a mere matter of legalities. Perhaps *she* could afford the farm. The idea was intoxicating, adding to her already-foggy thinking.

And then she saw Hugh Hutton differently. Her host might also be her rival in a bid for her family's property.

He pushed the paper closer, a thin parchment nearly flattened from being carried in his vest. A will?

Oddly, she didn't want to know what it said. It would only confirm what grieved her so. "Have you read this?"

He shifted in his chair and looked over her shoulder toward the parlor. "Yes."

"Where, exactly, did you find it?"

His tanned face paled a little, and his Adam's apple bobbed. His voice dropped even lower than its customary well-depth. "In the desk."

That meant he had already searched through it like she did yet had stood there watching her do the same.

"What is it?" A wasted question, but if he knew, she wanted to hear it from him. Somehow it made her feel like she wasn't completely alone.

"It's a will. Old-fashioned, hand-written, but it looks legal to me. Names you as heir to this property."

Her breath caught. She fingered a decorative button on her blouse, staring at the ribboned paper and stalling. Was it good news or bad to be named an heir? She could be in crushing debt, depending on the mortgage.

As she slid the ribbon from the parchment and unrolled the document, he let out a long breath. He was right about it being old fashioned—even her parents' wills had been processed by typists. This looked old. And it was, dated the day of her fifteenth birthday, April 11, 1903.

The year her aunt and uncle had homesteaded in Colorado. Rebellious tears fell, robbing her vision and clarity of thought. She pushed the parchment toward him. "Would you read it to me, please."

His blue eyes went soft, but his jaw tightened. Compassion seemed a painful conflict for Hugh Hutton.

He cleared his throat again. "We, Ernest Edward Dodson and Bertha Agan Dodson, being of sound body and mind, hereby bequeath to each other all the property in our possession. Upon the death of the last survivor, our 1,280-acre farm twelve miles north of Cañon City, Colorado, including the house and furnishings, barn and outbuildings, wagons, buggies, and farming implements found on the property, is bequeathed to our niece, Mary Agan McCrae."

Birds chattered outside. Tiny feet scratched beneath a cabinet. Mary's pulse beat a rapid counterpoint, and the man across the table watched her with worried concern.

Breathe. She opened her mouth but nothing entered against the ragged cry that escaped.

She slumped into herself, covering her face with her hand, and he was suddenly beside her, enfolding her in strong arms. She turned into him, pressing into his warmth, the rough fabric of his vest, and the scent of clean chambray and sunshine.

He held her as if he would never let go.

~

Hugh hadn't held a woman in his arms since the night Jane died. He'd clutched her lifeless body and cried like the baby at her side, praying that he could die with her.

That was his last earnest prayer—until the pit a week ago when he'd prayed he could get Mary McCrae out of it without killing her. He'd held her then, not knowing who she was, and carried her into the ranch house. But this—alone in the emptiness of a vacant home—this was different. He felt her sense of abandonment, the weakening of her steely resolve, her need for his strength.

His need to hold her.

He was losing his mind.

As her sobs faded, she pushed away from him, wiping her eyes with the heel of her hand.

He had grabbed a clean bandanna along with a clean shirt that morning, so he gave it to her. Not as fancy as she was probably used to, but she took it and pressed the red fabric against her face.

"Thank—*huh*—you."

He rolled the will and slid the ribbon around it but left it on the table. It was her property, not his, and he already felt like a heathen for having it.

In fact, the whole place was her property. If she had money to pay the debt, she could sell it off and high-tail it home to Pennsylvania.

Or keep it herself and stay.

He didn't know which would be worse.

She stood, and he scooted his chair out of the way.

"I'd like to go back ho—I mean, to your ranch, if you don't mind."

She left the kitchen and walked into the parlor.

He grabbed the will and shoved it in his vest again, catching up with her as she opened the front door. He stayed beside her on the porch steps, then handed her up to the wagon.

She didn't look at the house again, nor at the outbuildings, not even the cottonwood tree where redwing blackbirds raised a ruckus.

He rubbed Barlow's head as he walked around the mare, then climbed to the bench seat beside Mary.

She stared straight ahead as they turned out of the yard and onto the wagon path toward the Rafter-H. Not a whimper. Not a word.

CHAPTER NINE

Mary skipped the noon meal, appeasing Helen's motherly concern by accepting a slice of buttered bread. Ignoring the family's—well, *familiness*—was something she simply could not do in the midst of them, and she was too torn to try.

The day was warm and the shaded swing in the big cottonwood tree beckoned, low enough to the ground that Mary could sit in it without holding to the ropes. She looked toward the ranch house, pleased that no westerly windows gave the occupants a view of her whereabouts. But she knew her position was clear to anyone watching from the parlor.

She wrapped her left arm around one rope, turning in time to see the thin parlor curtain fall into place. Surely the boys were peeking on her.

The back screen door slapped three times.

That meant three hungry little Huttons had bounded inside, popping her conjecture like a circus balloon. Perhaps it was Helen who had spied her through the curtain.

Mary fingered a dab of butter and stuck it in her mouth. Creamy and smooth, but not nearly as good as an Ayrshire could produce.

Heat climbed her neck as she licked her finger clean. Of course it wasn't Helen behind the curtain.

She'd never felt more of an outsider than she did at that moment. Things had turned out so differently than she'd expected when she set a course for Colorado. She'd been emboldened by her aunt's and uncle's love, assured of their welcoming embraces and warm smiles, and she had relished the thought of being away from Lewis and his grumping.

Now she almost missed him.

Now she had no one and nothing.

Well, not exactly nothing, according to the will that Hugh had discreetly left on the bureau in her room when they returned.

Surely, a judge would rule in her favor on the property when presented with the will. But there were still taxes to pay and several months of mortgage payments of which she didn't even know the amount. She must find out as soon as possible how much was owed. Hugh might know, but he wanted the farm himself. That fact set them at odds with each other, though she had to admit, he'd not felt at all like an opponent when he held her in his arms in Aunt Bertie's kitchen.

A squirrel chittered near the barn, interrupting her musing with its insistence. Not a bushy-tailed tree squirrel like they had in Pennsylvania, but a dull creature sharing the same color as the dirt from where it scolded her.

Mary bit off a piece of bread, laid the slice in her lap, and tossed the bite toward the gray-brown creature. Greedily it gathered the bread and sat holding it in its tiny paws, nibbling and watching her as it did so.

It soon skittered closer, tail flicking like a hairy whip and its nose reaching along the ground. Another chirp, and it came a step closer.

Mary repeated her gesture with a more generous offering, and the squirrel scampered away with its prize. Perhaps it had a family to feed.

She felt as beholding as the squirrel, a position she did not at all relish. For more than a week the Huttons had housed and fed her, not to mention nursed her back to health. It was high time she was on her way to—where?

The thought of returning home to Pennsylvania and Lewis's

certain efforts to marry her off appealed not in the least, yet she had no other options. Other than the farm.

She sat a little straighter on the swing, instinctively pushing against the sling binding her right arm. Enough of it. She worked the knot on her right shoulder until it loosened and she could hold one end in her teeth and pull the other free. And free was exactly how she felt as she drew the black cloth from around her neck and arm. She rolled her right shoulder with a grimace, but inactivity had stiffened it as much as anything. Lifting her elbow, she felt like a bird trying its wings for the first time, then reached shoulder high to grip the rope. She toed the ground and pushed back, swinging her feet forward, and the sense of freedom increased.

"Should you be doing that?"

The deep voice startled her to a stop, and she gripped too tightly with her right hand. A sharp pang shot up her arm and into her shoulder, but she refused to cry out and clamped down on her bottom lip.

Hugh came around in front of her, concern pinching his brows.

"I am quite capable." Her comment came higher pitched than she preferred and no doubt gave away her discomfort.

"I never said you weren't."

He dropped to his haunches and picked up a twig with which he scratched in the dirt. A capital H paired with a second one, then a peaked line above them both. Rafter-H. Of course. The Hutton brand.

"Do you hope to add that brand to my aunt and uncle's barn?" Immediately she regretted the childish question. "I apologize. That was uncalled for."

He straightened and rubbed out the sketch with his boot. "I'd hoped to, but things have changed."

That was the last thing she expected him to say, and it left her speechless, a condition with which she was not at all familiar.

He looked her in the eye then, his expression beyond her ability to interpret. "Did you notice the buggy in their barn? A farm wagon too. I'll clean up the buggy for you, get it in working order. You can borrow one of our older mares. We've got a couple out to pasture that should be true enough."

No, she hadn't noticed. She'd merely fallen into a hole and apparently lay there until he'd rescued her—however he'd managed to do that. She was quite sure she didn't want to know.

"Why would you do that for me?"

He pushed up the back of his hat and rubbed his head before resettling it. A broad-brimmed affair it was. Different from what Pennsylvania dairymen wore.

"Why wouldn't I?"

That was the second time in two days he'd responded to a question with a question. She regrouped with another.

"How much are the property taxes on the farm?"

He looked off down the rutted path they'd driven that morning as if dollar signs danced across the open range. "Two hundred and twenty-five dollars."

She squeezed the ropes. That was a little less than the money she had with her, but the mortgage added to the debt. If the will was not recognized, she could be outbid at the auction. Yet even if she managed to win it, how would she afford to bring her breeding stock out from Pennsylvania? Or purchase equipment. Or even buy food or start a garden for herself.

The questions shot quickly through her mind, and she realized that she'd already decided to stay. In fact, she'd made the decision the morning Celia's family came for her stock, but hadn't fully acknowledged it until now. Somehow, she would make it work, even if she had to borrow the money—an idea that rubbed against every nerve in her body.

She glanced up to find Hugh Hutton's blue gaze stuck to her like the butter on Helen's bread that she'd flattened against her skirt. "What?"

"I won't be workin' on the buggy tomorrow." He waited, leading her on to ask why.

She refused.

His eyes snapped with unvoiced laughter, as if applauding her for a well-played chess move. "It's Easter."

~

It took everything Hugh had in him not to swear at breakfast Monday morning. Not only because he'd never hear the end of it from Helen, but because his sons were watching. He didn't want them picking up his bad habits.

And they'd all gone to church yesterday. Mary had sat on the other side of his boys and sang the entire song about a solid rock, not once looking at the hymnal Ty held for her. Hugh remembered the song from his days going to church with his folks, but he wasn't a singer and hadn't attended much without Jane.

The whole idea soured him, but he always gave in to Helen on Easter and Christmas if it wasn't snowing.

This morning, Mary sat to his right and passed the platter of fried eggs and bacon to Ty, who perched beside her like a peacock.

"I've taken advantage of your kindness for too long and should be on my way." Mary flicked a look in his direction. "At least a mile or so. Is that about right, Hugh?"

He opened his mouth but didn't get the chance to say.

"My aunt and uncle's home sits empty, and I might as well move in and clean it up while I'm here. Before the auction, I mean. And Hugh has offered to see to the buggy left in their barn so I'll have a way to get around."

Three pairs of little-boy eyes slid his way as if he'd just kicked a puppy.

Mary was as bad as Helen when it came to commandeering a conversation. Even Helen stared at her, fork suspended, dripping egg into her plate.

"But, Miss Mary, we'll miss you if you go off to the Dodson place." Kip's chin began to quiver. Hugh shot him a warning, but it didn't stop the other two.

"We could at least help out over there, clean up around the place and do chores for you." Ty glanced Hugh's way. "Right, Pa?"

Of all the addle-brained ideas he'd heard of, Mary moving into that run-down old place was the craziest, but he was in a corner for sure. How could he say no to his boys helping her?

Mary smiled, and three little chins lifted. "That is very sweet of you, Ty. I would so appreciate help from each of you, but don't you boys go to school?"

"It's been out for spring roundup," Jay offered. "We go back next week, doggone it."

"Watch your language, young man, or you'll be darning socks until summertime." Helen's grit assured the boy it was so.

"Yes, ma'am. Sorry, Miss Mary."

Mary held a napkin to her mouth, and from the sparkle in her eye, she was laughing.

Hugh slugged down his coffee. Since when did he notice a *sparkle* in anyone's eye?

He gathered his plate. "Thank you, Helen. I'll catch Sassy and get her trimmed and ready to go.

"Sassy? That ol' mare up on the ridge?" Kip said. "What are you gonna do that for?"

"For Miss Mary, dufus." Ty made a face at his brother.

Hugh flicked the back of the boy's head. "Don't be callin' names."

He made for the sink before he joined his sons in falling apart over Mary McCrae moving out.

For the life of him, he couldn't figure why.

He'd had what he thought was the best of intentions when he offered to clean up the buggy for her. But he hadn't intended on her leaving.

The angry slap of the screen door against the house drove the first nail in his chest.

He saddled Shorty, grabbed an extra lead, and set out for the ridge. Its crest bordered the Rafter-H on the south end and offered an unobstructed view of the long valley beyond. A peaceful place, where Cale had always ridden to get away. They used to ride there together when they were kids, but over the years it became Cale's spot and Hugh let him have it.

Now Cale was gone, with Ella beside him, and Hugh had ridden up there more times in the last six months than he could count. That's how he knew where to find Sassy.

The old black mare was right where he expected her to be, but he rode on past and sat for a time looking across the valley. Pine jays scolded and magpies squawked. Ground squirrels and rabbits dashed into the cedars, and the blue sky covered it all like a glass bowl.

Hugh filled his lungs with the mountain air, pure and peaceful with no sounds of humanity interrupting. The western range bared its rocky spine above the valley, and the Crossett Ranch stretched around two lower hills and disappeared off toward the Arkansas River.

Shorty reached for a mouthful of course grass, and Hugh let him take a bite before pulling his head up.

Jane had loved this country. Loved it all her life. She'd grown up on her folks' land one ridge over, and the first fall day she attended the section school house on Crossett's place, Hugh knew he'd marry her. A bold assumption for a boy of ten, but he set his course.

If he'd known she'd die bearing his son …

He turned Shorty away, and cedars gave up their perfume as he pushed through a clump, brushing his chaps against their blue berries. Jane's favorite fragrance, she'd once told him. Now he couldn't bear to smell it.

He rode back to Sassy, and she lifted her head as he

approached, whiffling out a greeting to Shorty. It was no chore fashioning a figure-eight rope halter around her without dismounting, and she fell into step as he rode down to the barn.

Mary was ready when he got there.

Of course she didn't have much to do to get that way, but she'd put on her green traveling suit like she was really going someplace. He snorted but kept it low so she wouldn't take offense.

As if he cared what she did and didn't hear.

He bristled at his mood, dismounted at the hitch rail, and looped Sassy's lead around it. Ty and Jay came out of the barn with a curry comb and a bucket of oats like they'd been waiting on him, and Kip made his way from the house holding Mary's carpet bag handles with two hands, kicking it every time he took a step. From the looks of its bulging sides, Helen had donated a few things.

He took it from Kip and set it in the wagon bed, then hitched up Barlow.

"Sassy doesn't look very sassy."

He hadn't heard Mary approach and he turned.

She took a step back.

Did he look that bad?

He rechecked a harness buckle for good measure, then gave Sassy his full attention. "She used to be, but over the years she settled into a solid mount. She's getting long in the tooth, but unless you intend to enter her in the chuckwagon races at the rodeo, she'll do fine with that buggy at your aunt and uncle's."

Mary cocked an eyebrow at him.

If he didn't quit running off at the mouth, he'd get his foot caught in it for sure.

"I'll keep that in mind." The eyebrow lowered.

He brought a leather halter from the tack room and switched it out on Sassy, then tied her to the tailgate before loading a sack of grain, his leather tools, saddle soap, and a few other things he might need. Last of all, he forked in a pile of hay at the end of the bed.

His sons stood like three frowning totems as he handed Mary up to the seat.

"What?" he said.

Ty elbowed Jay who elbowed him back and then pulled at his own shirt front.

"Can we go with you, Miss Mary?"

"No."

All three slumped at Hugh's bark, and he felt Mary giving him a cold glare. They'd asked her, but he was driving, and it was his wagon, and he didn't want her leaving either.

"Maybe tomorrow."

They brightened, but not much.

"Thank you, boys." She reached down from the seat, and they closed in to take her hand. "I so appreciate your eagerness to help, but like your father said, maybe tomorrow. I'm sure there are chores here at the ranch that will keep you busy today."

The way she looked at his sons twisted something hard in his gut and he had to turn away.

The screen door slapped, and Helen came around the corner of the house with a picnic basket on one arm and a napkin-covered dish that looked suspiciously like a pie.

"I've packed some things for you, Mary, since you probably won't be baking or cooking for a few days. See that Hugh chops some stove kindling for you. I've put in a jar of lamp oil that should hold you for a day or so but let me know if you need more before you can get into town."

Helen hefted the basket and pie into the wagon bed. A whiff of baked peaches wafted under Hugh's nose.

She reached for Mary's hands and gave them a squeeze. "Whatever you need, let us know. We've been blessed to have you with us. I wish you'd stay longer, but I'm sure Hugh will be checking on you. And don't overdo. I'd wager the boys will badger him into taking them over to help you with chores."

Hugh hadn't been so ganged up on since he punched

Tommy Hunter for pulling Jane's braids in the fifth grade.

CHAPTER TEN

Mary fought against tears at the sweet send-off from Helen and the boys. Her heart tore a little at leaving them, but the Rafter-H was not her home. She had no call to such an attachment, such a desire to stay.

Hugh stood off from the others, frowning and running his hand across his face. Apparently, he had no such misgivings. Did he detest her? Resent her presence?

A shiver spidered up her spine as she recalled his piercing gaze at the swing—and the way he kept glancing at her during the singing in church yesterday. Casually. As if she couldn't tell. She'd finally closed her eyes on the last hymn and sang it from memory. *My hope is built on nothing less than Jesus' blood and righteousness.* How could she not remember her mother's favorite hymn?

She pulled composure around her like a shawl. She'd pay him for the use of Sassy, and that would be the end of it. The end of seeing Hugh Hutton every morning, noon, and night, reminding her that she was imposing on him and his family.

The wagon tipped as he stepped up to the seat. He released the break and flicked the reins. The next leg of her journey west, but this time to her own home, she prayed.

Lord, please make it so.

Only the creak of the wagon and Barlow's plodding broke the tight silence between Mary and her—guardian? He'd taken on that roll perhaps out of necessity, but she did not appreciate him questioning her choices and actions. Another mile or so, and she'd be rid of his scowls. *And strong arms.*

"I wish you wouldn't move off out here by yourself."

His sullen profile matched his gruff voice. Did the man read minds? Or had she misheard him?

"Excuse me?"

He kept his focus straight ahead, but sitting so close, she had a clear view of the muscle in his jaw hard at work.

"Where would you rather I move? To town?" *To Pennsylvania, no doubt.*

"It's not safe. There's no telling who might wander around in your yard with less than good intentions. A lot of people know that land is up for grabs."

"Hmph." She was not intimidated by land-grabbers. She had a will, after all, and it would soon be seen by the bank and, possibly, a judge.

Barlow's steady plodding carried them on in silence until Hugh plunged in the knife.

"Somebody dug that pit."

The back of her neck crawled.

She deflected the blade of doubt with facts. "Helen told me about the grizzly that had all the ranchers on alert last year. She said you and Cale killed it."

"Cale shot it. I helped drag it back."

"Couldn't my uncle have dug that pit as a precaution in case the bear showed up on the farm?"

Hugh looked at her then, a pit of his own cutting between his brows. "You were in it. You think your uncle dug that?"

He had a point, but she didn't have to like it.

She arranged her skirt as much as possible to give her hands something to do. "Do you really think someone would go to such lengths to scare me away from the farm?"

He slid his jaw sideways as if working out a kink. "Someone didn't know there was a you and they still dug it. Imagine if they'd known."

An involuntary shudder swept through her. *Thank you, Mr.*

Hugh Hutton, for the comforting words. She worked her own jaw, clamping down on what she wanted to say, knowing it would not ease her nerves. But she'd not be scared off her rightful inheritance. Hugh Hutton wanted that land too, and he might be using every trick he knew to get rid of her.

She stopped short of accusing him of digging the hole himself. Mother had taught her not to be rude and unkind.

"And no, I didn't dig it."

The front left wheel hit a hole and the wagon seat bounced her forward.

He reached around her waist and pulled her back, then quickly let go.

Flustered, she drew in as much air as possible and tugged at her jacket sleeves. "I'd never accuse you of such a thing."

"But you were thinking it." The left side of his mouth pulled thin.

Was he laughing at her? In profile, she couldn't read him clearly, but she'd bet her jar of lamp oil that he was.

As they drove into the barren yard and stopped in front of the house, everything looked the same as she remembered—desolate. Hugh offered his hand, and she accepted it, climbing down on her own, unlike the last time he'd helped her from the wagon.

"I'll take your things inside, then I'll be at the barn, working on the buggy."

"Thank you." Such a flimsy remark, but what else did she have to say?

Hugh was as good as his word, a nagging reminder that he'd been nothing less since she first saw him more than a week ago. He drove over to the barn, then turned Sassy into the small corral, and set a bucket of grain in front of her before disappearing into the shadowed interior with a box of tools.

Mary walked inside the house and stopped in the parlor, suddenly overwhelmed at the immensity of work that lay before her. This time she saw things differently—as if it were *her* house. Dust laid thick on furniture, dirt covered the floors. Rugs needed to be beaten, windows washed, traps set for mice that had nibbled at anything of fabric. And upstairs? She didn't even want to look.

Helen's basket occupied the kitchen table, as cheerful as a vase of flowers, and next to it, the pie plate covered with a blue-and-white-checked napkin. Hugh would enjoy that for lunch. Surely, he'd be hungry in a few hours.

She tried the hand pump at the sink and rusty water spewed. But it soon ran clear, or close to it, and she rinsed a kettle and a coffee pot, filled them both, and set them on the stove. A kindling box held half its limit, enough to get the water boiling. She laid it in the fire box, using past months from the wall calendar as starter and a match from a box atop the warming oven.

How strange to begin housekeeping in a home that seemed untouched since its occupants had disappeared. As if they'd simply vanished, leaving everything behind them for someone else to use.

A bit of melancholy settled around Mary like the dust around the sugar bowl on the table. She found rags and a wash pan, and with a few soap flakes from a box in Helen's basket, she added the heated water and set to cleaning every surface. Then the cabinets.

She washed her aunt's dishes and pots and pans, used her broom to sweep the floor, and scrubbed it clean with a hard brush from the broom closet. Time stood still as she cleaned and boiled and cleaned some more, poured oil from Helen's jar into a lamp on the counter, and emptied the basket of its treasures— a lavender soap cake and udder salve that brought a smile to Mary's lips. She knew well that people often used their livestock medications on themselves.

The basket gave up a loaf of bread, a small cooked roast, even a large knife and a tin of cookies. A small wire basket held a clutch of eggs, and two half-quart jars offered kerosene and bacon grease in turn. A set of clean sheets lined the bottom. Helen had thought of everything.

Gratitude mixed with melancholy, and Mary dropped into one of the kitchen chairs, weary and lonely. Tears were mere minutes away, and she closed her eyes against the loving gifts from a family that wasn't hers. With a heavy sigh, she laid her head on her folded arms. A moment's rest, and she'd be almost good as new.

~

The buggy was in better shape than Hugh had hoped. The seat wasn't torn, the beams were solid and uncracked, and the wheels sound. He pushed it into the daylight where he could see things better and went to cleaning dirt out of the leather seats. He polished everything that would take a good rubbing, then soaped the harness he'd found on the wall. He easily repaired a couple of dry, weak spots in the leather, and by the time he was finished, Mary had a smart-looking rig. With Sassy's black coat, Mary McCrae would cut a fine figure driving into town.

His stomach knotted. She didn't need to be cutting a fine figure anywhere, especially in Cañon City where every man with two legs knew the Dodson place was up for auction.

He poked around in the barn, found shovels and pitch forks, and left undone anything his boys could do.

Beyond the corral, a wood shed harbored a half cord of wood and a dull axe. He took the axe to the wagon, where he traded it for his own. This evening, he'd put an edge on the Dodsons', but right now he needed to fill a kindling box.

An hour later, with more than enough kindling, he headed for the house with an armful. He went around to the back porch, determined to sound pleasant when he asked Mary to open the door for him. But then he saw her through the clean door glass, head on her arms at the table. He set half the load on the porch floor and eased the door open.

The floor was a brighter color than it had been before, and the kitchen smelled like soap and vinegar. Every square inch had been scrubbed, including the window above the sink. Through it, he saw the top of the Rafter-H windmill peeking over a small rise to the west. There was another chore that needed doing—checking out the windmill here. He didn't want Mary climbing up to replace a fan blade or doing some other fool thing on her own.

He quieted his steps to the wood box by the stove, laid the kindling in it, and fairly tiptoed to the table. Mary's jacket draped the chair, and her braid had come undone from its coil. Stray hair stuck to her face like it did when he found her in the pit. His hand itched to push it back, but he folded his arms instead and backed toward the door. A floorboard groaned and stopped him in his tracks.

Mary sat up. Didn't see him where he was standing, almost behind her. She pushed her fingers through her hair and flexed her neck and arms, then turned his way and gasped.

His hands shot out in front of him. "I'm sorry. I didn't want to wake you. You looked like you were tired, and after cleaning the place up like you did, I figured you needed to rest." He indicated the wood box. "I've laid in some kindling for you and left more on the porch."

There he went again, flapping his gums.

"You startled me, that's all. I didn't expect you so soon."

"Soon?"

"Yes. I thought you wouldn't come in until dinner time."

He glanced out the window and, judging by the sun, knew it was closer to two.

She followed his gaze and stood quickly. "Oh—it's later than I thought."

She wavered and gripped the edge of the table.

He took a step forward, but she shot him a green warning.

He stepped back.

"I stood too fast, that's all." She pushed at her hair, then shrugged as if she couldn't do anything about the way she looked. "Helen sent a meal for us. I'll get things set here if you'll give me a few minutes."

He went out for the remainder of the kindling which was more than the wood box could hold and spoke through the screen door. "I'll leave this on the back porch so it's close at hand if you run out before I get back."

"Get back?" She sliced through a loaf of Helen's bread and laid two pieces on a clean plate that must have been her aunt's.

"Yes, ma'—I mean yes. Uh, the boys have their hearts set on helping you, so I'll bring them over tomorrow."

She looked at the overflowing wood box, and a smile edged in around her mouth. "Thank you. I'm sure there's enough until you and the boys return."

There was enough until winter returned, but he didn't bother pointing that out.

She slid her cutting board and the bread and meat away from the sink. "You can wash up right here it you'd like. I don't remember seeing a tub and pump outside like you have at the ranch. You can use that bar of soap in the dish, and you'll find a towel in the second drawer."

Helen always made him wash. So had Jane. He came inside, feeling as easy as an elephant in a china shop. Or was it a bear in a china shop?

Mary set two plates on the table along with the pie, a knife, and two forks.

Hugh sat down smelling like a danged flower.

When Mary joined him, she folded her hands in her lap and bowed her head.

He just sat there.

"This is my first meal in this house, and I'd like to thank the Lord for it." She didn't look at him, but kept her head down. "If you can't say grace, then I will."

Over his dead body. He cleared his throat and tried to remember what Helen always said.

When Mary looked up after his brief, fumbling prayer, it was with a smile. "I forgot about coffee," she said. "I found some old tea bags in a tin in the larder, but I threw out the coffee. The beans looked like they'd been chewed on."

"Good call," he said before trying the food he'd blessed. "I'm sure Helen has some extra. I'll bring it tomorrow."

"Thank you." She pulled the pie plate closer and sliced two generous helpings. "I'll never be able to repay her thoughtfulness and generosity."

She laid a slice on his plate, and her cheeks pinked a bit. "Or yours."

When he drove out of the yard an hour later, Mary watched from the front porch. Her braid hung over her shoulder like a bronze rope, and she waved as he took the turn to the wagon road. There was plenty more to do at the farm, and he'd bring the boys tomorrow.

At the ranch, all three of them came running, and Ty took hold of Barlow as Hugh whoa-ed her in the yard.

"I want you boys to unhitch the mare, brush her down good, and give her some oats before you turn her out. I've got something I need to do. I'll be back in a while."

He saddled Shorty and set out for Cale and Ella's over a rise at the north end of the ranch. They'd gotten a cow dog last fall and bred her to Tug. The pups had turned out to be good looking dogs. Seemed to have Tug's cow sense and their mother's quick moves. He was sure they'd give him a pup for Mary, and while he was at it, he'd bring one home for the boys.

Tug wouldn't be around too many more winters, but he wasn't so far gone he couldn't start a pup. It'd give the boys something to help ease their loss of Mary.

The thought sneaked up on him and left him wondering what he was gonna do to ease *his* loss.

CHAPTER ELEVEN

Cleaning the upstairs bedroom was more than Mary had energy for after Hugh left, so she pushed and pulled the parlor settee out onto the front porch and beat it with her left hand until the puffs of dust were more like a frosty breath than plumes of smoke. After pushing it back inside, she set it facing a front window, which she cleaned with vinegar water, then spread a sheet over the settee for the night. It was a little short, but she didn't care. She could lie with her feet up and watch twilight slip over the farm and night settle in.

Hugh had been so different at supper, unlike the man who had driven her to the farm. She could not figure him out. One minute he was scaring her with tales of ne'er-do-wells, and the next he was making sure she had what she needed for the night. He'd cut enough stove kindling to last until January, and she suspected it was the result of nervous energy.

However, his remark about the pit and others wanting the farm had her up rummaging through kitchen drawers for keys to lock the doors. She found one for the front in the rolltop desk, and she wiggled the handle of the small, locked drawer again, frustrated that she couldn't force it open.

A task for another day.

And another day came all too soon the next morning.

Waking stiff and sore, she sat up on the settee, her neck protesting a night with her head bent. Both shoulders complained, especially the right one, as she rolled them awake, but sunlight peeking through the parlor window cast a glint of hope until she saw movement at the barn.

For the first time in her life, she wished she had a gun.

She knelt at the edge of the window and waited for whatever was out there to move again. But the only movement came from the corral, where Sassy nosed a small pile of hay and another horse did the same. It looked like Shorty, Hugh's gelding. Unsaddled.

At that moment, he stepped from the barn's shadowed doorway and into the light. A small spotted dog followed him on a length of twine, not at all happy with the constraint.

She watched, enthralled, as big, tough, blustering Hugh Hutton dropped to his haunches and rubbed the dog's back and ears, then pushed on its little behind until it sat on the ground. It jumped up, but he repeated the gesture and stood holding his hand out over the dog. Then he reached into his vest pocket and gave the dog something that set its stub tail to wagging.

Hugh tugged on the rope and the dog resisted. Again he went through the previous routine, rewarding the animal for its choice, and Mary laughed aloud at the way it wiggled its whole behind. This time when Hugh tugged on the twine, the dog followed.

Amazing.

They were making their way to the house.

She ran to the kitchen where she pumped water into the sink and splashed her face. Then she filled the kettle, fed the banked coals in the stove, and searched through her carpet bag for her comb and brush.

She must look a sight, and she didn't want him seeing her like this, though he'd seen her far worse. Still, this was different.

Thankfully it took as long for him to reach the porch with the dog as it took her to comb and braid her hair. No time to coil it at her neck, so she let it hang down her back with a green ribbon holding the end.

He knocked on the front door.

Her heart pounded out a reply.

"Get ahold of yourself, Mary McCrae," she scolded in a hushed whisper. "It's Hugh Hutton at the door, not a suitor. He wants the farm. *Your* farm." Her pulse settled at the brutal reminder, and poise returned to her movements. Calmly, or close to it, she walked to the front door and turned the key.

"Good morning."

The dog had other ideas and jumped up on her skirt, its tiny bottom wiggling furiously.

"No—down." Hugh yanked the twine and the dog fell back.

"Oh!" Mary went to her knees, drawing the squirming creature onto her lap and laughing at its eager kisses. "It's just a puppy, and so adorable. Wherever did you find him?"

She scooped the pup into her arms and stood, lifting her face away from his eager little tongue. "What a bundle of energy!"

"He's a she," Hugh said, helpless against the grin that forced its way across his face. "And smart as a whip."

"I could see that. She responded so well to your—" Heat stung Mary's cheeks as she realized her blunder, confessing that she had watched him working with the dog. "Um, what is her name?"

Hugh dragged his hand across his face, clearing all trace of his thoughts. "Doesn't have one yet. I thought I'd leave that up to you since she's your dog."

Mary blinked. "*My* dog?"

"Uh, yeah. You need a dog here with you. Someone to sound an alarm if coyotes get too close. Or snakes. She'll be a good watch dog for you. And a companion. Sort of."

He shuffled his feet and reset his hat.

Mary stepped aside. "Please, come in."

He took the pup and tied her to one of the porch uprights, then gave her another treat from his pocket with a firm command. "Stay."

Mary chuckled. "She doesn't have much choice, does she?"

Hugh came inside. "But she'll connect the word with the restraint. When she's grown, she'll stay without being tied."

His boots made a comforting sound as he walked through the house to the kitchen. The reassurance of a man on the premises, someone with strength and, well, strength. She'd never heard that comfort from Lewis's footsteps. Of course, Lewis left his barn boots on the back porch. Papa would have skinned him if he'd tramped manure into the house.

Mary's stomach rumbled, and she went immediately to the stove, where she pulled a skillet to the front and fed the fire. She washed three eggs from the clutch Helen had sent, spooned bacon grease into the skillet, and added small chunks of meat sliced from the roast.

"I brought you something."

He hadn't been carrying anything, but she looked over her shoulder hoping for salt pork or potatoes.

Coffee beans.

Hugh grinned like a little boy. "Helen had plenty to spare, and I remembered the grinder on your wall there by the stove. Shall I?"

"Please do."

Suspicion filled her thoughts as she filled the coffee pot with water. Had Hugh's twin brother, Cale, shown up this morning, playing a joke on her in her ignorance? She'd never seen Cale, but Helen said the two looked exactly alike, aside from the gray at Hugh's temples.

Mary stole a quick glance and noted silver in his sideburns but not in the dark stubble shadowing his jaw. She recognized the vest and also the hat. But she didn't recognize the man *beneath* those outer trappings. He was so changeable, and she longed to know what caused him to be gentle and kind one day and brusque the next.

She sliced three pieces of bread, diminishing the loaf considerably, transferred the eggs and meat to plates, and warmed the bread in the skillet.

Without asking, Hugh came up beside her, added ground coffee to the pot on the stove, and set it over the warmest spot. Of course he would know what to do.

~

Standing so close to Mary while she worked over the stove set Hugh on edge, and he moved to the window. The yard behind the house had seen better days, but inside Mary had already made a difference.

"Things are different in here. Feels homey." He stretched his neck and flexed his shoulders.

"Thank you. There is still much to do, but it's a start." She set two plates on the table with forks and a couple of napkins Helen had wrapped things in for the basket.

"I wish I had more to offer, but this will break the fast."

A meager smile followed, then she took her place at the table.

Maybe if he waited for the coffee to cook, she'd start without him and he wouldn't have to say grace again. But standing in the kitchen like a scarecrow while she sat with her hands in her lap was not a comfortable proposition. He hung his hat on the other chair and planted himself.

He would not reach for her hand. Nor would he close his eyes. If God was listening, Hugh figured he wouldn't mind him watching.

"Thank you, Lord, for this food. And for Mary cooking it." There was more, but he had to chisel it from his throat and the act cost him double what he was willing to pay. His voice came out thin and brittle. "And thank You that she has this place. Amen."

When he looked over, she was staring at him like he had a frog on his head. Ignoring her, he forked an egg onto each slice of bread on his plate.

She went for the coffee and two china cups, filling one for him first and then her own.

"I don't have cream or milk, but there's sugar here on the table. I'll get a spoon."

"No need, other than for yourself. I take it horned and barefoot."

"Excuse me?" She set the pot on a folded towel on the table and took her seat.

"Black. I drink it black."

"That's what *horned and barefoot* means?"

He grinned. "I heard that when I was a kid, and always liked the sound of it. Means nothing fancy or extra. Just how things come natural."

"Oh."

They ate in silence, which suited him fine but also made him twitchy. No telling what was going on in her head, especially after he spilled that bit about the farm. He didn't like it, but he knew if he didn't say it, he wouldn't be able to eat, whether it was true or not. And he was hungry.

"You were here early this morning." She tore her bread in half and took a small bite, cutting him a sideways glance.

"I, uh, wanted to bring the pup. I'll be going back for the boys. They're itching to come over and help you. Plenty of work for them in the barn."

"Yes. I imagine there is." She cut into her egg. "Why didn't you bring them when you brought the pup?"

He frowned at his eggs. What was this, the Inquisition?

"How did you sleep?"

His fork stopped halfway to his mouth. "Now wait just a minute—"

One fine brow arched above her green gaze and interrupted what he was about to say.

"You have a piece of straw stuck to the back of your vest. I don't imagine that happened when you fed the horses."

She laid down her fork and picked up her coffee cup. Before it reached her lips, she paused. "And Shorty isn't saddled."

Hugh's collar got tight and he shoved the forkful into his mouth. Blasted woman was smarter than she looked. Not that she looked weak-minded. She looked anything but that. But catching him at his ruse set him on his heels. He'd better be watching his back trail.

"You didn't have to do that, you know."

Mid-swallow with his coffee, he gulped. "Do what?"

"Sleep in the barn."

"I've slept in worse."

"Where?"

He set his cup down too hard and slopped coffee on the table. "Dadgummit it, woman, I don't want you out here by yourself with no clue about what goes on around here, no one to look after you, and not even a peashooter to defend yourself with."

"Are you finished?"

"No, I'm not—"

"With your breakfast." She reached for his plate. "If you leave a little, then Finley will have something to eat."

"Who in blazes is Finley?" He was losing his mind. Again.

"Why, the dog you brought me. And a most appropriate name I've given her. It means fair warrior, since she's to be my defender."

"She's a puppy. She won't be defending anything for a while."

"Then why did you give her to me?"

Hugh clinched his jaw hard enough to grind the rest of the coffee beans and pushed from the table. Mary McCrae was worse than Helen, and that was saying something.

He tromped out the door and headed for the privy he'd noticed set back in a clump of scrub oak. The way his day was going, it'd be caved in and full of rattlers.

~

Mary watched through the window above the sink as Hugh beat a path to the necessary. She'd had to take the lamp with her last night. At least he had daylight.

She set the dishes in the sink, smiling to herself. It was fun to banter with someone as if she had the energy to live life. She hadn't felt this good in quite some time, in spite of needing clean clothes and a bath, and she recalled a tin tub hanging on the porch wall out back. Likely Aunt Bertie's bathing tub.

Vitality surged through her arms as she washed, rinsed, and dried. Put the breakfast scraps in a cracked bowl, scrubbed the table, and filled a pail with hot water and a few soap flakes. Next on her list was the bedroom. As much as she hated going through her aunt and uncle's things, it must be done. Sooner was better than later.

The door opened, and Hugh stopped on the threshold, filling the entire frame. She'd not taken account of how big he was. Bigger, it seemed, than he appeared in the log ranch house.

"If there's anything you need, give me a list and I'll take it to Helen. I'll be at the barn *saddling* Shorty."

As he turned, she clapped her hand over her mouth. Laughing at his antics would be completely out of line. But he was behaving more like his sons than his sons.

A yap from the front of the house reminded her that she had another mouth to feed. She took the bowl of scraps to the front porch, where Finley was stretched to the end of her tether toward the barn, whining for Hugh.

"Finley, you dear little thing. Don't look so forlorn and forgotten."

The puppy bounded onto the porch, charging for the dish in Mary's hand, and she lifted it higher.

"Sit, Finley." Determined to be as disciplined as Hugh had been, she waited until the pup sat.

"Good girl, Finley." She knelt and set the dish in front of the puppy, who inhaled every scrap in the bowl.

Mary rubbed the pup's back and neck, patting her affectionately and repeating her name over and over. "You're my dog now, Finley. He didn't forget you, but you need to be with me now. I need you, Finley, to live up to your name and be my fair warrior."

The pup was not convinced and returned to the end of her

twine, where she watched intently as Hugh saddled his horse.

So did Mary. Things had changed between them, had become—friendlier. More familiar. The term stirred a warning from her mother. "Be formal, friendly, or familiar as the situation may call for. But remember, familiar is reserved for *family*. Take care becoming familiar with a man. Not all of them can be trusted."

Sobered by the memory, she shook herself free of the idea and went inside to write a note.

At the rolltop desk, she yanked on the little drawer again, then sat down and found a pencil nub and some small squares of paper.

Milk or cream. Butter.

She hated asking for dairy products that she had produced and sold at home, but it would be weeks, possibly months before she could ship her breeding stock here. And a year after that before she had milk from them. Provided she could pay the taxes and mortgage. Everything depended on that.

She added a few more items, then took a ten-dollar bill from the unstitched seam in the bottom of her carpet bag and wrapped it in the notepaper.

Hugh knocked on the door frame, and she realized he was keeping his distance from Finley.

"Come in. You don't have to knock every time you come in the house. I didn't knock at yours."

"That was different." He removed his hat and held it flat against one leg.

Not different to her way of thinking, but she was not going to argue about it. Some things were worth arguing over—knocking was not one of them. "All right. Let me know you're here and then come inside."

He held her eye. No comment.

She offered him the note but snatched it back before he touched it and went to the desk, where she added one more item. Then she folded it again and returned to the kitchen.

He unfolded it, and his brows dipped to a frown.

"That's for Sassy. I'm paying you for letting me use her."

He laid the money on the kitchen table. "No, you're not."

She picked it up and held it out. "Yes, I am."

He put his hat on, tugged on the front of the brim with a curt glance, and walked out the door.

Still holding the money, she hurried through the house to the parlor window and watched him ride away. Stubborn man. That was two arguments today he had dominated. He was as bad as Lewis.

No! The bill crumpled in her fingers. Never. Not even close to Lewis. Hugh Hutton and Lewis McCrae had absolutely not one thing in common other than their gender.

CHAPTER TWELVE

"**N**o, you cannot bring the pup." Hugh had a poke full of things from Helen tied to his saddle and all the boys stacked on Barlow—he didn't need a half-grown dog in the mix. "Tie him to the lilac bush in front of the house. Tug can babysit."

"Kip can tie him. He's already over there cuttin' flowers for Miss Mary."

Hugh took a second look and found only two boys on Barlow's back. Sure enough, Kip was trying to cut branches with one of Helen's kitchen knives.

"Hold on there."

"But, Pa, I want to take her somethin' pretty."

"Hold on, I said. One of your bloody fingers isn't going to be pretty for anybody. Here, let me help you." He flicked his pocketknife open. Good for cutting twine, apples, and bull calves. It could handle a bunch of lilacs.

"When am I gonna get one of those?" Kip asked.

"When you're tall as the top corral pole."

"Pa-*aw*. That'll take forever." Dark eyes looked up at him with an earnest plea.

"Show me which flowers you want, then tie the pup to the base of the bush so it doesn't follow us."

Kip pointed out several bunches, then gathered the puppy. It was a dead ringer for Mary's Finley, other than its undercarriage.

When they arrived at the Dodson place, the boys jumped

off Barlow and ran toward the house.

"Hold on, all of you!"

They all stopped and turned to see what he wanted.

"You leave your brains at the ranch?"

They stared at him, the flowers in Kip's hand hiding most of his face.

"Take care of your horse first. It's a law."

"Whose law?" Jay risked asking.

"Mine."

Jay turned Barlow into the corral. When he came out, Hugh handed him the bag from Helen. "Wait here and don't drop it. There's a jar of milk in there."

He unsaddled Shorty, pulled off the bridle, and the gelding walked through the open gate toward Sassy, who was already whiffling a greeting.

"Ty, fork a little hay in there for them, but make three separate piles."

"I know, Pa. Shorty doesn't share good."

Hugh waited until Ty finished and took the fork to the barn. "All right. You all ready?"

"Yes, sir." They had unison down to a T.

"Don't run. The pup is tied to the front porch, so go quiet and easy."

Mary came out of the house looking like she was glad to see them. She picked up Finley and stopped in front of the steps.

"Hello, boys!" A smile lit her face that made Hugh wish she was talking to him.

Ty took the dog from her, Jay handed her the poke, and Kip stopped at the bottom of the stairs and waited.

Reminded Hugh of himself.

Mary stepped around the commotion and waved Kip over. "What do you have there?"

Hugh's throat got tight knowing how the boy felt.

Kip took the stairs careful-like, as if he was carrying the jar of milk. At the top he handed the flowers to Mary. "These are for you. I thought you might like something pretty in your house."

Mary knelt down to his level. "Oh, Kip, you're going to steal my heart."

The boy stepped back. "Oh, no, Miss Mary. I'd never do something like that. I just want to make you smile. These flowers smell real good. They're lie-lucks."

"Lie-lucks?" Her brows knotted, but her eyes smiled.

"That's what Helen calls 'em. If you don't lie, you have good luck. Lie-lucks."

Mary rolled her lips and glanced toward Hugh. "I see. What a thoughtful thing for you to do." Taking the flowers, she added, "Will you please open the door for me so I can carry them and the bag inside." She threw Hugh an inviting look and jerked her chin toward the house.

Kip's chest puffed out as he walked past his brothers who were wrestling with Finley. The boy was uncommon for certain.

At the threshold, the smell of soap and vinegar hit Hugh again, and he looked the place over. Mary McCrae had been busy cleaning like she planned to stay for more than a few days. Part of him sulled at the thought, as if she was moving in on what he wanted.

The other part wanted to jump up and down like his boys. He patted his vest to make sure what he'd brought was still there.

He turned to his sons. "All right, boys. The chicken coop needs cleaning. So do the barn stalls. Rake everything old into the wheel barrow in the barn and dump it around behind the house for Miss Mary's garden."

"Isn't Kip gonna help?" Jay could be counted on to divvy things up fair.

"He'll be right out."

As they ran off toward the barn, Finley whined and strained at her tether.

"Sit."

The dog looked up with her head tipped sideways, but her bottom hit the porch boards.

"Good girl." Hugh gave her a piece of jerky from his vest pocket, rubbed her back, then let her loose.

At the sink, Kip pumped water into a mason jar and Mary dug through the bag Helen sent.

She glanced up. "Do you know if there's a springhouse? I didn't even think to look for one."

"On it," Hugh said, and opened the back door. "When you're finished there, Kip, go help your brothers."

The boy nodded but didn't look his way, intent on the task.

How was it Mary McCrae could have four fellas working on her place without her even asking?

He walked out around the garden patch, making note to repair the wire fence and sagging gate, then headed for a grassy rise no taller than Kip. Sure enough, on the other side of it was a path that led a few feet down to a heavy door barred shut. Not a springhouse, a root cellar.

He propped the door open and stepped inside, where it was cooler, almost cold. Shelves of canned goods lined one wall and boxes took up the other, half full of potatoes, onions, pumpkins, and such. The milk would keep down here. He barred the door when he left.

He raised his hand to knock on the kitchen door frame, but instead, rapped on the glass with his knuckles and opened it. "Anybody home?"

"Of course. Come in."

The mason jar sprouted lilacs in the middle of the table. Mary was busy peeling and cutting potatoes and dropping them into a pot of boiling water on the stove.

"No springhouse, but I found a root cellar. And it's nearly half full. Left over from last winter—" He didn't need to spell it out.

"Thank you." Mary pushed hair from her face with the back

of her right hand, then dropped more potatoes in the water.

The room smelled of coffee, so Hugh helped himself to the cupboard. "Want a cup?"

"That sounds good."

He filled two, set one on the counter, and took a seat at the table. Remembering she liked sugar, he took the sugar bowl over and spooned in a heap. "Hope that's not too much."

Her green gaze caught him through hair that was losing its battle with the steaming pot. "You can never have too much sugar."

His hand raised but he dropped it before he pushed that unruly hair aside. No telling what she'd do, holding a paring knife and all. "You didn't put that on your list."

But he did get one other thing she'd requested. Now wasn't the time to give it to her, so he laid it on the windowsill. She'd find it.

~

Mary chided herself for allowing *familiar* to worm its way in. But it was hard *not* to feel familiar with a man who was inching his way into her life—especially in her own house with his boys out front, a dog on the porch, and hope for a future.

Her breath cut short. Was that what had oppressed her so on the dairy, a lack of hope?

Her pastor often spoke about the God of hope who filled His people with joy and peace, yet she'd not connected those things to her daily life. They had been mere concepts. But here, in Colorado's high country, she was beginning to taste it all.

She puffed a breath with her lower lip, aiming for her errant hair. Perhaps Ella had the right idea, cutting a fringe that kept it from her eyes. Then again, she must be forever trimming it. Six o' one thing, half dozen of the other, Aunt Bertie would have said.

Mary hadn't heard Hugh sit down again, so she glanced over

her shoulder and found him at the window opposite. Legs spread in a wide stance, coffee in one hand, the other in a pocket. His hat hung on a chair.

He looked so natural there, as if this were *his* farm. That had been his plan all along and might still be. Why should he change his mind? She might be doing all this work for him and not for herself.

Her fledgling hope fell like a bird from a nest.

"What are your plans?" A double-edged question to be sure. She knew the long-term answer—one she had so abruptly interrupted by her arrival. But she wanted to know his plans for the day.

"The boys are working in the barn."

"The barn?" Her words pitched higher. "Isn't it dangerous with that gaping hole?"

He turned at the waist and gave her a curious look. "I covered it, remember?"

"Oh. Yes." Deflating fear lowered her voice as well. "That's right." Blushing, no doubt, she turned to the boiling pot. She wasn't thinking clearly. Was it from falling in said hole? Or was it Hugh Hutton's overwhelming presence in her small kitchen and runaway thoughts?

She laid her knife aside and wiped her hands on her apron. "I'll be right back."

"Where you goin'?"

It really wasn't any of his business.

"I'll be right back."

Descending the back porch stairs, she heard his boots on the boards. Let him watch. She should head for the necessary and embarrass him for being so nosey, but she didn't want to over-boil the potatoes. What she wanted was a clear, fresh breath without him taking up all the air around her. Angling away in a northerly direction, she rued her failure to ask him where the root cellar was.

"A little more to your left," he called behind her.

Blast. Not only was he watching her every move, but his colorful speech was infiltrating her thoughts. If he followed her to the cellar, she'd bean him with an onion—if there were any. A potato would work just as well. She'd always been a good shot, even Lewis admitted it.

The tall grass ahead of her flattened into a narrow path, and she followed it around a small rise. On the opposite side, a heavy, barred door was set into the bottom of the hillock, and a large rock nearby provided a doorstop for holding it back.

She propped the door open and stepped inside. Mary could eat until the following winter, based on what she saw before her. And as she had suspected, a box of onions took up a corner beneath jars of canned goods—peaches, cherries, beans, apples, pickles.

Hugh was right. The larder was more than half full. Her eyes pricked at the evidence of Aunt Bertie's hard work in preparation for a winter she didn't survive. Mary filled her apron with four onions and added a jar each of peaches, apples, and pickles.

When she returned to the house, Hugh was gone and she let out a deep breath—oddly disappointed, but relieved at the same time. She couldn't very well ask him to make himself scarce, but the less she saw of him, the easier it would be to distance herself toward friendly. Formal would be difficult with the boys, but she really needed to set boundaries.

Hard to do with a man who had lifted her from certain death and later held her in his arms as she wept.

Helen had sent fried chicken. Mary made potato salad, complete with diced pickles, then opened the jar of peaches, and set it all on the table. A simple cloth she'd found in a drawer served as a covering, and she squeezed five place settings around the little square table. Two brothers would have to share a side.

She searched the house hoping to find chairs she had overlooked but found none. Heavy boots on the porch drew her to the front door.

"These were hanging in the barn. Thought they might come

in handy."

Hugh held four ladder-back chairs, two in each hand, surely throwbacks from Uncle Ernest's family trade of furniture making. But too cumbersome for the kitchen.

"Exactly what I needed, thank you. Leave them on the porch and we'll eat outside."

Which was the lesser of the two evils? The familiarity of casual dining or the crowdedness of close quarters inside?

She went with her first instinct. It was too nice a day to spend crammed into a tiny kitchen when blue sky and sunshine ruled outdoors.

Little-boy stomachs had a way of knowing when food was being laid out, and three Huttons came running for the house.

"Hold on," their father ordered. "Go wash at the barn, then line up at the door here."

Off they went like a human tornado, brightening Mary's mood. How could she not smile at their unbridled enjoyment?

She filled five plates, rolled forks into five mismatched napkins, and took a wet cloth outside to wipe off the chairs.

"Looked for a porch chair or rockers but haven't found any yet." Hugh removed his hat and rubbed his forehead with his sleeve.

"These will work perfectly." Mary wiped each one down, revealing its natural woodgrain that had been hidden by dust and dirt. "My uncle's family trade was furniture making. The craftsmanship of these pieces is evident, but they would more than fill the kitchen. Would you please bring out one of those chairs to go with these?"

"Yes, ma—. All right."

That was where she'd gone wrong. His use of the customary address would have kept things between them a bit more proper. But she couldn't very well retract her request.

She chose three jars to serve as drinking glasses for the boys, then filled Hugh's cup and her own with coffee and set them all on the porch railing. A table would be handy and beyond Finley's reach, but Mary would hunt for one another day.

The boys lined up like stairsteps by the front door and held their hands out for inspection. Bless Helen.

"You have done admirably, boys, and I want to hear all about your work today as we eat. You may follow me inside to the kitchen where I have your plates ready and waiting."

Like obedient soldiers, they dogged her steps and each took the plate she offered with a sincere "thank you."

Mary carried the two remaining plates outside and handed one to Hugh, who stood apart from the chairs he'd set randomly across the porch.

As a good hostess, she took the one closest to the door.

While seated, the boys all dragged their chairs toward her until a scowl from their father stopped them.

Mary bit her lip.

"Be careful with the plates," Hugh warned.

"Yes, sir," chimed out like a chorus. Three plates found three laps and three pairs of hands folded.

Mary looked at Hugh, who was still frowning. Why did he so resist asking grace? She bowed her head and opened her mouth to do so herself when his deep voice rolled over them like a welcomed summer storm.

"Thank you for this food, this place, and this family. Amen."

Mary could hardly breathe.

The boys dove into their dinner as if they hadn't eaten in weeks, but Hugh's inclusive prayer had stymied her reflexes. It was not eloquent, nor did it address the Almighty, but he had offered gratitude for the things he appreciated. Had he deliberately made it sound like they were all family? Herself included?

No. Certainly not.

Of course he was grateful for food. What man wouldn't be? But he wanted "this place" for himself, and his family included the boys. Not Mary.

Hope took a deeper dive, dragging her appetite with it.

Did Hugh Hutton have plans of his own that involved getting the farm for himself at any cost?

~

Near suppertime, Hugh sent the boys and Barlow on ahead, then saddled his horse. He wasn't keen on leaving Mary by herself. It didn't set right with him, and he couldn't shed the worry over a third, unknown party having been there.

That person could be someone who planned to bid on the place. Would he do whatever possible to get it, including hurting someone who lived here?

Mary waved from the front porch like she had before, and Hugh rode around the house and headed for the ranch.

After chores were done and dark had settled, he returned beneath a hazy half-moon, riding up on the backside of the barn so Finley wouldn't raise a ruckus. He turned Shorty into a stall and spread a bedroll just inside the open barn door. With his Colt beneath the saddle skirt and his rifle tucked beside him, he dozed to the off-tune chorus of coyotes and distant thunder signaling an evening storm.

Sunup found him riding to the ranch through wet sage and cedar.

CHAPTER THIRTEEN

Sunlight peeked through the bedroom window and shone on scattered pools of water in the yard below. Morning had always lifted Mary's spirit, encouraging her to face with fresh strength what she had struggled with the day before. The lifelong tradition had blessedly followed her to Colorado, and she turned from the window with new resolve.

Her traveling suit settled on her hips a bit looser than it had when she left Pennsylvania, but it fit well enough—better than sweet Helen's dresses. Mary finished pinning her hair and looked one more time at the handgun she'd found in the bottom bureau drawer. It wasn't that she didn't know how to handle a gun, she'd simply never had her very own and never expected to. But she'd never expected to inherit her aunt and uncle's farm either, yet that had also happened, or was about to. She arranged a spare petticoat over the pistol and removed the box of shells before closing the drawer. Lifting the corner of the bed's mattress, she slid the box beneath it.

Aunt Bertie's Bible lay on the small nightstand, and Mary brushed a thin layer of dust from its black cover. Conscience urged her to spend a few minutes in its pages drawing strength from God's promises. But she was in a hurry this morning. Too much so to settle and drink in what she should. She'd read later this evening when there weren't so many issues roiling around in her head.

The narrow stairway down to the kitchen pressed against

her on the outside as her sense of urgency pressed from within. She desperately needed several things from town, personal and otherwise, as well as information, and with the means to get there on her own now, she intended to do just that. She patted her skirt pocket where the will bulged. Surely, it would be enough to cancel the auction. But how much were the taxes? And how much was due on the mortgage payments? Could she afford to pay them and still have money to ship her breeding stock and improve the barn with stanchions for milking?

Dousing those thoughts as she filled the coffee pot with fresh water, she focused on what she would do next in the house. A new cloth for the table would brighten the kitchen, and perhaps matching curtains. Glancing toward the window, she noticed a small paper sack on the sill. She'd not seen it the night before, nor the thin tubular package beside it.

She opened the sack and poured its dried contents onto the table, laughing as she unwrapped the long thin package. Hugh Hutton had indeed brought her everything she'd written on her list, including the peashooter she had hastily scribbled at the bottom. She'd be prepared for him the next time he showed up. Which would not be this morning.

She'd not mentioned that she planned to drive into Cañon City today for fear that he'd insist on accompanying her. Not that she couldn't resist his over-protective assertions. But if she was going to do things on her own, then she was going to do things on her own.

The unmistakable perfume of recent rain greeted her, and she dodged shallow pools on her way to the barn. Harnessing Sassy was as easy as working with Lettie, and she felt quite accomplished as she drove the black carriage down the farm's lane. Before the juncture of the road to town, she stopped and looked back. The house seemed not as forlorn, but that perhaps was due to personal ownership. Straightening the shutter that still hung askew from a front window and adding a fresh coat of paint would certainly improve appearances. And bulbs planted along the porch would brighten the yard next spring. The thought lifted her spirits.

The outbuildings were in fairly good condition, but the barn needed work, and she wanted to fill in that dreadful pit, not merely cover it. How would she do it all?

Rather than allow discouragement to root, Mary flicked the reins on Sassy's shiny back, eager to see Cañon City from a new perspective.

When she drove into town from the west end, horses and carriages shared Main Street with automobiles and bicyclists. The thoroughfare was wider than she remembered, and muddy from the recent rain. No doubt it churned with slush in the winter. But a spring rain symbolized hope for new life and fresh starts. Hers in particular.

She drew Sassy to a stop at the corner of Fourth Street and Main in front of a stately stone building with an impressive tower. Dropping the buggy weight and lifting a quick prayer for favor, she tugged on her sleeves and walked through the columned, corner entrance of the Fremont County Bank.

~

"Isn't my possession of the will proof enough?" A band of pain tightened around Mary's head, and she pressed her fingers against her temple.

"Miss? Are you all right?" The loan officer's voice tightened as well.

"Yes, I'm fine." Mary regarded the man, about her own age, hair slicked down, and a fine suit announcing his status. "This will should prove that I inherited the Dodson farm from my aunt and uncle, and I am here to pay the taxes and claim ownership of the property."

Again, he read through the document, and looked up at her with a frown. "You say you are—"

"Mary Agan McCrae, niece of Ernest and Bertha Dodson."

She reached across his desk and pointed to her name. "Right there."

"If you will excuse me one moment, please."

She watched the man scurry toward the back of the bank, where he knocked twice on a closed door before entering.

A balding gentlemen came out and preceded the younger man to his desk.

"Good morning, ma'am." He offered a smile and his hand in greeting. "I am William Rochester, president of the bank. And you are—?"

Did he not believe his employee? "Mary Agan McCrae, niece of Ernest and Bertha Dodson, Fremont County property owners recently deceased."

"Yes, well." He picked up the will and glanced over it. "This was drafted in Fremont County, I see, in 1903." Looking up with little change in expression, he added, "I was under the impression that the Dodson's had no descendants or heirs. When the taxes went unpaid, the property was put under lien. And of course mortgage payments are in arrears."

As if that changed the writing on the document he held. Mary's pulse increased, throbbing in her already painful temple. "The property was bequeathed to me."

"And you are from—?"

"Cumberland County, Pennsylvania."

"I see. We will need verification that you are who you say you are. Is there anyone in Cañon City who can substantiate your claim?"

"Excuse me?"

"I am sorry, ma'am, but we need proof of your identity. The property is under foreclosure and a tax lien and is to be auctioned off. When an heir appears contesting ownership, said heir has three years to redeem the property by paying overdue and current taxes. However, as I said, we would need proof of your identity. Preferably from a male next of kin."

She took the will from his hand, thanked him with as few

words as possible, and left. The distance to the buggy felt like miles rather than yards, and her jaw ached from clenching it. She didn't know what to think or feel—angry, insulted, cheated. She'd been so upset she hadn't verified what the mortgage debt was.

She must win the auction.

A new worry crawled up from the abyss. Could she even bid on the farm without a husband, brother, or father at her elbow? Apparently, property rights for women were as archaic in Colorado as they were in Pennsylvania. She'd expected better since Colorado had been an early supporter of women's suffrage. Women here may have had the right to vote earlier than most, but their rights of property ownership were no better off.

Mary marshaled her reserves and turned Sassy down Main Street. She could not afford to waste a trip to town and return home without the things she needed.

Home. The word cut through her like a hot knife through gravy. She'd thought it was home, but if it slipped through her fingers ...

Numb with new grief and frustration, she purchased the things she needed and drove to the farm in a daze. Chickens scattered before her as she entered the yard, and a crowing rooster jolted her into the present.

Where had they come from?

Hugh Hutton walked from the barn, and an odd sense of comradery washed over her, as if he were an ally, not a competitor. Tall and confident he was, yet caring, she knew. His expression bore relief that quickly gave way to a frown. He'd better not scold her for going into town. She was in no mood for another man telling her what she could and could not do.

He took Sassy by the bridle. "You were right."

She laid the reins over the bar and reached for the sack on the seat beside her, wary of his casual comment. "About what?"

Hugh took the sack with one hand and offered her the other

as she stepped down from the buggy. "About knowing how to harness a horse and drive yourself to town."

Biting back the pain she wanted to blurt out, she gave him a drole look. "You're serious."

He was fighting a grin and had no idea how lucky he was that he conquered it.

"Where are the boys?"

Disappointment swept his features at her question, but he went around and grabbed the box of groceries. "I sent them home. Helen had chores for 'em. They weren't happy about it." He shot her an appraising glance. "Wanted to see you."

She nearly cried and rolled her lips to keep from it. Those three little boys would have been a bright spot in her dreary day.

~

Hugh expected Mary to be pleased with herself for driving into town and getting what she needed. But she was sulled up and quiet. Rather than holding a spark, her green eyes were flat and dark, and they misted at mention of the boys. Had she gone to the bank? He itched to know everything she'd done, everything that she'd said or heard, but it wasn't any of his business.

Rather than charge ahead with her stores, he waited and followed her inside. It was *her* house, not his. He set the box and paper sack on the kitchen table, caught by the empty window sill. Maybe she was mad about that. Not used to his brand of humor.

"I'll fix us something to eat if you'll take care of the buggy and Sassy."

He heard the request tucked beneath her brave order. Something was up. Bad news about the farm, he'd guess. But what could make an open auction in a couple of months any worse than it was?

He lifted his hat. "Yes, ma—"

She stilled at the slip, watching him from the corner of her eye. Dadgummit, he needed something else to replace that

115

overused phrase. "I'm on it."

When he returned, she had pork n' beans on the table, with more canned peaches, what was left of the bread Helen had sent, and hot coffee.

"It's not much, because I haven't cooked anything." She rubbed her hands down an old apron, likely her aunt's.

"I've had worse."

She stared.

Blast it, he was short on manners as well as words. "What I mean is, it's good solid food, and that's what matters." He pulled a chair out and hung his hat on the back. She needed a hat tree or a set of antlers on the wall. Come to think of it, he had a rack mounted in the barn that would do just fine.

Watching the way she pushed at the knot of hair at her neck, then brushed strays from her face, he doubted she'd want something so *ranchy*. Jane used to primp like that, as if she cared what she looked like in front of him. Especially when something was on her mind and she didn't want to come right out and say it.

This time he was ready when Mary sat and folded her hands, and he offered a brief prayer of thanks. A little easier than last time.

He'd spoken his mind for so long that he didn't know to conversate his way around to what he wanted to ask her. She stared at her empty plate until he couldn't stand it any longer, so he scooped a pile of beans into the middle of it.

She looked up at him.

He locked on her, helpless to do anything about the pools rimming at her lashes.

She blinked and quickly swiped at a runaway tear.

"How 'bout some coffee?" A prize-winning line if he'd ever heard one. He escaped to the stove for the pot and returned with two cups.

"Thank you." She pressed her apron hem against her face. No napkins folded at the plates this time. She really was in a fix.

"I haven't been a very good hostess."

He set the pot on the stove and took his seat. "No need. I'm not a guest, Mary. I'm a friend."

He was winning the jackpot, surprising himself as well as her, and this time the tears tumbled out faster than she could catch them. His arms ached to do what any man worth his salt would do, but she wasn't his wife or his intended. Wasn't even his sister—thank goodness.

He reached across the table, palm up, hoping she'd give him her hand. "You can tell me what happened in town."

She didn't say a word.

As he drew his hand back, she quickly laid hers in it and held tight. A strong grip for a woman. Strong and warm like her, but trembling.

He closed his fingers around hers, wishing it was his arms around her instead.

"He doesn't believe I'm who I say I am."

What? "Who?"

"The banker. He said I need proof that I'm the niece of Bertha and Ernest Dodson. Somebody to verify it since I'm not from around here. Preferably a male relative."

Hugh never wanted to spit and swear more than he did right then, but he shoved down both impulses and held on to her hand.

"Don't you have a brother?"

She scoffed.

Not a good sign.

She pulled her hand away and held the apron to her face again, speaking from behind its thin curtain. "I'll wire him, but I wouldn't be surprised if he refused to answer, much less verify my identity."

When she lowered the apron, her steel had hardened. Shoulders back, chin up, she stared across the room and into the past. "He was not happy at my coming here. Said it was a harebrained notion he didn't approve."

Her voice softened and her gaze fell to the table. "He didn't even say goodbye."

Hugh understood sibling warfare, but he and Cale hadn't been that cold to Grace when she followed a wild hair and lit out with the Wild West Show.

Mary cut into her pie but didn't take a bite. "He's tried to marry me off to every bow-legged, single dairyman in Cumberland county ever since our father died last year. He wants to *improve the herd* without any regard to my wishes."

She said it as if it were a crime and part of him wanted to side with her brother. A very small part of him that he quickly throttled.

"Anyone else?"

Her shoulders relaxed and her face softened. "My best friend, Celia and her husband would vouch for me. But I don't know if that would count."

"Your birth should be on record at the county courthouse." He hoped. He really didn't know about such things, but he had to say something that would bring the light to her eyes. "Is there anything here in the house that your aunt and uncle left behind that might help? A letter? A picture—"

She drew a quick breath and looked as if she might choke. "A locket!"

"A locket?"

"A locket. I gave it to Aunt Bertie the year they moved out here. It has a miniature portrait of me inside. They never had children of their own, and I wanted her to have a remembrance of me."

"I don't know if that will help, but we'll hunt for it right after dinner."

The look she gave him nearly undid him, and he slugged down his coffee in self-defense.

"You would do that for me? You would help me prove who I am, even though you want this farm for yourself?"

Dadgummit, she could get under his skin and muddle his

brain. Stalling, he filled his mouth with beans to give his mind a minute. Of course he'd help her. He wasn't a complete heathen. Close, maybe, but not full-blooded.

CHAPTER FOURTEEN

Hugh Hutton was a man who backed up his words with action—Mary knew that for certain. But he was so contradictory. Gruff and detached one minute, kind and thoughtful the next. She'd never known anyone quite like him.

Leaving the dishes in the sink, she joined him in the parlor.

"Is there any place you don't want me digging into?" He stood in the center of the room and pivoted from wall to wall, taking in the clutter often found in homes of older people with no children to help them.

His perusal stopped on her, eyes darkening to an evening blue as he read her face—and heart, she feared. He must never suspect what feelings he prompted within her. But helping her prevent his purchase of land he wanted tore down nearly every barrier she had erected. It made no sense.

"No. You can look anywhere."

His brows rose and one side of his mouth tucked up.

"Except the bureau upstairs." Heat crawled her neck and she fingered her chignon, turning to make her own evaluation of the parlor. "I've already been through the chest of drawers and trunk upstairs. It makes sense that Aunt Bertie would keep the locket with other personal items but, of course, I didn't find it. I cannot imagine what she did with it."

Hugh cleared his throat, a nervous tic she'd come to recognize. She prepared herself for the unexpected. If that were even possible.

"Do you think she might have been wearing it when she was …"

Mary anticipated the next word and covered her mouth with both hands. The thought horrified her. But it *was* a possibility. However, it made no difference. She would not take any steps in that direction.

"I'm sorry." Hugh's words were gentle and deep. "Forget I mentioned it."

Clasping her hands against her chest, she drew a sharp breath. "I dare say, that is impossible to do, but thank you just the same."

He looked as if she'd whipped him, a startling observation of a man as grizzled as he. Would she ever begin to understand him?

"Well, this room is as good a place to start as any," he said.

They worked until dusk, when Mary lit a lamp in each room. But the light wasn't enough to brighten every corner or behind every knickknack, and she finally fell onto the settee with a sigh. "We've looked everywhere."

Hugh dropped his large frame onto a parlor chair, and she waited to hear it split beneath him. At the moment, she didn't care if it broke or not. The deeper they searched, the more discouraged she became. Where else could they look?

"I can't believe she wouldn't have kept it." Mary pushed sweaty hair from her temples. "We've searched the parlor, the kitchen, pantry, and dining room."

Hugh ran his hands through his hair, and Mary could easily imagine him putting his feet up on a footstool at the end of the day and relaxing. Or sitting on the back porch watching the sun sink behind the mountains. With her.

Dashing the thought, she returned to the parlor. "I'm going to look upstairs again. You are welcome to come and go through my aunt's trunk—maybe I missed something." Shocked by her own invitation, she chalked it up to fatigue. She was beyond caring about propriety, and that was a dangerous position to be in. However, she trusted Hugh.

Was that wise?

He went to the desk and ran his hand over the curved top. "I want to try this again. There may be a hidden compartment. A spot of mismatched wood that could reveal a secret drawer."

"Or another locked one."

He smiled, tired but determined.

Her emotions stirred in more than a neighborly way. "Go home, Hugh. You've been here all day, and the boys and Helen will be wondering what happened to you. I can start looking tomorrow morning when daylight lends a hand."

He stretched one arm across his chest and then the other, loosening a tight back, she suspected.

"I'll bring the boys tomorrow. They'll think it's a treasure hunt, and I'll have them look in the tack room, chicken coop, and shed."

Her expression drew a weary laugh from him. "I know. Your aunt wouldn't have hidden a special piece of jewelry in a shed, but the boys don't know that. It'll be an adventure for them."

He went to the kitchen, returned with his hat, and stopped by the front door. "We'll find it, Mary." His voice rolled out deep and warm, and suddenly Mary didn't want him to leave.

She wrapped her arms around herself, holding in a sense of loneliness. "Thank you for your help. You really don't have to spend every spare minute over here helping me look for an elusive piece of jewelry."

An idea shot through her like a dart and she cringed.

"What is it?" He took a step toward her, as if she were in danger, and she could feel the heat of him.

"What if she hocked it? What if they fell on hard times and needed the money? Is there a store in town where they could have pawned it?"

Concern creased his brow, and he shoved his hat on. "It's possible. Let's finish looking here, and if we don't find it, I can ride in and—"

She unwrapped her arms and fisted her hands on her hips.

Hugh raised one hand and reached for the door with the other. "All right, all right. *You* can ride in and ask Pete McKain if he has it."

His chuckle drew her own, blessed relief after a fruitless day, and she followed him out to the porch and picked up Finley. "Be careful riding home. It's nearly dark."

He came back to her, laid a hand on Finley's head, and bent close enough for his whisper to tickle her neck. "I could find my way home under a new moon with my eyes closed and my hands tied behind my back."

Tense and tingling from the nearness of him, she said the first thing that came to mind. "Humble, aren't you?"

His grin flashed, then he strode down the steps and across the yard to the barn.

Missing him more than she cared to admit, Mary dropped into one of the chairs on the porch and watched the barn until he emerged and rode past the house. He tipped his head in her direction and touched the brim of his hat before kicking Shorty into a lope.

She listened to the sound of the horse's hooves fade into the night, then tucked Finley beneath the porch, went inside, and locked the door.

She should have been locking her heart instead.

~

Hugh had felt Mary tense up when he bent close enough to kiss her. That was what he wanted to do, but his folks didn't raise no fool. A current had ebbed and flowed between him and Mary all day, but not in a bad way. More like the expectancy that stirs between a man and his wife.

Lord, help him.

Helen had supper on the table when he got in, and the boys were bubbling with questions. He promised they could go with him tomorrow if they behaved, and the three of them quickly fell into their choir-boy routine. He still didn't know where they learned to do that.

Too wakeful to sleep, he returned to the barn and double-checked the horses, corral poles, water buckets—anything he could think of. As it turned out, it *was* a new moon and darkness settled on the ranch and buildings like a heavy blanket. Even the stars seemed pale in the night sky, but for a glow on the eastern horizon.

The moon rising.

No. The moon wasn't rising. It wouldn't show all night.

Quicker than he could think to tell Helen, he saddled Shorty and rode hell-bent for the Dodson farm. Guilt spurred him across the open range. He shouldn't have left Mary alone. He should have stayed or gone back after chores like he had before.

Fire haloed the sky, rising over the barn, and he was off the gelding before it came to a complete stop behind the house. He kicked the kitchen door open and ran up the stairs to Mary's bedroom. She wasn't there, and a perfect view of the barn through the window confirmed his worst fears of where he'd find her.

Plunging down the stairs and out the front door, he ran for the robed figure frantically working the corral pump and shoving buckets beneath the flow. As she hefted one and headed toward the barn, Hugh came in behind her and wrapped an arm around her waist, whirling her away from the roaring flames. The barn was hopeless. Old, dry, and brittle, it raged as timbers cracked and fell, scattering sparks and embers. How could she possibly think she could save it?

Mary fought like a wild cat, screaming at him to put her down and help her with the buckets.

He set her on her feet but turned her into him and held her

against his chest, determined she wouldn't escape. He couldn't lose her. Hang the farm, the barn, and every blade of grass on the blasted property. He'd lost one good woman, and he wasn't about to lose another.

She pushed against him, and the glow of the flames lit her face as she watched in horror, tears washing tracks down her sooty cheeks. When she weakened and went slack, he scooped her into his arms and carried her to the house.

Far enough away from the barn that they were safe, he sat in a porch chair and held Mary on his lap. She didn't resist him, but watched as the fire spread to the corral, consumed the chicken coop and woodshed, and everything in its path. Each building lit a new torch in the black night. Fire fingered into the grass that was green with spring moisture and soon burned itself out, embers winking into darkness. The air was heavy with smoke and ash, and the taste settled on his tongue.

A total loss.

Mary turned her face into his chest and her voice broke with weeping. "Sas-sy."

His chest tightened at the thought of the old mare burning to death. Horses feared fire more than cougars, and he'd seen their white-eyed panic before. "Was she in a stall?"

Mary bobbed her head and wept harder.

He pulled her closer and kissed the top of her head, tasting smoke and soot. Mary McCrae was worth more to him than a whole band of mares, and a wild memory raced through his head. Something his pa had once said about his mother being more valuable than rubies.

A whimper came from beneath the porch, and Mary raised her head. "Finley?" She looked at Hugh, eyes round with fear and regret. "I forgot all about her. Is she all right?"

Hugh whistled for the pup. She slunk from beneath the front steps and crawled up on the porch, tail tucked.

"Oh, you poor dear." Mary tilted in her reach for the dog,

and Hugh circled her waist. She was soft and warm, not trussed up like she'd been when he lifted her out of the pit. In spite of the night's disaster, his mind raced at future possibilities of holding her in his arms in a different setting.

He shook off the image and focused on the barn and keeping Mary upright while she coddled the dog. He watched until the last timber fell, and by dawn, the barn was a pile of smoldering rubble. The pup slept at his feet and Mary in his arms, her breathing even with an occasional quick intake, as if she saw the fire in her dreams.

He prayed that wasn't the case. She'd lost nearly everything that mattered to her, but losing hope would be the worst. He knew how that felt, and it made a body not want to live.

Mary had to live. She had to laugh and smile and argue with him again.

As sunlight spread over the smoldering destruction, a familiar whicker came from the opposite end of the porch. Hugh had figured Shorty had taken off for the ranch and it'd be a long walk home without Sassy and the buggy. But the gelding walked around the corner dragging his reins, followed by a limping, burn-scarred mare with pink flesh showing on her back. Deep gashes scored her front legs.

He must have flinched in surprise, for Mary jerked awake and pushed herself upright, blinking at him as if she'd seen a ghost.

"What—what are you—what am I ..."

He smoothed hair off her soot-covered face, now red, her lips swollen. She'd gotten too close to the flames, and the more he checked her over, the more damage he saw. Her robe and gown were burned off at the knees, her legs scratched and bleeding.

Finley yipped.

"Look at that," he said, hoping the sight would be a relief for the weary woman in his arms. "Sassy put up a fight and it looks like she won."

Mary turned, and at the sight of the horses, attempted to stand. She fell to her knees with a sharp cry, and he saw the bottoms of her blistered feet.

Again he scooped her into his arms. "I'm taking you home so Helen can look at those burns. Sassy will follow us and so will Finley. Don't you worry."

He clucked Shorty over to the steps, gripped Mary tighter with his right arm, then grabbed the reins and pulled the two of them into the saddle. It was a trick holding her, but he'd break his arm before he'd let her fall.

He'd picked this woman up once before and carried her to safety. If he had his way, she'd not be endangered again.

The sun was well above the horizon as they came into the yard at a slow walk. The boys and their pup ran out to greet them, a hundred questions and hugs for Finley. Judging by the shocked looks that quickly took over, he and Mary must be a sight.

"Jay, get a can of grain and coax Sassy into the round corral. Go easy with her. She's hurtin' and you don't want to spook her. Don't touch her."

"Yes, Pa."

"Kip, hold the reins, and after I get down, see to Shorty. Brush him good and throw him some hay in a stall. Ty, come over and give me a hand with Miss Mary. Help me hold her as I get down."

He shot a look at Mary to see if she'd willingly cooperate, but she merely stared at him.

He was nearly in shock himself.

Helen joined them with a quilt, and covered Mary as he and Ty got her down. Hugh carried her through the front door Helen had swung open, and into Cale's old room again. The woman had evidently been watching from a window, for the sheets were turned back and two pillows perched at the head of the bed. She was a saint.

The saint returned with a basin of water and cloths. "You look like you've been through a fire. Smell like it too." Setting the basin on the nightstand, she stepped between Hugh and the bed, his signal to leave.

"You're right. The Dodsons' barn burned to the ground. When I got there last night, Mary was trying to douse the flames with a bucket of water."

Helen tsked and wagged her head as she set to work on the most obvious burns and blisters. "She's a fighter, I'll give her that."

Mary just lay there. No resistance, no cry of pain. Nothing.

She was in good hands. He pulled the chair over by the door and turned it sideways to give them privacy.

But he couldn't bring himself to leave her.

CHAPTER FIFTEEN

"**S**omething's going on and I intend to find out what." Hugh sat at his brother and sister-in-law's kitchen table, slugging down his fourth cup of coffee, doing what he didn't want to do—leave Mary's side. But he had to, for her sake.

Cale was drinking nearly as much, and Ella—big as a barn—was keeping their cups full.

Hugh would be a lot more comfortable if Ella was at the ranch house with Helen. Her time had to be close. Or else she was expecting twins.

He kept his thoughts to himself, determined to be more mannerly, but it wasn't easy. Lately, nothing had been easy, and this affair with the Dodson place had consumed his brain the same way the fire consumed the barn.

"I was in that barn yesterday morning and evening. Nothing was out of the ordinary, and there was no lightning last night." His brother knew that—he wasn't blind or stupid—but Hugh had to say it anyway. "Somebody wants that farm more than I did and is getting mighty close to doing whatever it takes to get it."

Cale held his cup out to Ella for a refill. "But why? There's got to be more to it than good grazing land." He stopped with the cup halfway to his mouth and gave Hugh a hard look. "What do you mean by 'more than I *did*'? Have you changed your mind about extending our acreage?"

Hugh shifted in his seat, not ready to expose himself just yet. But if Cale read him like he had since they were Kip's age, he already knew. Asking was merely Cale's way of dragging out the torment.

"I'll get into that later. Right now I want to cover every foot of that farm and see what we've missed. The Dodsons may have found something we haven't and didn't mention it to anyone. Something that wasn't even in the will."

"Will?" Cale and Ella said at the same time.

Dadgummit. "All right, you might as well know. The Dodsons left a will naming Mary as heir to their property. They had it written up nine years ago."

"And you know this how?" Ella pushed one hand into her lower back and laid the other on the table as support when she leaned in closer.

Hiding was hopeless.

"I read it. Found it one day when I was looking through a desk in the parlor. I figured the place was nearly ours anyway. After Mary showed up, and then *healed* up from her fall in that blasted pit—that's another thing that ain't right—I gave it to her. She had no idea. And that's not all."

"What?" Again, Cale and Ella spoke as one. Danged if they didn't sound like Hugh's boys.

"She took the will to the bank, and they said she had to prove who she is since she's not from around here. She has a brother in Pennsylvania who may help her—another story for later—but there's a locket she gave her aunt when they moved out here that might serve as proof. Has Mary's picture in it. We tore the house apart looking for it yesterday and it's nowhere."

Ella finally sat down and took a load off Hugh's mind.

"This is sounding more and more like a dime novel," she said.

Cale cut her a side glance. "You read dime novels?"

Ella waved him off, then squeezed his arm in a tender way.

Made Hugh hurt all over again, and he pulled in a breath. "Will you ride with me?"

Cale covered Ella's hand on his arm, and his face softened as he considered her. "I will if Ella goes down and stays with Helen while we're gone."

"It won't take more than a day," Hugh said. "I've never heard of gold in these parts. No caves or mines, and I don't think the streams are worth panning."

"No, I doubt it's gold. We're not on the right side of the mountain for that. But there's something. Barns don't burn down for no reason."

"And pits don't open up on their own."

Cale nodded. "I'll help you find it, and while we're huntin', you can tell me more about *than I did*." His grin said he meant every word equally.

"We can start at the northwest corner and work our way from there. I'll come over tomorrow morning and we can head out from here."

Cale shook his head. "No need. I'll drive Ella down to the ranch house, with Doc in tow, and we can set out then. Won't be early." He leaned over and planted a kiss on Ella's cheek as if Hugh wasn't sitting across the table from them. "But it won't be late either. Ask Helen if she'll pack dinner for us."

"She will, you can count on it."

Ella pushed up from her chair, and it seemed more effort than it should. "I'll go gather some things. It may take me the rest of the day, as slow as I'm moving."

She waddled out of the kitchen and into their bedroom not more than ten steps away.

Hugh leaned across the table and spoke low. "You sure she's all right with you leaving? Looks like she's gonna drop a foal any minute. No offense."

Cale chuckled and looked off in the direction his wife had gone. "She swears it's not her time, but I wonder about it like you. If she's with Helen, she'll be better off than she is here with me."

The comment blew through Hugh's stomach as if he'd been gut shot.

Cale saw it. "I'm sorry, brother. I didn't mean it like that." His face blanched with regret over his off-handed remark.

Hugh stood and tugged his hat on. "Don't worry about it. I happen to agree with you. I'll see you tomorrow."

Bile churned into Hugh's gullet as he rode down the hill toward the ranch house. When Jane's time had come with Kip, Hugh had been no help. Helen wasn't there with them in those days, but it was Jane's third birthing. They'd both thought everything would be fine.

It wasn't.

Halfway to the barn, he bailed off Shorty as the bile rose. It burned his throat on the way out the same way the memories burned through his heart.

~

"I seem to remember being in this position once before."

She sounded far away, even to herself. Detached, though she *did* remember. It had been her introduction to the Hutton family—one preceded by disappointment, shock, and pain. Was a pattern forming? Would it be like this forever?

Helen's lips smiled, but not her eyes, as she applied cold, wet rags to Mary's legs for the second time that morning. "You look like you've been dunked in scalding water."

"I *feel* like I've been scalded."

Helen gently patted Mary's skin dry, then applied whipped egg whites to the reddest areas as well as the bottoms of her feet. "I've got some petroleum jelly here that I want you to rub on your face. Only don't rub it. Smooth it on gently."

She handed Mary a small glass jar with the cork removed.

Mary knew the amazing powers of the so-called jelly, and had used it on cows' udders, along with Bag Balm. At least Helen hadn't given her that for her face!

Finished with her ministrations, Helen leaned back in her chair, wiping her hands on her ever-present apron, the patience of Job in her expression.

Mary's feet were so tender, she knew she couldn't jump up and walk out of the room, and after all of Helen's care over the last two weeks, she could at least cure the woman's curiosity.

"You're very kind, Helen. Thank you for taking such good care of me. Again."

"Pshaw." Helen swatted the air but didn't budge. "It's life on a cattle ranch. You tend to what comes up."

Mary looked out the window, seeing instead what had happened the night before. "I have a good view of the barn from my bedroom window upstairs. Faint light through the open doors made me think Hugh had decided to stay again."

A wave of embarrassment rolled through her as she realized the candor of her explanation. She glanced at Helen, hoping the woman didn't think her loose and forward. Nor did she want to paint Hugh in a bad light. But he had stayed in the barn on at least two occasions that Mary knew of.

"I know. I know that boy—man, I should say. But don't you worry. Yes, he spent a couple of nights at your place, sleeping in the barn. He worries about you over there all by yourself. Bad as an old hen, I tell you. But I'd expect nothing less from him. He's rough on the outside, but inside he's pure puddin'."

Mary felt a familiar warmth spread through her chest. It came with increasing frequency when she considered Hugh Hutton, and Helen's unconventional acceptance of the unconventional emboldened Mary to continue.

"Rather than dressing as I should have, I pulled on my robe and went downstairs, determined to scold him away. I don't need a baby sitter."

"Ha!" Helen's full girth bounced when she laughed. "Baby's got nothin' to do with it, honey. Go on."

"When I got to the barn, Hugh and his bedroll were not by the door—I'd seen the outline of where he'd slept on the mornings he'd left early, so I knew where to look." To hear the story out loud made Mary even more uncomfortable. What would Lewis think of her wild ways?

"I looked for Shorty, and he wasn't in a stall. Only Sassy was there." She dropped her head and whispered, "I should have turned her out."

"But you didn't know," Helen offered. "Don't torture yourself over something you couldn't have prevented and can't undo."

Mary picked up the glass of water on the nightstand and took a drink. "The light grew and as it grew, it flickered. I knew immediately what was happening and could think only of dousing the flames. I grabbed two pails and ran to the pump. The fire was in the corner stall at the back of the barn. I poured several buckets of water over it, but it wouldn't go out. It spread, as if following a path, and quickly climbed the wall."

Mary's breath caught and she closed her eyes against the vision.

Helen touched her arm. "You don't have to tell me anymore, honey. Just rest for a while. You can tell us later."

Mary set the glass on the stand and shook her head. "I kept filling the buckets. They got heavier and heavier, and the flames crawled higher and spread across the hay loft. I couldn't stop it—I couldn't stop it."

She fell against the pillows at her back, breathless. "Then Hugh was there, whirling me away from the flames. He wouldn't let go but backed us away from the barn, and we stood there watching it burn."

She fought to hold in the sobs.

Helen stood over her and smoothed her hair. "Sleep, child. Give yourself a chance to rest. Everything will be all right. It always is."

The bedroom door clicked shut, and Mary let the tears have their way. How could anything be all right ever again? Her barn was gone—the barn her aunt and uncle had given her. She'd endangered Sassy by not opening her stall door, and now she was in the Hutton home once again, unable to even stand. How much more could she take? How many more obstacles would she meet?

She had barely enough money to pay the taxes on the farm and must also pay the mortgage. But if she couldn't prove who she was and the farm went to auction, that could drive the price even higher.

And her breeding stock. Now she had no place for them even if she got the farm.

Do not despair. The words rose from a deep place in her soul, but the image of the burning barn flared against them. Hope for a fresh start, for her own home and farm, was fading, overpowered by glaring destruction.

CHAPTER SIXTEEN

Riding two square miles was not a major undertaking—unless you rode every foot of it and then some, searching bushes, rocks, and draws for anything out of the ordinary.

"Look for what doesn't fit," Hugh told his brother.

"You mean that needle in the haystack?"

Hugh snorted. Trouble was, everything fit, from scrub oak and sagebrush to creek-hugging cottonwoods. Rock outcroppings peppered the country, buttressing hills with craggy, wind-twisted cedars. Tall, straight pines cloaked the high points, and lush grass covered the lower parks. It was all there—everything a rancher could want in a mere twelve hundred acres, and most of it was prime grazing land.

Cale pulled up near a stream that ran out from a low rock face and around the edge of a meadow.

Hugh joined him. "This is good a place as any." He pushed his hat back and wiped his forehead with his sleeve.

"What did Helen put in that bag?"

Hugh stepped down and dropped Shorty's reins, then untied the flour sack and found a level spot. "We're about to find out."

They made quick work of beans and cornbread, washing it down with water from their canteens.

"No pie?" Cale looked like a hurt pup.

"You're kiddin' me," Hugh poked. "Does Ella serve you pie every day of the week?"

Cale grabbed the bag. "What's it to you if she does?"

Hugh laughed, leaned back on his elbows, and stretched his legs.

"You were holdin' out on me!" Cale tossed him a brown-paper bundle and opened one for himself. "Cookies."

"You're twelve, you know that?" Hugh sat up and unwrapped his bundle.

"So are you, old man." Cale shoved two gingersnaps into his mouth whole.

"By a minute." Hugh followed suit.

Fidgety, he stood and stretched his back. "We've got about six hours of daylight left, and we're only halfway through. I want to cover as much ground as we can."

"Not until you fess up about not wantin' this place for the Rafter-H."

Hugh dropped to his boot heels and pulled up a grass shoot. "It's not that I don't want it. I do. But it's Mary's. It's all she has of her kin, and they left it fair and legal to her. I can't bid against her at the auction. It wouldn't be right."

Cale considered him a long minute, finishing off his cookies. "You've changed. Time was, you wouldn't have cared."

Hugh's grit rose at the accusation, but he knew his brother was right. He'd soured after Jane's death. Blamed God. Blamed himself. Blamed everything he could blame. But the boys had somehow helped keep him going. And the Rafter-H gave him a sense of purpose. And he didn't like admitting it, but seeing Ella Canaday come along last year and lead Cale off to matrimony also had an effect on him.

Then Mary showed up and so did a second chance.

Not at first, but in time.

"I still want the grass, but that's all. We don't need a house and orchards and everything else. We've got enough to do taking care of what we already have. What we need is the grass. And I'm going to offer to lease it from Mary."

"As in pay her?" Cale stood and wiped crumbs off his mouth.

"If we pay her up front for grazing rights, it should give her enough to outbid everyone else at the auction—if she doesn't end up proving she's the rightful owner first. But either way, she could keep the land and we could keep the grass."

Cale took his hat off and scrubbed his scalp. "You're full of surprises, but I like it." He resettled his hat. "And I think you like Mary McCrae."

Hugh wasn't about to get into that, and he tied the poke closed and grabbed his canteen. "Toss me yours and I'll go fill it."

At the stream, he uncapped a canteen, knelt by the trickle, and leaned over. "Cale."

"Having trouble, big brother?"

"Quit your jawing and come over here."

Cale joined him and took the other canteen.

Hugh leaned over the stream again, then turned his head to look at his brother. "Does this water smell funny to you?"

Cale sobered immediately and leaned down. He lifted a handful to his mouth, then spit it out. "Tastes oily."

"Smells that way too."

They sat back on their haunches, looked at each other and then to the stream that rippled over smooth stones and around saplings.

Hugh walked upstream toward a low wall of granite topped with scrub and sagebrush, Cale right behind him. About a hundred feet from the rock face, a low spot opened on the other side of the stream. A dark low spot, as if something other than water was filling the hole.

Cale's voice dropped. "You thinkin' what I'm thinkin'?"

"Yup. We found it."

They gathered the horses and rode around on top of the rockface, where they could get a good lay of the land. The stream fed farther down into Four Mile Creek that curved off to the south east. It ran past the old Oil Spring where Gabriel Bowen had discovered an oil seep some fifty years ago. Men had scoured the area ever since, looking for their own pot of black gold. Wells had been drilled in the oil fields around Florence, east of Cañon City, but up in this country, every well drilled had gone dry.

Did old man Dodson know about the seep? Was that why he'd bought a second section of land when he didn't own a single cow, much less a herd?

Cale jerked Hugh from the questions stampeding through his head. "Somebody else knows about this."

Hugh threw him a dark look. "You're speaking truth. And I intend to find out who it is."

"And how are you going to do that without letting the whole town know?"

"I'll figure something out."

On their way home, they cut through an apple orchard close to the house and stopped abruptly at the west end. Two grave markers took the place where a tree should have been.

"If that don't beat all." Cale shook his head.

"Mary will be glad to know where they are." Hugh heeled Shorty into a lope and they rode home silently, each lost in their own thoughts.

Hugh knew if word got around, it would shoot the auction sky high. Everybody would bid on this land whether they could afford it or not. If Mary could prove it was rightfully hers, she'd end up with enough money to build ten barns. And a new house.

He scrubbed his face, dragging such thoughts from his head. He was getting way ahead of himself. Ahead of everything.

At least Cale had agreed with him about leasing the land. Hugh couldn't bid on the land and feel right about it. Weren't people held accountable for what they knew?

That sword cut both ways, because he intended to hold the mysterious *someone* accountable for nearly killing Mary—twice. His brother was right. Somebody knew, and the sooner they discovered who it was, the safer Mary would be.

They didn't make it to the barn before Hugh's boys ran out

to meet them, jumping up and down and waving. Kip and their pup ran ahead of them all, Finley in his arms.

"Uncle Cale, Uncle Cale! Miss Ella's birthin' a baby!"

~

Helen had given Mary two pairs of Hugh's socks, and she'd pulled them onto her tender feet, cinched herself for the second time into one of Helen's dresses, and then stripped her own bedding. Ella would not be having her baby in Hugh's room, and Mary refused to let Helen give up her bed. This was the only option, in Mary's opinion, and it was something she could *do*.

She had not seen a woman give birth, but she'd helped plenty of first-year heifers. Only one had carried twins, but she was huge, and Mary suspected the same condition in Ella who, for lack of a more delicate description, was as big as a cow.

"Don't push yet," Helen said. Seated at the foot of the bed, she coaxed Ella who had braced her feet against the footboard, knees high and draped.

Mary held her left hand—rather, Ella squeezed the life out of Mary's hand while Mary squeezed water from rags with the other and arranged them across Ella's forehead.

"I can't not push. I *have* to push!"

"Pant," Helen commanded, perspiring as much as poor Ella. "Pant like a dog. A tired dog. A thirsty dog. *Pant*, I tell you."

Ella closed her eyes and groaned.

Mary swabbed the young woman's sweating forehead, thankful they weren't in the heat of summer.

"It won't be long now," Helen said with remarkable restraint. "I see the baby's head, but it's not quite time. Keep panting."

Mary started to pant herself, and Ella looked at her, frowning. "I can't help it, Ella. Pant with me. We'll both pant."

A moment later, Ella arched off the bed with a guttural cry, nearly crushing Mary's hand.

"Push!" Helen cried.

In two shakes of a calf's tail, the baby gushed into her waiting hands, and that fast, a new little human entered the world.

Mary blinked, trying to keep her vision clear.

"Hand me the dry cloths," Helen ordered.

Ella's hand had relaxed enough for Mary to withdraw her own that was numb and nearly useless. She passed cloths, towels, and string to Helen. Next came scissors and carbolic acid that Helen had set on the nightstand.

"Pour the acid over the scissors, both sides. Hold them over that extra pan as you do, but don't dry them. After I tie off the cord, hand them to me." She looked at Mary. "Unless you'd like to do the honors."

Mary's lungs locked, and she stared at Helen.

"Well, make up your mind. We can't wait all day."

"Yes—yes, I will." She sterilized the scissors as instructed and went to the foot of the bed.

Helen had tied string in two places on the pulsing cord and pointed between them. "Cut here."

Mary told herself this was no different than pulling a calf, except it was. Very different. Steeling herself against the intensity of the situation, she placed the scissors and snipped. The baby didn't cry out. Ella didn't either.

But she arched off the bed again, groping for Mary's hand.

"Lord, help us." Helen quickly wrapped the babe in a towel and shoved it into Mary's arms. "Here, hold him."

Him? Mary held the precious child up so Ella could see him, but Ella's eyes were screwed tighter than the lid on a canning jar, and she screamed.

As if recognizing his mother's voice, the baby squalled—a good sign, Mary knew. So tiny his cry compared to his mother's that could have moved a mountain.

Mary watched Helen's face, seeing the exact second the next baby came.

"Sterilize these again." She passed the scissors to Mary, eyes on Ella who had gone suddenly still.

Mary cupped the babe in her arm, held the scissors with that hand, and poured the acid over them as Helen finished tying the second knot.

No invitation this time. Helen simply snipped the cord, wrapped the second child, and handed it to Mary. Then she took the remaining towels and pressed them against Ella, all the time watching her face.

"Is everything all right?" A babe in each arm, Mary couldn't help but remember how Helen had made that very promise to her the day before, and she prayed desperately that everything *would* be all right for this mother and her babies. *Oh God, please, please make this right.*

Helen moved to Ella's side, gently lowering her draped legs, then feeling for her pulse. A gush of air escaped from Helen's lungs, and her shoulders slumped in relief. With the back of her hand, she swiped her forehead, then squeezed out the rag Mary had used earlier and laid it on Ella's forehead.

She reached for the second baby. "Here, let me have her. You go bring the kettle in and add some hot water to this basin. Then get some fresh cloths. You'll find them next to the sink, second drawer down."

Her. A boy and a girl. Mary's eyes watered as she made her way through the dining room and into the kitchen, where she found Hugh and Cale sitting at the kitchen table, scared stiff as statues.

Cale shot from his chair, staring at the bundle in Mary's arms.

A second cry came from the bedroom, and Hugh jumped up.

"Congratulations, Cale. Meet your son. Your daughter is in the next room."

He took the baby in his big hands, dwarfing it against his chest, and a smile broke out on his face that would be the end of Mary if she didn't look away.

"Hugh," she said, laying her hand on his arm. "You are an

uncle. Twice."

He looked at her as if she were a miracle worker, but the miracle had taken place without her doing a thing. She gave his arm a light squeeze, then grabbed the kettle from the stove and escaped before she started blubbering at the sight of a grown man standing in the kitchen like a little orphan boy.

CHAPTER SEVENTEEN

When last Hugh had seen Cale, his brother's buttons were about to pop off his shirt.

Hugh beat a trail outside and just kept walking. Past the corrals, the barn, through the pasture poles and out into the open meadow where he could fall if the rope cinching his chest finally cut off his air.

He was happy for his brother, and proud—near proud as he'd been when his boys were born. But the process had worn him down, and his hands ached at clenching them for so long. Fear had raked him like a bronc rider on a rank horse. What if the baby didn't come right? What if Ella needed a doctor? What if Helen couldn't handle things?

It was Jane all over again. *What-if* was nearly the spurred-hide death of him.

He'd left the kitchen without his hat, and he ran both hands through his sweaty hair as he reached the end of the pasture. A buck and rail fence cut off the west side, and he straddled a low pole, heaving a long sigh. A whipped dog had more strength.

He thought of the grizzly he and Cale had dragged out of the pasture last summer, nearly as big as the wagon they'd dragged it into. It had tormented cattlemen for more than a year. Now it was a prop for the Selig Polyscope movie folks who'd talked him and Cale into selling the carcass.

But what Hugh had just been through in the kitchen—sitting by helpless as a kitten, listening to a woman's muffled groans and then screams—was worse than dragging ten bears from the pasture.

His insides were wore clean out.

In the late afternoon light, the sky was a clear blue dome over the country. He looked slowly around at the ranch his folks had left him, his brother, and sister. A good stout barn and house. Outbuildings, corrals, solid fences. Water.

Raising beeves was supposed to be easy. Turn 'em out, watch 'em get fat, and haul 'em to market—if a grizzly, winter storms, summer drought, or rustlers didn't get 'em first.

He spit.

Nothing came easy. Pa had told him and Cale that, but young bucks don't listen to their fathers like they should. They gotta learn things the hard way. He prayed his boys would be smarter than that.

There he was, thinkin' about praying again. He pulled in a deep breath of mountain pine and sweet grass. He'd prayed more in the last couple of weeks than in the last seven years, and most of those prayers had to do with females of one sort or another.

Suddenly weary, he stretched out near the crossed supports of the buck and rail fence and covered his eyes with one arm. He was too tired to walk back. He'd lie there for a bit, taking in the scent of life around him.

An owl hoot jerked him awake and he sat up, hitting his head on a pole. He swallowed a swear word and pulled himself to his feet, looking around at dusk lying on the ranch just waiting to be tucked in. Another owl answered the first call, and he turned for the house, where a yellow glow warmed the windows.

That house had been his home since he was born, and he'd figured he'd grow old with Jane there. Get their portraits made for the dining room wall.

That wouldn't be happening.

As he slid between the corral poles, he saw someone coming through the settling dark, someone in a skirt, moving slow. *Mary.*

He'd had a lot of thoughts about Mary McCrae lately. Homing thoughts, but after today's reminder of what childbirth entailed, he wasn't so sure he wanted to risk it again. She was a tiny thing, barely came up to his chin. But she came all the way up to his heart, and he didn't know how he was going to reconcile the two.

"Hugh." She stopped a few paces off and folded her arms against her waist. "I wondered where you'd gone."

Her voice was soft as the evening. No edge. No scold. He walked up close enough to see real concern on her face, but before he could do or say anything, she moved into him and wrapped her arms around his waist.

She felt good and fit him, tailor-made.

"I'd guess you're thinking about the boys' mother."

Reflexively, he stepped back, unable to withstand the heat of her words against his chest.

She gathered her apron and folded it around her hands but didn't stop talking. "And I'd guess that's why you have a hard time praying."

Dang, if she didn't know how to hit hard.

"I'm so sorry."

Her whisper nearly doubled him over, and words fell that he never intended to say out loud. "I begged God not to take Jane. But He did anyway."

"Maybe God didn't take her."

His lungs seized. How could Mary say such a thing? She didn't know anything about it.

"Maybe He *received* her."

The idea struck dead center, fissuring through his chest and spreading into his brain. She could be right, but he needed time to consider the new perspective, and now wasn't that time.

He couldn't do this. He couldn't let Mary see his pain, his weakness. What kind of man showed his bloody wounds to a woman he cared for?

He turned the light on her. "What are you doing out here with those blistered feet of yours?"

She cocked her head to the side, as if wondering either why he changed the subject or why he sounded so dang tight and high-pitched. But she didn't answer him. Just folded her hand into his and turned for the house.

"Supper's on, and Helen and the boys are waiting."

~

Mary's feet were tender all right, but she wasn't about to let Hugh know it. Nor was she about to complain, not after what she'd witnessed today.

While he stopped at the washstand, she went inside, a sense of home engulfing her with the aroma of fresh coffee and a rich stew. The boys sat at the table like ants on a sugar cube, and Helen dished up a small bowl for each one.

"You can sit by me," Kip offered, suffering kicks from his brothers across the table. He sat board straight, glaring at them. Helen shook her head as if she didn't have the strength to cuff them.

Mary helped set the bowls around. "Thank you, Kip. I'm so pleased to see all of you waiting like perfect gentlemen."

Ty and Jay hung their heads, not looking up until their father came in.

Hugh's hair was wet and slicked back, his sleeves were rolled up, and water spots dotted the front of his blue shirt. The sight of him shamed her for speaking so boldly, for *acting* so bold, and she hoped the flush she felt in her cheeks would be blamed on the cook stove. It was almost too warm an evening to serve hot food, but Helen had cooked for this family long enough to know what they needed and liked.

After everyone was seated, Hugh held out his hands. Sitting to his right, she took his and then Kip's. It was the first time she'd seen Hugh do such a thing, and she prayed her hand held steady.

The customary throat-clearing followed. His boys would probably grow up thinking it was the preamble to saying grace.

"Thank You, Lord, for Your help today, for the two healthy babes and for keeping Ella safe." His voice cracked, and Mary squeezed his hand, regretting it immediately.

"Thank You for this food and Helen and Miss Mary's help today. Amen."

As she attempted to withdraw her hand, he held it fast and tightened his fingers briefly, as if in answer to her gesture. If only she could hide from the probing questions of curious little boys.

"You can sleep in the barn tonight."

Helen's remark stopped everyone mid-bite, and five pairs of eyes looked her way. To whom was she speaking?

"Really?" Jay said.

"Really."

Well, that answered that question.

"Your dad's going to take your room, and Miss Mary will sleep in his. Ella and Cale are staying here tonight."

Of course they would, but Mary was the newcomer, the uninvited guest. She should be sleeping in the barn.

"You know, boys, my brother and I used to sleep in our papa's barn when we were your age, and the cats would climb into the loft and purr themselves and us to sleep."

Breathing in through her nose, she revisited the innocent childhood days when Lewis was more a friend than an overlord. "It smelled *so* good up there. Like sweet hay and milk."

"Not manure?"

Jay snorted and stew sprayed his bowl.

"Yeeeeeew!" Ty scooted as far away as he could, and Helen thumped him on the head.

Kip looked about to cry, and Mary couldn't let that happen. "Yes, manure too, Kip, but in the loft, the smell of hay was stronger."

Hugh kept his head down, but she saw the smile that

interfered with his chewing. So different a reaction. A few days ago he would have snapped his boys' heads off with a hard rebuke.

After supper, he disappeared with his sons, helping them get settled in the barn while Helen and Mary washed dishes.

"You were a big help today, and I thank you for it, especially with two babies." Helen folded her apron and laid it over a chair.

"You are most welcome." Mary didn't feel like she'd done much, but she supposed an extra pair of arms did help somewhat.

"I imagine you've been in on birthings before—bovine or otherwise."

Mary sensed the statement was more of a question intended to draw her out. "Yes, a few first-year heifers, though only one set of twins."

Hugh came inside but left the door open with only the screen in place.

Helen squared herself. "Well, I do believe I'll turn in early. It's been quite a day." She made a show of checking the kitchen, then patted her hands on the dishtowel lying on the counter. "Blow out the lamp when you're done, please, Mary. Good night."

Immediately the pressure in the room changed. Mary looked at the lamp, and Hugh cleared his throat again.

"If you have a few minutes, I need to talk to you." He indicated her chair from supper.

She shouldn't have said—or done—what she did outside. How forward to wrap her arms around him like that and prescribe what lay behind his hesitancy at prayer. But helping in the rigors of childbirth had shifted something inside her. Given her a deep sense of home and longing, and the desire to comfort a man she knew was hurting.

But squeezing his hand during prayer. What had she been thinking?

"Would you like a cup of coffee? It won't take much to

warm it up."

He ran a hand over his jaw and glanced at the stove, clearly as nervous as she.

With heat flooding her veins, she turned away from him so he couldn't see her humiliation.

"Sure. That'd be good." His chair scraped the wooden floor as he sat.

She added a few pieces of kindling, gathered two cups, and prayed a hole would open in the floor. She felt his eyes following her every move and ridiculed herself for such foolishness. How could she feel such a thing? But she did, and it made her jittery as a June bug.

He went to the cupboards that ran along the opposite kitchen wall, brought out a silver sugar bowl she'd not seen, and set it on the table before retaking his seat.

He was doing it again—showing another side of himself. If it weren't for the gray at his temples and the fact that she'd heard Cale talking to Ella in the bedroom, she'd wonder which twin was here with her.

More than nervous when she brought the filled cups, she concentrated on not spilling coffee on the table, then took her seat. Humiliated beyond belief, she wondered what he had to say. Was he going to tell her to go home to Pennsylvania? Not that he had any right to say where she should go, but she'd been soured by her brother in such matters.

Or maybe he was going to recommend she mind her own business and take a room at the hotel in town. Her confidence shriveled at the thought of leaving the Hutton family behind. But the bold way she'd acted tonight certainly warranted such a call on his part. She had interfered where she was not invited.

She added sugar to her cup, then held her hands in her lap, hiding their trembling. "What did you need to talk about?"

Another pass of his hand over his chin, followed by a long draw of coffee, and he leaned forward, arms on the table.

She leaned back ever so slightly.

"I have a proposition for you."

Oh dear. She'd made herself out to be a floozy, but she never dreamed he would—

"I'm not going to bid on your aunt and uncle's farm."

Tired blue eyes watched for her reaction.

It took a few heartbeats to review what he'd said. How had that been a proposition? Uncertain of his intent, she began with his last comment. "Why not?"

"Because it's your place. Your family left it to you, and you should have it." The blue gaze never left her, but it darkened.

"I haven't found the locket," she said. "And I don't know what Lewis will do. It would be like him to not reply to my telegram at all." Which drew her to a humbling request.

"May I borrow your wagon, or a horse, to go into town tomorrow and wire him?"

His gaze slid down the draping of Helen's dress, to Mary's socked feet, and back to her head.

She had no change of clothing, and her feet were still tender. She should go home and get herself together first before going into Cañon City.

Embarrassed, she shifted in her chair. "I know. I look a sight. I should go to the house first, but I hate to ask for so many favors. You and your family have already done so—"

"Mary." Deep as a well, his voice splashed all the way down to her toes. "It's no favor. It's what neighbors do. I'll take you in the wagon tomorrow if Helen doesn't need your help with Ella and the babies. And I'll take you to town if you let me."

If she *let* him? Mary looked at her lap and rolled her lips, holding in her hidden conflict. Ungratefulness was an ugly attitude, Mama had always said. A prideful one. Mary was definitely prideful, and the burning sensation in her chest was indication of that pride being purged.

"Thank you."

"But that's not all."

She risked reaching for her untouched coffee before looking

his way. "It's not?"

"Cale and I found a couple things on the farm you should know about."

Her nerves were gnawing holes in her bones. Why didn't he spit it out like he used to? His kindness was killing her, but she waited for him to finish.

"We found your aunt's and uncle's graves."

The gnawing stopped and her bones went weak.

"They're buried at the west end of the apple orchard nearest the house, markers facing east."

"The sunrise," she mumbled. "Aunt Bertie always said people should face the sunrise in their final resting place."

"Why's that?"

"For the Lord's return, of course."

He looked away. "Of course."

Questions pummeled her weary mind, such as who buried them? And why there? But she was too tired to carry on a rational conversation, and she longed to go to bed and save everything for tomorrow.

Hugh made no move to leave. There must be more.

He finished the last of his coffee and set the cup down with uncharacteristic ease. "What I'm about to say has to stay between us—you and me."

Oh no …

"Don't mention it to *anyone* in town. Not the telegraph operator, not your brother when you wire him. No one."

What was he saying? Keenly revived by his intensity and gripping gaze, she held her cup with both hands, bracing herself for something she did not want to hear.

"Go on."

"We found what's on your property that some people would do most anything to get."

CHAPTER EIGHTEEN

Sleeping in Hugh's bed was almost more than Mary could bear. No one had thought of changing his bedding, for everyone was focused on Ella and her twins, as well they should be. The scent of him had enveloped Mary and held her through the night, and she would not soon recover.

Discussion at breakfast had consisted of the Hutton boys—younger siblings and older twins—arguing over what the babies should be called. Helen ended the fray by declaring that it would be Ella's decision.

Every male pouted.

Helen had also come to Mary's rescue by tucking and pinning an old dress on her that Helen had saved for quilt scraps. She added a shawl, stockings, and a pair of shoes that were too big, but Mary's gratitude overrode any misfitting. At least she was presentable enough to be seen in town.

When Hugh handed her up to the wagon, one of the shoes fell off.

He retrieved it, but rather than give it to her, he held it low as if waiting for her to slip her foot into it.

She was not Cinderella.

She reached for the shoe, and he pulled it away, raising both eyebrows in an infuriating way.

"M' lady?"

Honestly. Did he really think she would raise her skirt to his so-called *princely* offer?

She glared as fiercely as she knew how, a look she'd often used on Lewis when he was trying to get his way over something in the house. But Hugh Hutton held his ground. And his grin.

"Oh, very well." She hiked her skirt above her ankle, which was the length of her own dresses anyway, and slid her foot into the waiting shoe.

Hugh held onto the old lace-up with both hands until she looked at him. "Comfortable?"

He was mocking her, and she wanted to kick him in the chest. But that was unladylike, and ungrateful, and unlikely to get her to town.

"Perfectly so."

He circled around in front of the horse looking entirely too satisfied for her liking.

At his flick of the reins, a similar scenario rose in her memory.

"My life is repeating itself." She folded her hands in her lap with not even her small purse to occupy them.

"How's that?"

"A ride to the farm."

"We're going to town first."

"I know that, but still. And I will repay you for the cost of the telegram."

He focused on the mare now rather than her foot, ignoring her offer of repayment.

Making two trips to the farm was pointless, so she'd agreed to Helen's creative clothing in order to wire Lewis first and then return to the farm. Which suddenly concerned her.

She would be stranded there. The buggy and wagon had burned to ash and she had no horse, nor a barn or corral in which to keep one.

Dependency fit her more poorly than Helen's shoes.

"What's wrong?"

Hugh's question surprised her out of her wool-gathering. "Nothing."

He snorted.

"I beg your pardon?"

"Why, what'd you do?"

She called upon every Christian thread of her being to not unravel right there in front of God and the wild country around them. Hugh Hutton was the most infuriating man she had ever met.

She stiffened.

He set the mare to a trot, which bounced the rough-riding wagon even more so.

She would be black and blue by the time they got to town.

"I'm horseless."

"What?" He looked at her with true curiosity.

"You asked, I told you. I'm horseless, that's what's wrong."

"You're right, you are."

If she jumped from the wagon seat, she'd lose both shoes and be hard-pressed to walk to the farm through sharp grass, sagebrush, and cactus.

"Don't worry, I have a plan."

Unable to resist rolling her eyes, she sighed. "Oh, I'm so grateful."

He chuckled and slowed the mare. Barlow was its name if she recalled. Poor Sassy had been seriously burned.

"How is Sassy?"

"She's going to be fine. I've salved her burns and wrapped her legs. The boys are keeping her stall clean. It'll be a while, and she probably won't pull in harness again, but she'll make it."

Mary burned with regret for not letting the mare loose when she first saw the fire.

"It's not your fault, you know."

How did he so easily know what she was thinking? Was she that easy to read? She looked at his profile, strong-jawed but clean-shaven this morning. Granite resolve one moment, tormenting tease the next. How did Helen manage all these Huttons?

"Tell me about the fire."

With the horse's easier pace, she relaxed a bit. "What is there to tell? It burned the barn down and everything else but the house. Thank God."

His attention held to the road. "When you were in the barn and first noticed it, do you remember anything in particular about where it was and how it burned?"

"I mentioned that to Helen because it seemed odd to me. I know fire burns *up*, but this followed a narrow path up the back corner. It didn't spread until it reached the loft."

With his boots planted on the buckboard, Hugh rested his elbows on his knees. "Did you smell anything?" He glanced sideways at her, deadpan.

She tried to see the inferno again, remember what she heard and ... smelled? "I was terrified and trying to stop the fire. All I smelled was smoke and burning wood and ... "

He jerked his head her way. "And what?"

She rubbed her temples. "I don't know. Maybe nothing. I don't know."

He laid his hand on her shoulder, but gently, and his tone matched his touch. "It's all right. Don't worry about it. We'll figure it out."

We? Who did he mean by *we?*

By the time they rode down Main Street, Mary's head hurt from trying to smell the past. Hugh pulled up in front of the Denver and Rio Grande train station, set the brake, and came around to help her. Secretly relieved, she arched her toes to keep the shoes on as she climbed down, using his hand for support.

When she landed successfully, he didn't let go and enfolded her hand in both of his. "Remember." His voice dropped to an intimate level. "Not a word to your brother about what I told you."

She resisted her instinctive reaction to his husky tone and tried to look away, but neither would he release her gaze.

"Promise." He held on.

"I promise. But why?"

"Trust me." A quick squeeze of her fingers.

Could she? Could she trust this big, not-always-so-brazen cowboy with her future? Her inheritance? Her heart?

~

Hugh considered going into the Western Union office with her, but she'd likely have a wild horse fit. And wouldn't *that* keep the beans from spilling.

He leaned against the front wagon wheel, folded his arms, and watched her stumble up the platform and in the front door with a furtive glance over her shoulder.

He touched his hat brim and dipped his chin and could imagine her rolling her eyes.

At first, she'd made him crazy. Then she'd made him weak in the knees. Now he felt he needed to protect her from every money-hungry lecher who might get wind of what she had. He wasn't fool enough to think word wouldn't get out, but he prayed she didn't mention it in that blasted telegram. The whole town would know within an hour.

Couldn't have been ten minutes before she was out the door.

"That was fast."

"I didn't have much to say." She took off both shoes, held them under one arm and offered him her hand.

He managed to not laugh, grabbed her around the waist, and hefted her up to the seat. It was easier.

"Thank you." She set the shoes beneath the seat, adjusted her skirt, then folded her hands on her lap. Not a word about him manhandling her.

He clucked Barlow away from the train station and into the street. "You going to tell me what you said?"

"No. It is a private matter." Her chin was higher than it was on the way into town, and he figured the whole affair was putting a kink in her side. Kin had a way of doing that.

"But rest assured, I did not mention the—you know."

"Good."

Barlow clopped along, not at all bothered by the buzz wagons choking the street. Infernal things. There were more of them today than he remembered the last time he was in town at the sheriff's.

He'd like to tell the sheriff what he and Cale had found, but news of the barn fire would have to do. He drew up in front of the jail and looped the reins around the brake.

"I'll be right back."

"What are you doing?"

He tugged his hat low and gave her a cool look. "It's a private matter." He couldn't resist and was rewarded by her predictable indignation.

He was also rewarded by the sheriff's gap-jawed reaction to the fire, and tempted to tell him the whole story.

"That barn didn't burn itself down, Sheriff. You and I both know that's true."

Payton shifted in his chair. "I'll look into it."

"What're you gonna look into? A heap of ash and charred wood?"

The sheriff glared unappreciatively across his desk at Hugh's veiled insult. "I've got an investigator in town looking into other matters. I'll send him out tomorrow."

"What time?" Hugh didn't need some out-of-town snoop poking around Mary's place with her there alone.

"After dinner."

"I'll be waiting."

Ignoring the sheriff's puzzlement, Hugh let himself out and joined Mary on the wagon seat.

She ignored him.

Fair. He unwrapped the reins, looked behind them for rattletraps, and took his time sizing her up. He'd insulted her, like he'd insulted the sheriff. It wasn't his day.

"Any place you need to stop?"

She shook her head.

"I'll loan you the money."

"Thank you, no."

"Suit yourself." He flicked the reins on Barlow's rump and headed for the opposite end of town.

When he pulled into the fuel station, Mary looked at him strangely. "What are we doing here?"

Regretting his former remark, he walked around to her side of the wagon. "Helen needs lamp oil. I'm going to get another can, and that way we'll have two. No sense running short. You want a can?"

"No." She looked down at her lap. "But thank you for asking."

Danged if it wasn't easier catching flies with honey than vinegar.

He lifted his can from the wagon bed and met the supplier inside, who brought out a second can. Hugh loaded both in the bed and shoved them up against the back of the seat so they'd ride easier.

He pulled the money from his pocket and handed it over. "Thank you. Appreciate your help."

The man watched Mary as if she was a rattler. "You're welcome, uh—any time." He dipped his head at Mary. "Ma'am."

As they pulled away from the shop front, Mary turned around and leaned over the cans, her nose wrinkling.

Hugh watched long enough to see her face blanch.

"What's wrong? What is it?"

She gripped the edge of the seat and her knuckles went white. When she looked up at him, fear rounded her eyes, now dark as a forest at night.

"I remember. Tha—that smell. The cans. That's what I smelled in the barn."

CHAPTER NINETEEN

Disturbed by the direction her thoughts had taken—that someone had deliberately set the barn afire—Mary was unprepared to see the destruction in broad daylight. The house sat like an orphaned child, the only uncharred thing other than the orchard beyond. The skeletal remains of the barn and corral stood black and forlorn. She felt the tide rising in her chest.

Unwilling to weep in front of Hugh again, she gathered her shoes, jumped down, and ran up the porch steps in her stocking feet. He followed, ever the faithful guardian.

She didn't need a guardian. Didn't *want* a guardian. She wanted to be alone and turned on him.

"Please just leave me alone. Go back to the ranch and let me be."

Shock made an appearance, but only briefly, and male dominance quickly prevailed. "I'm not leaving till I tell you my plan."

If she were honest, she'd admit that it was pain washing his rugged features. Instantly she regretted hurting him, and she bit the inside of her cheek.

"Very well. Come to the kitchen."

He followed her like a pup, which brought Finley to mind. The dog was more the boys' now than hers.

Without coffee or anything else to offer Hugh, Mary sat at the table and waited. The sooner he left, the better.

He removed his hat, turned the chair around, and straddled it.

"I'll take the wagon home, unload the fuel, then return leading Shorty. The wagon and Barlow will stay here. You've got enough good grass that you can stake Barlow out. She won't stray. No reason the pump at the barn won't still work, but I'll check before I leave. I'll bring another bucket when I return so you can water her."

Every emotion Mary owned had jammed into her throat, and all she could do was nod. If she opened her mouth, she feared what might fall out.

"You won't be horseless for any longer than it takes me to ride home and back."

Blast his tenderness. If he'd simply yell or stomp or even swear, she could handle his outburst. But she couldn't wall up her emotions in the face of his kindness.

She bobbed her head again, but a sob broke unchecked. Covering her mouth, she stood, putting the table between them. If he took her in his arms, she would fall apart. She couldn't afford to do that. Not now, not ever.

~

Hugh left Mary standing in the kitchen looking fragile as a porcelain doll.

His sister Grace'd had one when she was little. When it broke, she cried for days. If he touched Mary McCrae right now, she might break like that doll, and he didn't think he could handle that.

He set his hat and crossed the yard for the burned-out barn, wondering if the timbers he'd laid over the pit had burned as well.

He was watching the ground, and a gut-check stopped him halfway there. Turning around, he placed his boots carefully in his own footprints and followed his back trail for what had caught his eye. In two steps, he found it.

A chill ran up his neck as straight and even as the two tire tracks in front of him. Not wheel tracks, *tire* tracks. Too fresh to be from Mary's Roadster. He read sign as good as the next fella, and these tracks were recent. Following them, he saw where they stopped near the barn, backed up and turned around heading toward the farm road.

Blood ran hot in his veins and throbbed in his head. If he got his hands on the varmint who'd ridden out here to see a burned barn, he'd wager he had the one who threw the match. And there was no telling how he might desert his Christian upbringing then.

Watching where he stepped, he made it to the pump and splashed water on his face and neck. He'd have that investigator take a look at the evidence when he came tomorrow.

Hugh had to make sure the man didn't ride—or drive— over the tracks when he got here. And there was only one way to do that.

Be here first.

~

Mary stood at the sink, taking in the open country west of the farm and the top of the Rafter-H windmill in the distance. It took Hugh longer than she expected to drive off, but when he came around the house, the sight of him leaving in the wagon pushed her over the edge.

She ran for the stairs, stumbling as her stocking feet slipped on the worn risers. Sobs stole her breath, and she flung herself across the bed letting everything gush out of her. All the pent-up anxiety. The pain, the fear, her resentment of Lewis. The loss of her aunt and uncle. Now she might lose their farm as well.

Grief swept over her in waves, crushing her beneath its weight. Where was hope and the promise of tomorrow?

Rolling to her back, her arm flung out against the bedside table and hit Aunt Bertie's Bible. Mary picked it up, drawn to its words for comfort but too tired to read. Too tired to hold the leather-bound book. She tucked it in against her and curled around it like a child.

~

Hugh did chores early, gave his boys instructions for helping Helen and Cale the next day, then tossed his saddle, bed roll, and a bucket in the wagon and unloaded the fuel cans. His mind worked like a windmill in a blizzard on a possible connection between the tracks he'd seen at Mary's and what she'd smelled at the fire. His good sense told him to let the investigator look into things. Instinct told him to ride back to town and grab that long-necked fuel dealer by the throat and ask him what he knew.

The screen door slapped and Cale ambled out.

"You goin' somewhere?"

Up close Cale looked like he hadn't slept in two days, and Hugh figured he hadn't. "I'm going to the farm. An investigator's coming out tomorrow and I want to be there."

Cale blinked a couple times, clearly not in the conversation.

"I took Mary to town so she could wire her brother in Pennsylvania. Then I stopped at the jail and told the sheriff what happened. He said he'd send a visiting investigator to have a look."

Cale rubbed the back of his neck, his head bent. "All right."

"But after I stopped at the fuel depot for the lamp oil, Mary bowed up like a scared colt when she smelled the filled cans in the wagon bed."

Cale looked at him then, a frown cutting his brow. "You think there's a connection?"

"I intend to find out."

Hugh tied Shorty to the tailgate and climbed to the seat. "Tell Helen what's going on. I'm not about to let Mary stay there by herself until this thing is settled."

Cale gave him a mock salute and meandered to the house.

Dusk was running in by the time Hugh made the farm, yet

no light shone from the windows. That worried him, but maybe Mary was sleeping and hadn't lit the lamps yet.

He had too much fire in his veins to even think about sleeping.

He pulled up next to the house, not crossing trails with the tire tracks, and staked Shorty and Barlow out past the root cellar where the grass was thick. He carried two buckets of water to them, then took his bedroll to the front porch.

Still no lamplight from the windows, but he'd give her an hour or so. The way she'd looked when he left, she might sleep for a month.

He set two chairs facing each other so he could sit in one and put his feet on the other. Darkness crawled the eastern sky and spots of light broke out. Soon the whole expanse was black as ink. Only the hand of God could scatter stars across something so endless. It was times like these he remembered his raising, and what his folks had taught him.

The prayer came gentle, easing out of him with a purpose all its own, asking God to cover him and Mary, his sons. Helen, Cale, Ella and the twins. His sister Grace.

"Give me wisdom, Lord, and a level head. You know I need that more than anything right now."

Intent on seeing that Mary was safe and sound, he set his feet down careful and checked the front door. It was unlocked, and he went in quiet, not familiar enough with the house to avoid the squeaky boards. But he made it to the stairs without knocking anything over and went up quiet as a cat.

She was lying on her bed, still wearing Helen's dress, and curled up like a kitten. He watched long enough to see her ribs move as she breathed, then crept down the stairs and out to the porch.

The wooden decking was harder than dirt beneath his bedroll, but he didn't care. He wasn't there for his comfort. He was there to be near Mary, and that was all that mattered. He intended to spend the rest of his life near her—closer than this—she just didn't know it yet. In fact, he'd not realized it himself.

Fingers linked beneath his head, he followed the stars and drifted off on ways he could convince her to marry him.

~

Glass broke, and Hugh sat up. Had he dreamed it?

Before he could figure it out, a rider raced past the porch, hunched over his horse, hell-bent for leather.

Hugh reached for his rifle, but a flicker of light turned his head to the north and sucked the air from his lungs.

He crashed through the house and took the stairs two at a time, hitting a wall of fumes at Mary's bedroom. Flames licked the curtains and followed a trail rolled by a rag-covered rock that had ignited the bedclothes. As consuming as the fire was, the rage inside him roared louder over what could have happened had he not been there.

He scooped Mary into his arms, including the book she clutched, and looked around for the small bag she carried. The will. Anything that would be of value to her. But the fire was growing.

He bolted down the stairs, kicked through the back door, and ran for the field. Mary squirmed in his arms, but he held her tighter.

"Hugh! What are you doing? Put me down!"

"Hold on, darlin'. I'm gettin' you out of here."

He ran past the wagon, to where the horses stood pulling against their stakes. He couldn't lose them now.

He set Mary on her feet and cupped her face in both hands.

"The house, Mary—it's on fire. But you're safe. Stay here while I get the horses."

"But my money. The will. The *locket!*"

He gripped her by the shoulders. "It doesn't matter. Do you hear me? Stay here, and I'll bring the horses."

Clutching what looked like a Bible with one hand, she

strained away from him.

He couldn't carry her and gather the horses both. "Mary!" He yelled her name and swung her around to see her glaring as if he was trying to rob her. "None of it matters but you. Stay here by the wagon. Better yet, come with me and get Barlow."

Mary shoved the book in his chest and broke free, running to the front of the house.

He dropped the book and caught her near the porch, where she fought him like before.

"The locket!" she screamed. "The locket has to be in the little desk drawer. The one that's locked!"

He gripped her arms and forced her to look at him. "How do you know?"

Panic washed her face. Even in the pale light flickering above them, he could see her desperation.

"It isn't anywhere else. It has to be there!"

He would lose his mind, but he'd not lose her. "Stay here, I'll get it."

Timbers from the roof crashed into the second floor, and smoke rolled out like storm clouds. Hugh ran for the kitchen, where he found a butcher knife and returned to the desk.

Mary was there, coughing and clawing at the drawer.

"Go outside—I'll get it. Just get out of here!"

He pushed her hands aside and shoved the knife blade behind the drawer edge and wrenched it open.

The drawer was empty.

"No!"

Mary's scream ripped through him. He dropped the knife and pulled her to the porch, where he hauled her over his shoulder and ran for the root cellar.

CHAPTER TWENTY

Hugh carried Mary to the top of the small rise and sank into the grass, holding her while she wept. Dadgum, if things didn't keep getting worse.

This was a nightmare he wouldn't wish on anybody.

Several pops sounded over the roar in quick succession, and he spoke close to her ear. "Was there a gun in the house?"

She nodded.

"A box of shells?"

Another nod, and she burrowed into him.

He wrapped his arms tighter, his chin on the top of her head. "You're safe, Mary. That's all that matters."

The house fell in on itself, and Mary flinched at the roar. Sparks and embers flew into the sky like a geyser, and Hugh thanked God for the recent rain—that this hadn't happened during a dry spell.

A noise that didn't fit drew his attention to the south, away from the burning house, and he separated himself from Mary and stood.

"What is it?" she choked, her voice torn from sobbing.

"Not sure. I'll be right back."

"No!" She gripped his leg like his boys had as toddlers.

Kneeling, he loosened her hands and smoothed her tangled hair off her face. "It's all right. I'll be close by. But it may be the—it may be a rider. I want to find out. Stay here."

Straightening, he felt for his revolver, silently cursing that he hadn't strapped it on. His gun belt and rifle were both on the porch. If he was quick …

This time Mary did what he said.

He ran for the south end of the house and cut back to the porch. His bedroll was burning, but the Winchester, gun belt, and saddle weren't. He sucked in a deep breath, pulled his neckerchief over his mouth and nose, and reached for the rifle. The metal burned his hand and he tossed it into the yard. The saddle was scorching, but he grabbed it and his gun belt and rolled off the porch as the roof caved in.

"Hugh!"

It wasn't Mary hollering, but he couldn't make out much more over the inferno. He pulled off his vest, wrapped it around the rifle, and hunkered down as he ran back the way he'd come.

Again, the call, but more familiar. He made out a horse in a close stand of scrub oak and a man running toward him. *Cale.*

"Thank God—" Cale slammed into him, gripping him in relief.

"How'd you know?" Hugh squeezed his brother's arms, happier to see him than he'd ever been.

"The boys slept in the loft again tonight, but of course didn't sleep. They saw the glow and woke me up."

Hugh made a mental tally to thank them. Reward them somehow.

"Where's Mary? Is she all right?"

Cold horror sank through him. She'd be anything but all right had he not been there. "Yes, for now. I've got her over on top of the root cellar." Hopefully, she was still there.

"The wagon," Cale said. "It's awful close."

"I know, but there was no time to hitch up Barlow and move it—and keep Mary from going back in the house."

Cale looked at him like he was crazy.

"She got it in her head that the locket we couldn't find was in a locked desk drawer. I went in to bust it open and she followed me. The roof was caving in, but we got out in time."

"Was it there?"

Hugh shook his head. "It's nowhere. I'm afraid her aunt may have been wearing it when she was buried."

Cale grimaced and looked toward the wagon. "Come on. If the wind shifts, that wagon's a goner. Together, we should be able to push it."

As dawn paled the eastern sky, they moved the wagon farther from the house. The fire was burning itself out. Mary's bed had fallen through from the upstairs and lay twisted in the debris. All that remained of her aunt's trunk were the metal bracings. The sink lay on the ground not far from the cookstove—the only things that survived intact. The rolltop desk was a pile of charred kindling.

Hugh kicked through some of the still-smoldering rubble.

"Doesn't look like there's much of anything left," Cale said. "You lookin' for something in particular?"

"Yes, and it's here, I'm sure." Hugh continued kicking at broken furniture and smoking boards. And then he found it.

He wrapped his neckerchief around his hand and picked up a lump as big as his fist. Still hot enough to singe his scarf, he tossed it away from the rubble.

"What is it?" his brother asked.

"The rock that went through Mary's bedroom window last night with a soaked rag around it. I saw it burning on the floor like a coal from hell when I ran up to get her. The sound of it breaking the window is what woke me."

"That's arson, not to mention attempted murder."

"I hope the investigator agrees. But that's not all."

Cale waited, worry distorting his face in the brightening day.

"The person who threw it rode past me like the devil himself was on his tail."

"Did you get a good look at him?"

"Not his face. But I did see he had the stirrups jacked up, ready for a fast trip."

~

Mary sat in the grass atop the root cellar, arms around her knees, watching Hugh and his brother walk through the charred remains of the house. Cried out, she was. Nothing pooled in her core but searing guilt. The farm was ravaged because of her. If she hadn't come west to Colorado, the barn and house would still be standing.

All that was left now were smoldering furnishings and door frames.

The will was gone.

Her money was gone.

Everything she'd brought with her and all Helen had given her were gone.

Even the locket was gone, likely melted into an unrecognizable lump, the picture ash.

The sun rose undeterred by the tragedy that surrounded her. Light spread across the fields and through the orchards as if the dawning day was like any other fresh start. But it didn't work for Mary this time. The light merely revealed the harsh reality that hope too was gone.

Remembering where her aunt and uncle's markers had been found, she rose, stiff and sore-footed, and walked through grass that Hugh valued so highly. So highly that he'd offered to pay her for grazing rights.

She scoffed. She couldn't even prove the land was her inheritance.

The orchard stretched beyond the house, untouched by either of the fires. Leafed-out branches held tiny apples, and at the western edge, two markers stood in the place of a tree, as Hugh had said. Not the ornately carved granite of her parents' graves, but two simple crosses, each bearing a name: *Ernest*

Edward Dodson and *Bertha Agan Dodson.*

Solitary they stood, nearly touching, symbolic of the courage that drew two loving people to brave their Western adventure together.

Mary's heart was stone, too heavy to carry, and she fell to her knees. "Forgive me, Aunt Bertie, please forgive me—for not knowing you were ill. For not knowing you'd left me your hard-earned farm."

A cry broke from her dry lips, and she sank into herself. "For not keeping it safe."

Footsteps brushed through the grass and a familiar hand warmed her shoulder. Hugh took a knee beside her and spoke in a gentle tone. "It's not your fault, Mary."

Soot covered his clothes and blackened his face, setting off his eyes like dull sapphires. She looked down at her clothes and arms, also black, but she didn't care. She may never care about anything ever again, least of all her appearance.

He wrapped his arm around her, bringing her into his side. More than an embrace. The bolstering of a friend. "Let's go home."

A wagon waited near the orchard. Hugh lifted her to the seat, then sat beside her, one arm around her again in unspoken support. With the other hand, he flicked the reins and the horse led out.

His brother rode beside them, leading Hugh's horse.

Numb in body and mind, Mary struggled to think clearly. When they made it to the ranch and Hugh turned in next to the house, the boys came running. Their names muddled together as he lifted her down.

"We prayed for you, Miss Mary."

New tears swelled.

"God answered our prayer, just like he did for Tug last year."

"We're glad you're home, Miss Mary."

Home. A strange word lately, with meaning that had shifted in form and place. Where was home? She once knew. Now she could not define it, but she let three little hands lead her to the ranch house as two pups bounced along with them.

At the door she stopped and leaned toward a large, flowered bush between the step and front window, breathing in the sweet aroma.

"Them's lie-lucks," the littlest boy said. "Remember?"

She didn't remember, but she touched his hair, leaving a black smudge atop his head. A bath. *That* she remembered. A bath was what she wanted most, and then sleep.

"Oh, for pity's sake." An older woman took Mary's arm as she stepped inside. "You must be worn thin as a bee's wing. Come in here and sit down while I heat some water and get you a bath going. You boys skedaddle." She flung her hands up as if shooing flies. "Go on, you can talk to Miss Mary later. Unless you want your own bath and me scrubbing behind your ears."

The boys turned as one, ran through the kitchen, and out a screen door that slapped behind them.

The smell of fresh coffee stirred memories of breakfast and late suppers in that very room. Taking a seat that felt familiar, she watched the woman—Helen, yes, that was it—who fetched a dusty bottle from a high cupboard and poured amber liquid into a tin mug before adding coffee. Then she set the cup before Mary and returned the bottle to its hiding place.

"Go on, now. Drink that coffee while you're waiting. I'll toast some bread to go with it after I get the water boiling."

Mary sipped the coffee.

Another woman, younger than Helen, came in holding an infant in each arm. She joined Mary at the table, her arms gently bouncing the bundled babes.

Mary's head hurt trying to fit the pieces, but the coffee was helping. She took another sip.

"I'm so sorry, Mary," the woman said. "But it's good to see

you here. This is the best place you could be, among this loving family, and under Helen's care."

"Don't overdo, Ella," Helen said. "You should be sleeping while those young'uns are. You're up all hours of the night with 'em, both you and Cale."

Ella. Yes. Mary remembered Ella, with her short dark hair and fringe. And she remembered being with her when the babies were born. She took a bigger sip.

Helen went out the screen door and a loud clanging soon filled the air. Then she came inside as if nothing had happened.

The boys must have been nearby, for they scrambled through the door, stopping short at seeing Ella with the babies.

"You three go find your father. Tell him I need him, and then go help your uncle do whatever needs doing."

They turned in unison—

"Wait." Helen's command stopped them cold. She went to the counter and picked up a crock, then held it out to the boys. "One for each hand. By age. Kip, you're first."

Kip. She remembered that name, but the others were foggy. She took another drink of coffee. It was the best she'd ever tasted.

"Have you named your babies?" she asked Ella.

The question brought a tender smile to the woman's face as she lifted the babe in her left arm. "This is Elizabeth, after my nana, but already I call her Beth."

Regarding the baby in her right arm, she pressed a tender kiss on his forehead. "And this is Caleb, after Cale's grandfather who was the first Hutton in Cañon City."

Mary's throat thickened and she blinked, dismayed by tears that regenerated so swiftly and came so easily. She glanced at Helen. "May I have more coffee, please?"

The screen door opened and Hugh stepped inside, quickly removing his hat. His forehead was white as snow compared to the rest of his soot-covered self, but his eyes—oh, his eyes— blue as the sky. For some reason, they turned her insides to jelly.

"Hugh, will you bring in the tub, please? You know where it is, hanging on the wall outside."

His gaze never left Mary and lingered even as his body turned for the door. "Yes, ma'am."

Helen started filling pitchers and large jars.

Hugh delivered a copper bathing tub, set it in the center of the kitchen, then retreated to the door.

"You're next, Hugh. Unless you want to go sit in the creek with a bar of soap."

Mary thought he blushed but wasn't certain due to the grime on his face.

"I recommend a bath, though. It'll do your bones good and soak out what ails you."

He glanced at Mary then and left.

She stood. She'd get her own coffee.

"I have some rose water that you can add to the bath," Ella said. "I'll lay these babies down and be right back."

Helen began filling the tub. "Close the door and draw the curtains over the windows. Then get out of those clothes and into this tub."

Helen asked for nothing. Even her request for Hugh to bring the tub had been more of a command. Mary had no choice but to obey, and gladly. Every inch of her body ached, and a warm, rose-scented bath was tonic for not only the body but the soul.

"More coffee first?"

"Later," Helen said with an odd chuckle.

CHAPTER TWENTY-ONE

Hugh was bone-weary, but the bath felt good, and he scrunched down in the rosy-smellin' water till it was up to his chin. The thought of Mary McCrae in this very tub helped keep him awake—a good thing. For he still had to ride to the farm and meet that investigator. After last night's fire, he had twice as much to tell him.

The women had vacated the kitchen to parts unknown but left him a towel and clean clothes. Helen was a God-send. She'd even left a sandwich on the table.

He ate it in three bites, and feeling some better, struck out for the farm. It would never again be the Dodson place, regardless of what happened at the auction.

The smell of charred wood met him before he reached the farmyard, but once he did, the sight hit him hard. No wonder Mary had reacted so emotionally yesterday when she saw the aftermath of the first fire.

He'd not lost any of his possessions or labors to a fire, and he thanked God for that. But to see anyone's loss kicked a hole in him. Especially since that loss affected someone he cared deeply for.

Why hadn't he told her how he felt? The better question might be, *when* could he have told her? If they weren't arguing, they were facing a disaster of some sort. Not finding the locket galled him as much as any of it. He'd wanted to do that for her—give her the thing that meant most where only things were concerned.

He ground tied Shorty by the root cellar, grabbed his rifle, and walked over to where he'd seen the tire tracks. They were still there, but not as clear. Wind from the fire had blown dust and ash into them. But if the fella coming out was worth his salt, he'd recognize them for what they were.

Last night's rider was another matter.

He walked the length of the house, but one set of horse hooves blended in with another. He picked up his good saddle, now looking like it'd ridden flank in hell, and took it over to the cellar. Then he carried his frustration out a ways on the farm road and sat down to wait against a fence post.

With his belly full, his muscles relaxed from an almost warm bath, and another sleepless night under his belt, he dozed, jerking awake every time his head bobbed. He didn't want to get too comfortable. Couldn't have that investigator comin' up on him unawares.

He squinted down the farm lane, judging by the sun that it was after noon.

Shorty whickered, and Hugh looked toward the farm. A lone rider was coming in from the north, between the burned-out barn and the house, watching the ground as he rode.

Rifle in hand, Hugh jumped to his feet.

He reset his hat and strode toward the man who stopped and watched him approach. No anxious moves. No reaching for his sidearm. The man crossed his arms on his saddle horn and held the reins loosely in his left hand.

As Hugh closed in, the man pulled one side of his vest back to reveal a badge. "Silas Graham. Colorado Rangers." A thick mustache hid his mouth.

Relief eased Hugh's hand from fisted to relaxed. "Hugh Hutton."

"Sheriff Payton mentioned you wanted to see me." Graham straightened in his saddle and gazed around the farm. "I can see why."

He stepped down, and Hugh offered his hand. "Thanks for coming out."

"Not much left, is there?"

"No, but I have a couple of things I want to show you." Hugh indicated the ground behind him and hunkered down.

Graham led his horse of couple of paces away, ground tied him, and joined Hugh for a closer look. "Do you own an automobile?"

"Nope. Had one here a few weeks ago, but these tracks were made day before yesterday. The day after the barn burned. Morning, actually." Hugh stood and pointed. "You can see where they stopped at the barn, backed up, and drove out toward the road."

Graham walked around, careful not to step on the tire tracks, which shot him up a notch in Hugh's estimation.

"Anybody could have driven out here to see what was burning."

True, but unlikely. In Hugh's mind, no one was here but the arsonist. He turned for the house, listening to see if Graham followed.

At the north corner where the porch had been, Hugh picked up the rock.

Graham was right behind him.

"I was sleeping on the porch last night when this went through the upstairs window wrapped in a fuel-soaked rag."

Graham took the rock, hefted it for weight, then cut Hugh a sharp look under his wide-brimmed hat. "And you know this how?"

"The breaking glass woke me, and a rider tore past like the furies were after him. I ran upstairs to get Mary out of the bedroom—did Payton tell you this is her family's farm?—and saw this lying on the floor in front of the broken window. It was wrapped in a burning rag and the smell of lamp oil filled the room."

"Did you get her out?"

Hugh's chest tightened. "Both times."

Stone-faced, Graham kept on. "What do you mean *both* times?"

"The barn fire. She was trying to throw water on it and I pulled her out of the barn. Later she told me the flames crawled up a corner like they were following a path. And she'd smelled lamp oil."

Graham rolled the rock into the debris, then took a note pad and pencil stub from inside his vest. "You spend a lot of time over here. What's your relation to this Mary—"

"McCrae." Hugh's hackles rose. "We're neighbors. She's alone." He couldn't make out what Graham was writing.

The ranger slipped the pad in his vest. "Sheriff Payton said this place goes up for auction in a couple months. You interested in bidding on it?"

Thorough, Hugh'd give him that. Bordered on insulting. But Hugh knew his nerves were stretched as tight as a fiddle string and he didn't need to come across agitated and angry though he was plenty of both. "I was, but not anymore."

"Why's that?"

"Mary McCrae's kin, the Dodson's, left the farm to her in their will. Now the will's burned along with everything else."

Graham watched him, waiting for a clue to break out. Hugh held his eye.

"If it was drawn up by an attorney, there should be a record."

Hugh remembered the attorney's name at the bottom of the will, T.F. Beckman.

"What?" Graham squinted, reading Hugh like an open tally book.

"There's more, but you have to swear you won't tell anyone. Not even Sheriff Payton."

Graham stuck his thumbs in his gun belt and his eyes turned cold.

Hugh tossed a scrap. "We think what I'm about to tell you is behind the whole mess—burning the barn, burning the house, digging the pit—"

Graham's hand shot up. "Hold on, what pit?"

~

Mary woke with a dry mouth and a strange taste on her tongue. Again she found herself dressed in an overly large gown, but this one had no sleeves. Its light weight was refreshing, as was the cool air from the open window.

Placing her feet gingerly on the floor, she looked around for a wrapper or robe—anything with which she could make herself presentable enough to leave the room—but she found nothing. She considered opening the drawers of a bureau at the opposite wall but resisted, remembering she was in Hugh's bedroom. He would not have what she needed in the way of clothing. Tiny embers fired through her veins and up her neck.

Crawling over the bed, she leaned toward the window screen, drinking in the fragrance of mountain grass and cedar, and the faintest scent of cattle. *Manure,* as Kip had called it one evening. A smile pulled her dry lips at the memory. Petroleum jelly—another memory. But that was in her old room where Ella was staying with the babies.

Her stomach grumbled. It must be well after dinner. With no breakfast and only Helen's wonderful coffee, Mary felt she could eat a dozen of the cookies the woman had given the boys.

A light knock on the bedroom door returned her to the covers. "Are you awake?"

Confident she wouldn't be exposing herself to one of the Hutton men or boys, Mary got up and opened the door to Ella, whose arms were full, though not with babies.

"Please come in. I'm not very presentable, but I have no choice."

"But you're ravishing in Helen's shift."

179

Mary tried not to pull her cracked lips but was relieved at Ella's lightheartedness. It reminded her of Celia, and she wondered if her friend had answered her postcard.

"I'm glad to see you up and awake. You look so much better," Ella said. "And your hair is absolutely stunning, though I do not envy the care such long tresses require." She shook her head, swishing her own hair from side to side. "I would bob mine again, but Cale asked me not to. If it gets as long as yours, though, I will be asking *him* to care for it."

"Please, sit down. You must be exhausted with the twins." Mary gathered her hair with a quick twist and pushed it behind her shoulders. It was moments like this that she sorely missed her tortoise-shell combs.

Ella emptied her armload onto the bed, revealing women's clothing in all its various layers, some of it quite nice.

"What's all this?"

Ella eased into the room's only chair. "These are some of my clothes that I may never fit into again. I sent Cale to the house this morning to bring them down for you." She gave Mary a steady once-over. "We are near the same size, though your girth is not even close to mine."

Ella laughed, such a pleasing sound after all the crying. Would Mary ever laugh again?

"How generous of you, Ella. I don't know what to say." Humbled beyond anything she'd experienced before, Mary cleared a corner of the bed and lifted the nearest item, a lovely pale-green skirt with matching jacket. Mother would have said it set off her eyes. The thought stirred more grief, and Mary coughed, forcing its retreat. She was weary of weeping.

"Let me get you a glass of water." Ella pushed from the chair but stopped at Helen's entrance.

"Sit down, Mrs. Hutton. You are on your feet entirely too much." Helen carried a tray with biscuits and jam, a teapot Mary hoped held coffee, two china cups and saucers, and a glass of water.

"Thank you, Helen. You have an uncanny knack of anticipating everyone's needs."

"Pshaw," Helen said, placing the tray on a bedside table that matched the one in Mary's former room. "Both of you will be up and around in no time, busy with your own lives, and I'll have no one to talk to about those Hutton boys. The taller ones included."

She felt Mary's forehead with the back of her hand, then leaned close. "God has a way of working things out—like bringing you into our lives at just the right time. What would I have done if you'd not been here to help me with the twins' birth?" Patting Mary's arm, she straightened. "You are welcome to stay here as long as you like. Remember that."

At the door, Helen paused. "You need something for your lips. I'll be right back."

"Petroleum jelly," Ella whispered.

"At least it's not Bag Balm." But balm was definitely what Helen had applied to Mary's bruised heart with her tender words.

Ella snickered when Helen returned, scolding, "I heard that."

After Helen left, Mary prepared two biscuits with jam for each saucer, then poured *tea* into each cup. *Drat.*

A baby cried out as if stuck by a pin. An innocent demand for Mother's attention. "It seems someone else has a keen sense of timing."

Ella pushed slowly to her feet. "That's Caleb. He is his father's son and wants to eat twenty minutes ago." She paused by the door, saucer in hand. "I'll take these biscuits with me— they're one of my favorites. And we'll visit later."

She glanced at the pile of clothes on the bed. "I do hope they fit. They shouldn't sit in my bureau when you could be wearing them. And if they don't suit you, I'm pretty handy with a needle and thread." A sassy smile accompanied her out the door on her way to a second baby's cry, distinctly different from the first.

Mary pushed some of the clothes aside and propped herself against the pillows, weary again. Weary in both body and mind. From great loss to great generosity, she'd been raked over coals of fire as well as humility. Both burned in their own way, and Mary simply longed to sleep.

~

Little-boy voices and the deeper tones of grown men spun their way into Mary's subconscious. Waking to near darkness, she sat up and looked outside. A pink glow radiated along the bottoms of low cloud banks, hinting at a setting sun she could not see.

She fell against the pillows, content to simply listen to the family sounds emanating from the kitchen. A biscuit remained on her plate, so she trimmed the lamp, added more of Helen's delicious jam, and filled her cup with tepid tea.

A knock at her door surprised the tea from her cup.

"Come in?"

A low chuckle.

Oh dear. She pulled the green jacket on over the shift and held it closed at her neck.

The door swung slowly in, and Hugh stood on the threshold with a grin. "You didn't sound so sure."

Oh, how sure she was. Sure that she wanted to see him. Hear his reassuring voice, soak in the strength of him. Such unreasonable desires, for her days were numbered at the Rafter-H, and she would no doubt leave soon for Pennsylvania.

If Lewis allowed her to return.

"I wanted to see that you were all right."

His concern stirred an inexpressible longing in her, and she was grateful the flush she felt in her cheeks was hidden in the lamp's thin light.

"I am. Thank you."

"I have something for you, but I'll give it to you tomorrow.

It's too late now and—"

"What is it?"

Shadows hid his eyes, making his expression difficult to read.

"I don't have it with me, but I believe you'll want it. It's from your aunt and uncle's house."

With an involuntary sigh, she released her hold on the jacket. "Please, not one charred piece of their home. I'd rather have nothing than a burned memento."

"It's not burned." His voice rolled out deeper than before, solid and true. "There's not a mark on it."

Her curiosity piqued and she sat up.

"Goodnight, Mary. I'll see you tomorrow." With that, he quietly closed the door to *his* room.

Where had he been the night the house burned? She hadn't thought to ask. Yet, if he hadn't been somewhere near, he would not have been close enough to save her. *Again.*

The pillows caught her in a soft embrace and tears trailed once more. How often Hugh Hutton had come to her rescue— each time a matter of life and death. How could she put herself in such compromising positions so many times?

Grief settled in beside her and nibbled into her core like a termite. She had no reason to stay in Colorado. She could not prove her relationship to her aunt and uncle, which was a moot point now without the will. And she had no money to bid on the farm at the auction.

"Lord, show me what to do," she whispered. "You have always been faithful, yet now I feel abandoned. Help me, please."

CHAPTER TWENTY-TWO

The sun broke over the eastern rimrock and washed the ranch in a golden light. Hugh positioned a long nail against a loose corral pole and drove it through to the upright.

Mary's grief last night had given him pause about what he'd found. He didn't want to add to her pain, but he believed she'd want it, especially now, after everything she'd been through. It bore no reminders of the fire, other than a faint hint of smoke, and he'd cleaned the cover with a saddle soap and wiped it dry so it wouldn't stain her clothes.

He huffed and picked up another nail. What clothes? Everything she owned had burned. But she'd had on some sort of jacket last night when he checked on her, and this morning at breakfast she'd worn a blue dress that Jane would have saved for church. It fit Mary well, and he figured Ella had something to do with it.

Surprised, he stopped pounding and looked out over the near pasture. This was the first time he'd thought of Jane without a knot twisting him in two. He still missed her more than he would air for his lungs, but the pain had lessened.

Maybe God didn't take her. Maybe He received her.

Something akin to hope had pushed in next to the pain. Something with hair the color of a blood-bay horse and eyes like a meadow after rain.

He breathed deeply, hoping to find that scent again. Another rain was what they needed. It had a way of healing over scars—his and those on the Dodsons' farm.

Yesterday after Graham left with a pocket full of notes, Hugh saw the book in the grass where it had fallen when Mary shoved it at him. Confounded woman made him crazy running into burning buildings like she did.

He'd picked it up, finding half the pages bent from the way it landed, and catching a fine gold chain that had probably been used as a marker. A fine gold chain with a thin locket attached.

His heart nearly stopped.

He pulled pieces of grass from the pages but left the chain where it was and slid the Bible in the back of his waistband. Last night after cleaning it, he'd set it on a high shelf in the tack room.

The screen door slapped and he tipped his hat brim up enough to see Mary walking around the end of the house toward the old cottonwood. The blue dress brushed her ankles, and Helen's old lace-up shoes didn't seem to fit the picture.

But he didn't care what Mary wore or who the clothes belonged to. He grabbed the box of nails and took them to the tack room. Mending the corral could wait.

She sat in the swing facing away from him, walking the swing, hands low on the ropes, not reaching to pull herself into the air. A coppery braid hung to her waist.

He held the Bible behind him as he approached. "Mary."

She toed herself to a stop and looked over her shoulder. "Hugh."

He wanted to hear his name on her lips the rest of his life. But this wasn't the day to ask. It was a day to heal.

He sidestepped his way around until he was in front of her. "You look nice."

He could win prizes with his speech-making.

"Thank you." She smiled a sad smile, and he wanted to kiss it from her lips.

She was completely still, hands on the ropes. Nothing to say.

He wanted to give her hope, bring back the light, so he took a step closer. "I found something in the grass behind the house yesterday after the ranger left the farm."

"Ranger," she said with resignation.

"Silas Graham, from the Colorado Rangers up in Denver. When I stopped to see Sheriff Payton, he said he'd send Graham. Turns out, he's interested in the case.

She glanced away, shrugged.

Another step brought him to her knees. He dropped to his boot heels and held the Bible over her lap.

Her hands trembled as she took it. Then she clutched it against her chest the same way she'd been holding it two nights ago.

The memory fired through him like the flames had the room.

Tears puddled at her lashes.

He waited, finding no words that were safe to say.

"How—how is it possible?" she whispered, eyes shining like dew on the grass.

"You were holding it when I picked you up off the bed and carried you downstairs. Do you remember shoving it at me outside when I told you to wait where you were?"

She shook her head, no evidence of the memory.

"Maybe this isn't the time to point out that you don't do what you're told."

She hiccupped a breath. "No, it isn't."

"Open it. Where it falls apart on its own."

It bulged slightly near the center, and with both hands, she turned back two sides of the well-worn book.

A sharp breath cut from her. She blinked, then blinked again. Slowly she lifted the thin gold chain until it tugged against the oval locket with a small bird engraved on the front. With trembling fingers, she pressed the clasp and the cover opened to reveal a miniature portrait of herself.

He'd thought it was beautiful. But not as beautiful as the real Mary Agan McCrae, warm with life and energy and a smile that melted his insides. He'd give anything to see that smile again.

Her whisper wavered as she read the inscription on the inside. "To my dearest Aunt Bertie, whose name I bear. I love you. Mary Agan McCrae, April 11, 1903."

As she looked across at him, eye-to-eye, the corner of her lip curved in a near smile. "Do you know why there's a bird engraved on the front?"

Of course he didn't know. He didn't know his own name right then. "Tell me."

Her expression became childlike, innocent. "When I was a little girl, I used to call her Aunt Birdie. That's what I thought Mama had been saying all along—Birdie. Not until I learned to spell did I realize the mistake."

"It's a perfectly understandable mistake," he said, thinking of Kip. "And it's your proof. The locket proves who you are, Mary, that you are your aunt and uncle's heir."

~

Numb from loss and disappointment, Mary struggled to make sense of what seemed so unreal. But she could feel the thin chain wrapped around her fingers. Hear the crunch of dirt beneath Hugh's boots as he shifted, smell coffee on his breath.

So close he was, she wrapped her arms around his neck. Was she dreaming?

"'Thank you' seems so weak a phrase. But I do thank you—with all I have."

His hands braced her back, and as she withdrew, they slid to her waist. He still hunkered in front of her, his hat tipped up, reminding her of pictures she'd seen of cowboys around a campfire. All he needed was a guitar.

His hands slid away, and she felt untethered without them. "Will proof of who I am matter now without the will? I can't prove my aunt and uncle left the farm to me."

"An attorney's signature was at the bottom of the will, so there should be a copy."

A spark flickered in Mary's breast. "Who was it? Do you remember?"

"T. F. Beckman. I don't know if he's still around, but we'll find out. The banker saw the will too. He should vouch for it."

She considered the locket, smoothing her fingers over the engraved bird on the front. "Do we have the slightest chance to stop the auction with this?"

"If you're up to it, we can ride in tomorrow and find out." He smiled, and the lines at the corners of his eyes tugged tiny strings attached to her heart. "Maybe there'll be a reply from your brother."

That afternoon, Mary sat in the sewing rocker in the Hutton's parlor with her aunt's Bible open on her lap. The locket had been there all along as a bookmark. If only Mary had read it when she should have, as faithfully as her mother and aunt had taught, what suffering could have been avoided.

The locket and chain marked Psalm 37. The verses continued from the lefthand page to the right, familiar lines that carried childhood memories of her mother reading to the family on winter evenings. The psalm held so many promises of God's provision, and so many warnings against harmful choices.

Mary's gaze fell first to "fret not," repeated three times in the first eight verses—an insistent reminder that worry accomplished nothing. Mary was an expert in that regard. All her fretting had done nothing but weaken her faith.

But also repeated was mention of dwelling in the land. Inheriting it. How tenderly those verses touched her, as if God had known all along what was going to happen.

The psalm also spoke of evildoers who wreak havoc and are envious of those blessed by God. Mary laid her head against the back of the rocker, amazed at how the ancient insight addressed her life so perfectly.

The screen door slapped the house and the lighter step of shorter males scattered across the kitchen floor.

"Miss Helen, do you have anything that will tide us over till supper?"

One of the older boys had spoken, because Kip stood at the parlor entrance watching Mary with a question on his face.

"Hello, Kip. What are you up to?"

"The business end of a milk cow, Pa says."

Mary clapped a hand over her mouth at the unexpected remark, desperate not to laugh at the serious little cowboy standing before her. She could easily imagine Hugh saying such a thing.

"Well, Kip, when I was your age, I was up to the same thing. We had a lot of milk cows at our dairy. Still do."

"Are you gonna marry us like Miss Ella married Uncle Cale?"

Evidently, Kip had learned quite well from his father how to speak his mind. Shocked into silence, she gaped a moment before gathering her chin.

"Excuse me?"

"We seen you huggin' Pa out on the swing, and Ty said only folks who are married do that. If you married Pa, then you could be our ma."

Mary's powers of concentration were beyond her reach in the face of such innocent honesty. In her spontaneity, she'd not considered curious little observers. She should have known better.

"It's usually the man who asks a woman to marry him, and your pa hasn't asked me. Not that I *expect* him to do such a thing, don't get me wrong." She was rambling to a seven-year-old. "Your pa might not want me to be your ma."

"Oh, he does. Me and Jay and Ty heard him in the barn one night, talking to Shorty about it. Sounded like he was prayin', but he don't pray much, so we figured he was talkin' to his horse."

Helen came up behind the boy, wiping her hands on her apron. "If you want a cookie, you'd best get one now before your brothers eat them all. And take it outside."

The youngster bolted to the kitchen without another word.

Mary also had no other words. In fact, she didn't know what to think much less say. Hopefully, Helen had not heard their conversation, but Mary would wager that the woman was blessed with the ears of a barn owl.

CHAPTER TWENTY-THREE

Mary had gotten little sleep with Kip's remarks running through her head all night. Mama had always said truth more often than not fell "from the mouths of babes." But was it truth the boy had shared or merely something he thought he had heard his father say when it was nothing of the sort?

Marry Hugh Hutton? She had avoided marriage for so long that the idea was difficult to swallow. Yes, she enjoyed his company—if she wasn't arguing with him—and she admired his raw strength of character and spirit. And yes, she'd been quite bold in reaching out for him. He drew her like no other man ever had. Her behavior would certainly knit her mother's brows into a frown, condemning her deportment as entirely too familiar. Flirtatious even.

But there was something about him.

Mary picked through her thoughts the same way she was picking through Ella's lovely clothes, overwhelmed once more by such generosity. Everything she could possibly need was here, other than a hat for her trip into town this morning, and a decent pair of shoes. Her stop at Western Union would involve more than checking for a response from Lewis. She would have to notify her bank to wire the rest of her savings. She could not continue living on the charity of the Hutton family, and if she didn't get the farm, she would need money to get home.

"I'm off, Helen. What do you think?" Wearing a simple rose-colored suit and white blouse, Mary stopped in the kitchen, where Helen was rolling out pie dough, and turned it from one side to the other.

Helen dusted her hands on her apron. "Stay right there." She hurried down the hallway, then returned with a wide-brimmed straw hat.

"Take this old straw of mine. It's not near fancy enough for that fine suit you're wearing, but you'll be fried as a fritter if you don't cover up. Just stuff it under the seat when you get to town."

"Thank you, Helen. You are the most thoughtful person I know."

From her apron pocket, Helen drew a small roll of paper. "If you would, I have a few things you can pick up for me at the general. Hugh won't mind." She pressed the paper into Mary's hand. "And there's a little extra for anything you might need."

"Oh, but—"

Helen laid a hand on Mary's cheek. "God has a way of helping us make do, don't you agree?"

The screen door opened.

"You ready?"

Mary squeezed Helen's hand and whispered, "I will pay you back."

Hugh entered, hat in hand, a fresh blue shirt and denims, clean boots setting him off finer than Mary had seen him. His vest had even been brushed. And he'd shaved.

"As I'll ever be," Mary said, tucking the rolled paper into her skirt pocket. It was much thicker than one piece of paper.

"Helen, you need anything from town?"

"I gave Mary a list." Helen folded the round of pie dough in half and laid it in a glass pan. "And while you're there, I wouldn't mind one or two of those bon-bons from Ott's."

She gave Hugh an under-the-brow look that Mary couldn't interpret.

He set his hat with a swift "Yes, ma'am."

Mary had heard the birdsong again this morning, and asked Hugh about it as they pulled out of the yard.

"Meadowlarks," he said. "Sing every morning, calling to one another."

She would not have guessed the song came from a cousin of such a familiar bird. "They're lovely. And so flute-like, not at all like the meadowlarks in Pennsylvania."

Grateful for the floppy brim of Helen's broad hat, Mary felt somewhat hidden from view and it suited her. Sitting beside Hugh was uncomfortable due to Kip's question. It only stirred several more questions of her own, such as what would she say if Hugh proposed?

She certainly had feelings for him, but could she stay now and not return to the dairy? She had entertained the option earlier, frustrated by Lewis's overbearing ways, but she'd rested on the comfort of Aunt Bertie and Uncle Ernest. And later, after learning of their will, she had determined to do so. But now, with the way things had turned out, could she remain in Colorado?

She was nearly destitute—at least temporarily. Would his proposal be merely an offer of home, hearth, and safety? Though too old to consider herself an orphan, that was exactly how she felt.

So much for doing things on her own.

Fret not.

The admonition fluttered through her as clear as the meadowlark's song. She'd been bolder coming West than she felt at the moment. Had she known what awaited her, she would not have come. She would have avoided the heartache, fear, and destitution.

And she would have missed Helen, Ella, and the boys. And their father.

Could he be part of God's design for her?

Her chest tightened a little as she remembered her bold embrace yesterday morning.

"You all right?"

Caught in her musings! She tugged at the hat, more grateful than ever for its floppy brim. "Yes, quite. Thank you. And thank you for bringing me to town today."

"We'll go to sheriff's and find out where the attorney's office is. Next, the bank, then fill Helen's order, and hit Ott's and Western Union on the way out of town. Sound good?"

He was actually asking her what she thought.

As if she had a say in any of this.

"You have the locket?" He bent over and looked under the brim at her, worry clouding the blue.

She fingered the gold chain over the neck of her blouse and revealed the locket. "Right here."

"Good."

Barlow clopped on a few more paces.

"The millinery is next to the general. They have hats."

Laughter bubbled up at his tone, and she lifted the brim and turned to him. "You don't like this one?"

As they rode into town, Mary removed Helen's hat and tucked it under the bench seat. The scratchy straw had pulled hair loose from her chignon, and she did her best to brush it from her face. Oh, for the combs. No doubt her mother's lovely combs lay somewhere on the open range between the farm and the Rafter-H, trampled by now.

At the sheriff's office, Hugh wrapped the reins around the brake handle and helped her down. Already the street was clogged with conveyances.

He opened the door and waited as she entered first.

"Ma'am." The sheriff's gaze flicked from her to Hugh, and he brought another chair to his desk.

"This is Mary McCrae, the Dodsons' niece," Hugh said, then looked to her. "Mary, this is Sheriff Payton."

She nodded once in greeting.

"Graham was by yesterday. Told me what he found out at the farm." Payton dipped his head. "My condolences, ma'am. He's got a theory, but he wouldn't share it. Tight-lipped fella."

Hugh asked about the attorney and learned his office was across the street from the courthouse.

Mary had the distinct feeling that Hugh and the sheriff were not on the best of terms.

Which was exactly how she felt about the banker who, twenty minutes later, held the opened locket up to the light and glanced between Mary and the small portrait several times. Then he read the inscription, closed the locket, and returned it to her. "Do you have the will?"

"It burned with the house." Mary burned with tension. *Fret not … fret not.*

"Is there a copy?"

"T. F. Beckman's office has a copy," Hugh said. "We were just there and they said they'd send a copy over." Hugh sat as solid as a pine beside her, and Mary silently thanked the Lord for his help.

"Mr. Hutton, do you have interest in the Dodson property?"

A muscle in Hugh's jaw flexed. "I'm here to see that Miss McCrae's rights are upheld as the Dodsons' heir."

The man adjusted his spectacles. "This is quite a unique case. A judge will have to review matters, but I do know that the auction is still set for June tenth."

"Does this evidence not prove my inheritance?" Mary's hands tightened into fists at her sides.

"We'll wait for the judge's ruling and let you know."

"And how long will that take?" Hugh's voice had hit rock bottom.

"I can't say. But we will let you know."

"Thank you." Mary locked her fingers into Hugh's elbow and stood, dragging him with her. Irritation rolled off him like steam off the milking parlor floor. She couldn't be sure that he would not climb over the desk and rearrange the banker's tie, which would be no help to her at all.

Outside, he handed her up to the wagon seat and quickly followed, his jaw tight enough to crack.

Worrying about his reaction pushed her own misgivings to the background. She touched his arm and felt steel beneath the fabric of his shirt. "Hugh—it will be all right."

Wasn't that what Helen had said weeks ago? Things had gotten worse, much worse, yet Helen was right. Mary was still alive and breathing. That counted for something. Plus the locket had been found.

Hugh's eyes were blue fire in his sun-browned face, and she squeezed his arm, hoping to bring him back from the edge of wherever he was.

~

The tables had turned so drastically that Hugh wasn't sure if he was afoot or horseback. Mary looked at him with worry all over her. How had she become more important to him than the Rafter-H and good grazing land?

He scrubbed his hand down his face, gathered the reins, and turned Barlow away from the bank. The sooner he got out of town and back to the ranch, the better.

"Don't forget Helen's list." Mary unrolled several bills wrapped in notepaper—Helen's way of helping her get what she needed. She didn't have a dime to her name now. But if the authorities agreed that the Dodson place was rightfully hers, she might have enough from that oil seep to buy the town. Depending on the quality of the seep.

He pulled in a keg of air and let it escape through his nose, hoping his pent-up anger went with it. He didn't need to be taking out his frustration on Mary. "Read it to me."

She lifted her chin and stared straight ahead.

"Please." He was pretty much snubbed to the post where this gal was concerned, and she didn't even know it.

"Four lengths of toweling. Garden seeds. Two bars of lavender soap. Comb, hairbrush—"

She stopped reading.

"What?"

Her voice went soft and drew him down closer. "Most of what is on this list isn't for Helen, and it's certainly not for you or the boys."

He pulled up in front of the general. "It's her way, Mary. Let her do it."

She curled the list into her hand, slump-shouldered, head drooping.

He set the brake and angled toward her. "Helen and her Ben never had children. Since she's come to the Rafter-H, she's had only us rowdy fellas to care for, other than Ella for a few months last year. She thinks a lot of you, and this is her gift. Let her give it."

Mary pressed her fingers beneath her eyes and sat up a little straighter. "She sounds a great deal like my Aunt Bertie."

Hugh stepped down and came around to Mary's side.

She stood and held out her hand, but he gripped her slender waist and lifted her to the sidewalk. Her hands rested on his shoulders, and he liked it. He liked it a lot. But they were in public. He stepped back.

Mary fumbled with the paper. "As soon as my money arrives, I'll repay her. Though money will never be enough to repay you and your family for your kindnesses."

"Don't fret yourself about it." He tugged on his hat. "I'll meet you here in an hour."

Hugh headed for the café a block west, where he found Graham at the back corner table.

"Mind if I join you?"

The ranger indicated an empty chair. "I could use the company."

Hugh hung his hat on his knee as the waiter brought coffee and a mug.

Crumbs on Graham's empty plate gave clear sign of apple pie, and Hugh ordered a slice.

The ranger nursed his coffee. "What brings you to town?"

The pie arrived, and the waiter topped off both mugs.

Hugh thanked the man and waited for him to make himself scarce. No telling how good his hearing was. "Found the locket."

Graham's brows rose—the most expression Hugh had seen on the fella. "In all that mess?"

Hugh filled him in on the discovery, near like a miracle to Hugh's way of thinking. "Like Providence had a hand in it."

He tucked in to his pie, not near as good as Helen's, but not much was. "We also found a copy of the will at the attorney's office. He's passed on, but it was in the files."

"Did you show the bank?"

Hugh's mouth was full as well as his gullet where the bank was concerned. He swallowed. "The auction's still on until we hear from a judge." It wasn't so much the loan officer, but the whole infernal situation that galled him.

"Can she bid on the farm?"

Hugh picked up his coffee. "Depends on how much money she has back home. Everything she had here burned."

Graham shook his head. "Dang shame." He pinned Hugh. "You gonna bid on it now?"

"Might."

That question had been skirting his brain since the second fire. And after talking to the banker today, how else would Mary get her family's farm if the judge dallied in his decision? If Hugh won the farm, he could lease it to her in exchange for grazing rights.

Or he could marry her and she'd be the heir again.

The idea caught him off guard. Why hadn't he thought of it earlier? But as quickly as it struck, it splintered. She'd think he was marrying her for the land, and that wasn't it at all.

He wanted to be with her. And from the way his sons were around her, he figured they did too.

The whole thing was working out backwards. Frustrating as a hobble on a huntin' dog.

But the auction was still set, and Graham knew about the oil slick.

"I've been thinking," Hugh said, "about who else will be at the auction."

Something flashed in Graham's eyes. "Sounds like we're ridin' the same trail."

Hugh nodded. The two of them together might be able to flush the son-of-a-gun out of hiding.

CHAPTER TWENTY-FOUR

A dollar and seventy-five cents.

Mary scrunched her toes in the new black low-tops, feeling like a decadent spendthrift. But she needed shoes, and she'd had just enough left after getting everything on Helen's list, plus a hat. An empress style, not too extravagant, but with a wider brim that Mary had become accustomed to.

When Hugh walked with her to the Ott Candy Store, Mary caught him looking at her feet. She'd also caught him paying for two small bags of bon-bons. One for Helen and one for herself.

She didn't know what to think. No man had ever bought her candy.

Or saved her life three times, or told her not to *fret*.

His wording hung on her ear the rest of the day, including at their stop at the Western Union office. The remains of her savings should be at the bank by tomorrow.

But her brother's reply to her earlier telegram rested in her hand as the wagon carried them out of town and around the bend at the Soda Springs.

> *You are my younger sister, Mary Agan McCrae stop*
> *Lewis Sean McCrae*

Mary stared at the impersonal paper, as devoid of feeling as her brother's words. She hadn't really known what to expect from Lewis, and frankly, was surprised he'd answered at all. A piece of her heart chipped off at his lack of familial affection. He had simply recited their birth order, as if recording a stock breeding record.

At least he had answered.

A sudden gunshot from above made her flinch into Hugh's arm as she looked up at the red ridge rising sharply beside the road.

"Backfire," he said without so much as a twitch.

"From what? And where?"

"Up on what they call Skyline Drive. Buzz wagons chug along the road up there carrying people who want to see the view."

She shuddered. "It's hard to imagine conveyances of any kind riding on what appears to be so narrow."

He chuckled. "Oh, it is."

Grateful that Hugh wasn't taking the wagon up the scenic route, she looked again at the telegram, and the biblical admonition came to mind once more. *Fret not.* Even here, with Lewis's brief reply, the command was a negative directive, instructing her to *not* do something. It was harder to not do than to do, and she couldn't help the quick comparison of Shakespeare's "to be or not to be."

She hadn't committed enough of Psalm 37 to memory, but she did recall several words of a positive nature concerning what to do, such as "trust in the Lord" and "delight in the Lord." She had read it more carefully this morning.

Weary of jostling by the time they made the farm road, Mary revived at the sight of three little boys running down the lane from the ranch house, waving their arms and hollering.

Hugh pulled up by the house and the boys dashed around to his side.

"Did you bring us anything, Pa?"

Kip held Finley and another pup by their rope leads, and the family's older dog stood off to the side, tail wagging a slow salute.

"I sure did," Hugh said as he helped Mary down. "I brought you plenty to help us carry inside."

Three faces fell, expectancy draining like water through a sieve.

"And I have a treat for workers who cheerfully take to the task," Mary added.

Not only did the boys brighten at her words, but Hugh's mouth quirked up on one side and he flashed her a blue glance that spoke of appreciation. For what, she wondered. Surely he wasn't counting on a peppermint stick himself.

General supplies were boxed, and Hugh hefted the biggest. Ty and Jay each carried a smaller one. Mary handed several sacks to Kip, who dropped the ropes to manage the bags. The pups followed behind like his shadow.

Inside, Mary helped Helen unload her kitchen order before going to her room with entirely too many items indicative of Helen's generosity. Her feet ached from breaking in her new shoes, and after she put everything away, she slipped out of her shoes and into an extra pair of Hugh's socks, washed and returned to her room in recent days.

She saved the other pair to wear tomorrow with Helen's lace-ups. A split riding skirt had been among Ella's hand-me-downs, and Mary intended to put it to good use on a ride to the oil seep. She wanted to see it for herself.

She socked her way into the kitchen, found an apron in a cupboard drawer, and looped the strings twice around her waist, ending with a bow. She and Hugh had missed dinner, and she wanted to contribute to the evening meal. Something that would stick to everyone's ribs.

"If you don't have dessert planned, I could make a bread pudding."

Helen looked up from peeling potatoes and wiped the back of her hand across her forehead. "That will hit the spot. I have a few currants if you want them and half a loaf of bread I was going to give the chickens tomorrow. Your idea sounds much more pleasing."

Mary eyed the scrap can, hoping the bread hadn't already been donated. Only potato peelings and carrot tops showed, so she rummaged through the kitchen and found the loaf in the pie safe.

That evening, the entire family gathered in the dining room rather than the kitchen, for the sweet aroma of cinnamon and sugar had drawn everyone out of hiding for the pudding. Ella sat closest to the hall so she could hear the babies if they squeaked from their bureau-drawer beds. So little they were, that they nestled in their bundling like dolls, each in a drawer set close to the bed.

"I don't want Cale going to the trouble of bringing the cradle from the house, since we'll be going home any day now," she said. "They should both fit foot-to-foot for a little while, until we can get a second crib."

Hugh's spoon stopped halfway to his mouth and a strange expression crossed his face.

"What?" Cale asked, always the first to notice the smallest change in his brother.

Hugh scooted from the table. "I'll be right back."

Cale watched him leave the room and slid his own chair over the floral rug, but Ella laid her hand on his arm and shook her head the tiniest bit. Cale frowned but paused to read what only he could see in her expression, then dug in to his dessert.

Amazed by the family's ability to communicate, Mary remembered an odd quote she'd heard as a child, attributed to St. Francis. "Preach always; if necessary, use words."

It had to be the love among all of them that sent feelings and sentiments flying on wings of subtle expression without the need for spoken words.

Everyone was nearly finished with dessert before the screen door opened, followed by a heavy thump on the kitchen floor.

Helen stood. "What in heaven?"

The boys fired from their seats in record time, and the last two piled into the first who had stopped at the kitchen door.

"A baby bed?" Ty asked.

Helen, Mary, Ella, and Cale gathered behind the boys, each nearly as surprised at the dust-covered cradle.

"It was in the loft. There are two of them." Hugh hunkered down to meet his boys at eye level. "This one belonged to your Uncle Cale." He wiped dust off the top of the cradle's lip that covered the head and traced a carved C in the wood.

"Where's yours?" Jay asked.

"I left it up in the loft. Each of you boys slept in it when you were the size of Ella's babies."

"We were *that* small?" Kip's eyebrows nearly rose to his hairline.

Helen squeezed around the group, rinsed out a towel, and returned to the cradle.

Mary joined her with another wet cloth, and they wiped it down until the fine cherry wood revealed skilled craftsmanship.

Ella covered her mouth with both hands, and Cale drew her to his side.

"Does yours have an H carved into the top, Pa?"

Hugh stood and roughed Kip's hair. "Yes, it does, son."

"Are you ever gonna use it again?"

Mary's breath stuck in her throat as she waited for Hugh's reply.

He bent to lift the head of the cradle as Cale picked up the foot. They made for the door, and Hugh's eyes caught hers. "I don't know, son. Maybe."

~

After setting the cradle in the bed of Cale's wagon, Hugh went to the wash stand and splashed cold water on his face. He had found the twin cradles one night after checking on the boys, covered with a tarp and stacked in a corner of the loft.

Burning with curiosity, he rubbed water on his neck and arms. What was going on in that pretty head of Mary McCrae?

When Kip had asked what he did, she looked like she wasn't breathing at all.

The screen door squeaked and Mary joined him on the porch, where she braced herself against the railing and stood looking up at the moon.

This could be the opportunity he'd been trying to fenagle.

He fingered his wet hair back and dried his hands before easing up beside her. Trying not to be obvious, he angled himself a bit so he could study her profile, the way her pale skin nearly glowed in the moonlight. He was close enough that he could run his fingers over her cheek—

"I want to see the oil seep."

His hand stopped and he shoved it through his hair again. Words jammed in his throat, and it took a second to clear his airway.

"What?"

"I want to go to the oil seep. I'd like to ride Barlow out there tomorrow."

He gave her a good once-over, from the hem of her pink dress to the white collar that framed her pearly throat.

He swallowed hard. "You ride?"

She laughed, light as the breeze. "You know I do. I was born on a farm, remember?"

Right.

So much for churning up sweet words in the moonlight. "I'll have the horses saddled and ready after breakfast."

"Horses?" She looked at him as if she didn't know what he meant. She was no fool—she knew exactly what he meant, and her innocent act made not one bit of difference. She wasn't ridin' out there alone.

The next morning, he was good as his word and had the horses ready. Helen had a picnic prepared. Of course.

She handed him the poke. "Can't have you getting feeble out there in case you don't make it home for dinner." The woman's gray eyes sparked, and she fought a grin like a yearling colt fights a halter.

"Thank you, Helen. That's very sweet of you." Mary was wearing the split skirt Ella had worn in the river-crossing for the movie scene last year. Helen's lace-ups showed beneath it, as did the top of Hugh's socks. He'd wondered where all his socks had gone.

He wasn't all that happy about this trip and had carried an uneasy feeling since sunup. He set it aside and tromped down to the boys' room for an old hat of Jay's he thought might fit Mary. When he returned, she was holding a rolled blanket. Helen's idea for sure.

"Let's go." He dropped the hat on Mary's head, then held the screen door so it didn't slap her southern quarter.

She marched out to Barlow and lashed the blanket roll behind the cantle as if she did it every day. The hat fit just right.

There might be more to Mary McCrae than he'd figured.

He tied the poke on Shorty's saddle, checked the rifle in the scabbard, then went to the barn for his gun belt.

When he returned, she was mounted, waiting for him to lead out.

They headed east toward the farm and she watched the ground as if reading sign.

"You lookin' for something?"

"My combs. I thought they might have bounced out of my carpet bag with everything else. At least I hope they did. If not, I'll never see them again."

Hugh felt fool-paint hit his cheeks. He'd kicked himself enough over tying her bag to Shorty, but if she was right, they might be something she could salvage from her losses. He started looking too.

"Describe them."

"They're tortoise shell with sterling silver scroll work on the tops. They were my mother's."

Great. Just great.

Riding with their heads down, it took longer to reach the farm. Hugh turned Shorty away from the yard and around the burned-out buildings. At hearing a sniff, he looked over his shoulder to see Mary swipe at her cheeks.

She caught him watching and tugged Jay's hat farther down.

Meadowlarks sang north of them, answered from not far ahead. Mary's attention followed their song, and her face lit with a smile. If he could make those birds sing all day, he would just to see that smile. Such a simple thing in all her loss.

The sun was at late-morning by the time they reached the meadow where he and Cale had stopped. "This'll be a good place to eat. Lay out the blanket, and I'll ground-tie the horses over in the taller grass."

He unlashed the poke and set it nearby, then led the horses away from the creek and into the edge of a small aspen grove. Purple columbines huddled in the shade, and he pulled up a few, knocking the dirt off their roots. Maybe he'd have a chance yet to ask her what he wanted.

A check in his gut sent him to Shorty, and he pulled the rifle from its scabbard. Too many times he'd been on this farm and something unexpected had happened. He wasn't gonna be caught off guard again, flowers or no.

He slowed his pace as he approached Mary and the blanket she'd spread, watching her set things out with purpose and arrange them just so. He'd missed that in a woman—the way they saw to how they wanted things done. He longed for what he'd once had. Sharing life and hard times. Drawing a woman close beneath the covers, feeling her breath on his skin. He thought he'd lost those things forever, but spending so much time around Mary stirred hope that there might be a chance. If she leaned at all the way he was leaning.

He'd done plenty of talking to Shorty and the Lord about it late in the night, and he counted on God listening better than his horse.

He tucked the flowers behind him.

Mary looked up, the hat shading her face, but he sensed her hesitation at the rifle.

"Are you expecting trouble? Maybe another bear?" No tease in her tone.

He laid the rifle on the blanket corner, then dropped down beside it. "It doesn't hurt to be prepared is all."

He offered her the flowers.

She seemed pleased and rubbed them against her cheek. "They're columbines, aren't they? The flowers you told me about."

"They don't smell like other flowers do." He watched her face, the way her lips curved a little on the edges.

"But they're beautiful, and I thank you."

She gave him a lazy gaze, and he knew swallowing today's meal would be harder than he'd thought with his air cinched off like it was.

"And prepared is exactly how you appear—with flowers and guns, armed for anything." A smile tilted the last word.

Beef sandwiches, cold tea in a jar, and a crock of bread pudding held down a checkered napkin in the center of the blanket. Mary gave him a saucer and spoon, then folded her hands and bowed her head.

This was going to be a regular event. Had been all his life, so it shouldn't be that hard but it was. He was talkin' to the Lord in private more lately, but in front of people, it was still a chore. He removed his hat and did the deed.

Mary's glance of gratitude was worth it.

Uneasiness nettled him and made conversation more difficult than usual. He couldn't explain it to himself and didn't even try to explain it to her. He cut the meal short. "I'll get the horses."

Her clear disappointment gouged him, but his gut was never wrong. He couldn't afford to dally like he wanted, alone with her and wanting to say certain things. As much as he liked the isolation, it was dangerous.

She had the food up and the blanket rolled when he got back, but no smile. Sadness haunted her, and she kept her head down, turned away from him.

As she grabbed Barlow's reins to mount, he stepped in close and covered her hand with his. "We can do this again if you're willing. But I'm uneasy about being out here, with all the things that have happened on the farm. I don't want to put you in danger."

She lifted her chin, and her green eyes met his with a longing he hadn't expected. Her lips parted and without thinking, he met them with his own. Warm and responsive, she touched his face, and he pulled her into him.

Lord A' mighty, he might be dying. Heaven couldn't be better than the taste of her sweet mouth and the soft curve of her waist.

CHAPTER TWENTY-FIVE

Grateful she had the horse to lean against, Mary took a moment to catch her breath. Nothing she had ever imagined could have prepared her to be kissed by Hugh Hutton. His reined-in passion stirred her, and the beat of his heart against her own mingled his sense of urgency with her surprise. The combination charged through her like an electrical current.

She'd thought he didn't want to be with her, didn't enjoy her company, despite the flowers, but that misconception melted like snow beneath sunlight. She must keep her wits about her, mind clear and alert, especially at his mention of danger. Such an unlikely concern in the meadow, bordered as it was by shimmering aspen trees and canopied by the clearest blue.

She mounted and joined Hugh as he rode along a nearby stream toward a rocky bluff beyond the trees. They crossed at a narrow bend near the granite wall, and Hugh reined in by a darkened low spot between the bluff and the stream.

Mary stopped beside him.

"There." He dipped his chin and she followed his gaze.

"That's it? That's the seep?"

"Fifty years ago, a fella found one like it not far from here, and it proved enough crude that the town of Florence grew into an oil boom. Folks have been looking for another one like it ever since. Seeps were found, but they all petered out after a few gallons."

He leaned over as if noticing something unexpected on the

Hope Is Built

ground, then urged Shorty back.

"How will we know about this one?"

"Come around here on my other side."

An odd answer to her question, and it made the back of her neck crawl. She squinted at the place that held his interest but saw nothing other than hoof prints.

He straightened and looked downstream toward a distant river valley. "We won't until someone comes out to test it. But until then—"

A gunshot hit the rock behind them.

Hugh grabbed his rifle and lunged from his saddle for Mary, taking her to the ground on Barlow's off side. The horses spooked across the stream.

Another shot sent rock chips flying, closer to their position.

"Close your eyes." He tightened his arms around her and rolled them into the cedars.

A third shot kicked up dirt near the seep.

With her arms pinned to her side and Hugh on top of her, Mary struggled for air. "I can't breathe."

He bent a knee to shift his weight but didn't move from her.

She drew her hands up against his chest and took a deep breath.

"Stay here," he whispered.

"What?" She'd heard him, but she knew what that command meant, and her fingers curled into his shirt.

"Stay here under the cedars, out of view. I'm going to get around him." He drew his revolver and pressed it into her hand with a look that tore her soul. "Use it if you have to. But let him get close enough that you don't miss."

He brushed his lips against hers, then rolled to his knees.

Scrambling through the brush, Hugh quickly disappeared, and Mary's confidence went with him. What if he was shot? How would she help him? Who was shooting at them, and why? Was it over the seep? Was it really that important?

Her ears strained to hear every movement, detect Hugh's

211

position and that of the shooter. Pushing up on her elbows, she held the revolver in both hands, solid and heavier than the .22 she'd used hunting rabbits. She cocked the hammer, sensing the weapon would put a hole through a man. No peashooter this.

The gunfire had stopped, and the horses wandered to the creek, but didn't drink. Instead, they blew and pawed at the water.

Based on what Hugh had said about the seep found earlier, this one could be the answer to her financial need. Or it could be the death of them both.

No wonder he had been so insistent she tell no one. Yet someone knew.

Silence surrounded her. No birds sang, no creatures chittered or scurried through the cedars. It seemed hours but must have been only minutes since Hugh left. She wanted to get up and search for him, find him well and sound, feel the strength of him within her arms.

"God, protect him." Her blood pounded louder than her whispered prayer.

Tight with tension and anxious over Hugh's safety, she noted the sun had moved beyond the trees along the creek. Her fingers ached from squeezing the butt of the gun, and she relaxed them until the snap of a twig sent her pulse soaring. Holding her breath as tightly as the revolver, she squinted into the brush toward the sound.

"Mary."

At Hugh's voice, she nearly wept. "Here."

"Don't shoot me."

Relief fired through her veins leaving her weak and shaky. She rose to her knees, still holding the gun, but her finger not on the trigger.

Crouching low, he pushed through the brush and dropped to his knees before her. He slipped the gun from her hands, eased the hammer down, and pulled her against him.

His shirt was soaked with sweat and struck through with

cedar and dirt. Nothing had ever smelled sweeter. She could stay there forever.

~

Hugh's thoughts raced as hard as his pulse, but one decision outran them all. No matter what happened with Mary's land, the oil seep, or the Rafter-H, he wasn't letting her go.

He cupped her head beneath his chin and anger surged at the scent of her fear. He swore he'd find the shooter no matter how long it took. God help him if he found the man alone.

He had turned back at the sound of hoofbeats carrying the culprit downstream toward Four Mile Creek, and in his mind, he saw again the rider that had run by him the night of the house fire.

In time, the land around them came to life. Jays squawked. Ground squirrels chirped. With Mary beneath his arm, clinging to his side, they gathered the horses. They took no easy pace home and made the ranch in what felt like half the time. In the empty yard, he dropped the horses' reins. The boys were at school.

Mary insisted on untying the poke and taking it inside.

"What in the world?" Helen gawked as they fell into chairs at the table, dirty, flushed, and out of breath.

Mary clutched the sack. "Someone shot at us."

Hugh longed to draw her close again, but Helen's concern intervened, and she came nearer.

"What do you mean someone shot at you?"

"Just that," Hugh said as he went for two cups and the water pump. He filled both and set them on the table.

Mary took the tea jar out of the poke, full of columbines, and set them root-down in her cup with a glance his way.

He pushed his cup toward her and got another.

Helen brought two plates and the remains of a canned peach pie, giving each of them a hearty serving and a fork. "Neither of you appears to be bleeding, so eat up, then tell me what happened."

~

Mary lay atop the bed, still wearing her riding clothes, and staring at the ceiling. She might never sleep again.

By her count, she had been in Colorado four weeks, and her life had been threatened four times. Was God trying to tell her something? Was this whole trip a foolish mistake? Should she have stayed in Pennsylvania and married the next dairyman her brother invited to Sunday dinner?

The worst thing that had happened to her there was being kicked into the wall by a cow. She'd never been shot at, burned out, or snared.

Yet if she hadn't come west, she would not have known about her aunt and uncle's passing, their farm going up for auction, or the oil seep that could possibly be productive.

And she wouldn't have fallen in love with a gruff, blue-eyed cowboy who took her breath away. Not to mention three lovable little boys who had stolen her affections at first sight.

"Oh, Lord, you're all I really have. All I've ever had. Everything else can be taken away." Grief spilled from the corners of her eyes and into her ears, and she sat up, irritated by such a ridiculous sensation in the midst of her self-pity.

A knock came at the door. "Miss Mary?"

Kip, she guessed. The boys were home from school. Throwing her legs over the edge of the bed, she straightened her blouse. "Come in."

His blond head poked around the door and he entered holding her columbines arranged with several lilac twigs in a crystal vase. "Miss Helen said I could bring these to you if I was real careful."

She stood to take the vase and planted a kiss atop his head. "You are most kind, Kip, and I thank you very much. These are my two favorite flowers."

He beamed and his little chest puffed out.

She looked behind him for his siblings, but they were elsewhere, possibly Helen's doing to protect the vase.

"What about right here?" she asked, setting the lovely crystal on the bedside table. "That way I can smell the lie-lucks when I wake up."

Without a word, he wrapped his arms around her and held tight, then he dashed down the hall, through the kitchen, and out the screen door with a slap.

"You've turned his head."

The deep timbre of his father's voice surprised her as much as Kip's sudden departure. Hugh stood at the threshold. Ran his hand around the back of his neck and cleared his throat.

Oh no. He was either going to pray or say something she didn't want to hear. Would it be rude to feign fatigue and close the door in his face?

"Can we talk?"

She stared. Looked for silver at his temples. Checked his belt and boots. Yes, it was Hugh, not Cale.

"Talk?" She'd rather kiss him than talk to him.

Shocked by such an inappropriate thought, she blushed from her toes to her forehead. "Of course. Perhaps in the parlor."

"That's what I was thinking."

He moved away from the door, making room for her exit and offering a few blessed moments for her mortification to recede.

She escaped to the sewing rocker near the window.

He sat across the room on the settee, dwarfing the formal couch.

The last time they'd been alone together, they had been in each other's arms. Was he thinking the same thing?

He cleared his throat again. "I'm riding into town tomorrow to see the sheriff and Silas Graham about what happened to us."

Mary revived, intrigued by such a conversation.

"Alone."

She swallowed, uncertain she'd heard him correctly. "Alone?"

"Alone."

She folded her hands, commanding her hackles to lie down, and she forced her countenance into a pleasant but neutral pose.

Blue scrutiny held her.

She'd long suspected Hugh had the ability to see through her facade and right into her hidden motives and desires. If that were the case, she needn't say a thing.

He scooted to the edge of the settee, as if trying to get closer, leaning toward her, elbows on knees. "I can't *make* you do anything. But I'm asking you."

Ridiculously uncomfortable, she crossed her arms at her stomach. "Asking me what?"

She'd never seen a man's eyes beg, but if there was a word to describe the pleading in the sky-blue depths of Hugh Hutton, that was it.

"Please—stay here while I'm gone."

No command. Rather, an earnest plea. The river-deep tone nearly swept her away.

"All right."

"I know you want to— What did you say?"

Moved by his loss of composure, she gripped her elbows and squeezed. "I said all right."

"You will?"

He was impossibly charming with that little-boy look on his face.

"Yes, I will."

He came for her. No little boy. Slowly, deliberately he moved toward her, hands out in invitation.

She took them and stood.

He drew her into his arms, cradling her head against his chest, filling her with the rhythm of his heartbeat.

"Thank you, Mary."

The protective caress of his hands on her back quickened her breath, and his words sank down inside her, spreading to every fiber of her being.

She heard much more than what he'd said.

CHAPTER TWENTY-SIX

The next morning, Hugh found Silas Graham at his regular table at the café and joined him.

The ranger set his brew down. "From the looks of things, I'd say you've got news."

Hugh accepted a fresh mug from the waiter and took a long draw. "Ambushed yesterday, out at the seep."

"How many?"

"One rifle. Got away on horseback while I was workin' in around him on foot."

Graham pushed his finished plate to the side. "Anybody hurt?"

"Nope, other than a few rock chips hittin' the horses. But it was dang close."

"Who was with you?"

Hugh took a minute to unclench his mug and cool his anger. "Mary."

Graham commented on the ancestry of a man who'd shoot at a woman, then drowned it in his coffee.

"I'm gonna camp out there."

Graham raised one hand off the table, low. "Hold on. I don't need to be bringing you in for murder."

Hugh would gladly take the charge if it kept Mary from danger.

"I know you're fired up about this, but I want to catch the weasel. Could be he's got a few other dealin's under his belt I don't know about. That's usually the way it works."

"He rides a bar-shod horse. Right front."

"You know this how?"

"I saw fresh sign at the oil seep. He was there right before us. We might have flushed him out."

"You tell the sheriff yet?"

Hugh shook his head, slow-like, eyes nailed on the ranger. If he was as savvy as Hugh suspected, he'd hear what wasn't being said.

"Let the farm go to auction like we talked about. We'll run this fella to ground. If we're lucky, he'll sing like a dance-hall canary."

Hugh was bitin' bullets by the time he left the café. He turned Shorty east down Main Street away from the sheriff's office and toward the livery. If anybody would know, it'd be Frank Schultz.

The man was at his fire, sweat running off his bearded face despite the doors wide open and cool air drafting through.

"Mornin', Hutton." Frank wiped a beefy arm across his brow and pulled his tongs out of the fire pinching a horseshoe with one side bright orange. At the anvil, he hammered it a couple times, turned the shoe over and gave it a couple more "taps," then dunked it in a bucket of water until it stopped hissing.

"What can I do for you? I know it's not shoein' since you do your own work out at your place."

He offered a work-creased hand and genuine smile.

Hugh countered with the same. "But you're the expert around here, and I have a question for you."

Frank unbuckled his leather apron and took a seat on a tall stump set aside for that purpose. "Shoot."

Hugh bristled at the familiar remark. It'd never caught quite like that before. "Do you have any customers with a horse wearing a bar shoe on the right front?"

Frank scratched his sooty jaw. "Come to think of it, I do. A couple of 'em."

The blacksmith knew as much as a bartender in a town this size and was just as cautious about what he shared.

Hugh hedged his bet. "I saw a track out in our part of the country and didn't recognize it. We don't have any barred shoes."

Frank rubbed his jaw again, shot his gaze off toward the stalls. "Well, I doubt the librarian would be toolin' around out your way with her buggy mare, Daisy, but the way things are today, you can't be too sure."

He slapped his thigh at his own joke.

Hugh ground his teeth but pulled a smile while doing so.

Frank hefted himself off the stump and grabbed his apron. "But Oscar Thornbeck? Well, he's got himself one of those devil wagons now. Hardly see him anymore. I put a bar shoe on his old gelding a couple months ago. Had a sizable crack in its right front hoof."

"Thornbeck? I don't recall the name."

Fastening the stained leather around his girth, Frank lumbered over to his forge. "No, you probably wouldn't. He's new around here, 'bout a year now. Took over the fuel station at the east end of town."

~

Hugh had thought finding the Bible with Mary's locket in it was an act of God. But the closest he'd come to out-and-out, bona fide miracle material was riding west out of town on Shorty and not stopping until he hit the ranch road.

It took every grain o' grit he had to not go back and grab that yellow-livered, egg-suckin' dog at the fuel station by the throat and talk to him by hand.

A bar-shod horse *and* an automobile. A beating was too good for him.

It was God and Graham's rationale that kept Hugh in his saddle till he made the Rafter-H, where he went straight to the woodpile and laid in enough firewood to last through Christmas.

He was shirtless, wringing wet, and fit to be snubbed to a post when he heard a discreet cough behind him.

Mary stood a few yards away, wide-eyed and pretty as a filly in a flower bed.

He snatched up his shirt but it didn't go on easy, sweatin' like he was.

"Beg pardon." He turned away and fumbled with the buttons.

"Dinner's on."

She moved closer.

The smell of him would probably scare her off any minute.

"Would you like to eat outside under the pine tree? It's not too hot, and it might be a nice change."

A nice change was exactly what he needed, along with a good dunking. He'd have to simmer down before he could talk with her like a civilized human being. He forked his hair back. "Sure."

She hooked it for the house, barely keeping under a run, and he prayed he hadn't scared her off for good.

~

Mary stopped at the washstand by the back door and braced both hands on the sink. If she didn't know Hugh Hutton as well as she did, he would have frightened the stuffing right out of her. He looked completely capable of taking on that rogue grizzly they all talked about with his bare hands. What in the world had happened in town?

She pumped cold water into her hands and splashed her face and neck. Have mercy! The sight of his muscled chest and arms sent an aching clear through her. She dried herself with her apron and fingered loose hair into her bun. She didn't need Helen asking embarrassing questions because Mary had only embarrassing answers.

Hugh came around the corner of the house, and she fled

through the screen door.

Cale and Ella had taken their wagon and the babies home this morning, and the boys were at school, leaving Helen and Mary alone at the ranch house.

She had welcomed the quiet at first but became increasingly curious about what Hugh was doing in town. It had not been easy granting his request, but she knew it carried a weight of importance between them. Whatever had happened, it evidently had not gone well.

"Since it's just us chickens, I'm going to rest and read some. I'm sure you can handle dinner for yourself and Hugh."

Helen's attempt at casually making herself scarce endeared the woman even more to Mary.

She gave her a hug. "I'll bring you a tray if you like."

Helen waved her off as she left. "I've got a cup of soup here. I'll be fine."

Mary stood in the kitchen, keenly aware of its emptiness. It took her back to her kitchen at home and how lonely she had been as a girl after her mother died. Even more so when her father passed.

The Hutton family had filled a void in her life, and with the sudden realization rose gratitude. They had become her family in a sense, and the thought of leaving them broke her heart. If she didn't have enough money for the mortgage, she'd have no chance of winning the auction either. It all depended on the judge's decision.

Hugh's boots on the porch quickened her from her melancholy. She picked up the bundle she'd already prepared and with her other hand grabbed a pitcher of lemonade.

The screen squeaked open. "I'll carry that."

Hugh took the pitcher from her and stepped aside as she went out. The scent of lye soap, sweat, and wet hair met her as she passed—the close scent of a man. Something she'd known very little about until coming to the Rafter-H.

He followed her to a bench that was not really a bench but two stumps and a long board set against the big pine. It would serve her purpose, which was to seat them both with dinner in between.

"I hope you're hungry. Did you have breakfast in town?" Such blatant fishing should be beneath her, but she was starving for information.

He surprised her by rubbing both hands over his face and hair with a great sigh. What burden did he carry? Would he not share it with her?

She'd prepared two plates with roast, potatoes, and gravy, and managed to stack them between small jars without spilling anything. Fresh bread and jam would serve as dessert, but she'd made another bread pudding for supper later since Hugh had liked it so much the last time.

He held his hand out, completely surprising her. She took it and bowed her head.

"Father, thank you for helping me keep my head today. And thank you for this meal and for Mary." His grip tightened. "Amen."

Somewhere she'd misplaced her breath and it took a moment to find it.

"This smells great and looks even better." He dug in, and silence settled around them like goose down.

As much as she wanted to hear about his morning, she relished the easy comfort there in the yard—even more so than their picnic. He had been so tense then, so hurried. Yet it turned out that he'd had good reason. She shivered.

"You cold?" He drank in every inch of her from head to toe and back again, warming her with his unbridled observation.

Cold, indeed.

"No, just thinking." She didn't want to bring up bad memories, and being shot at was about as bad as one could get. Nor did she care to mention the way his perusal affected her.

"Can I ask you a question?"

"Certainly." But not about shivering.

His eyes gentled as he glanced at her, but he didn't hold her in a scrutinizing gaze, Instead he kept eating, setting her at ease.

"You came out here for more than a visit with your aunt and uncle. Can you tell me why?"

She'd expected the question for quite some time, but hair-raising events kept interfering with casual conversation. Except the answer wasn't very casual and cut near to the bone. She sliced her meat into tiny pieces as she considered how best to lay herself bare. "I was lonely and weary of grief. Mama died when I was fourteen, and Papa passed last winter. Lewis had my life planned out according to his wishes without any consideration of mine. I wanted to choose for myself."

She peeked up to find him watching her in that way that saw clear through to her soul. But she had nothing to hide any more. Perhaps she never had. Hiding wasn't what she wanted. Acceptance and love were what she'd come west for, certain she'd find both with her aunt and uncle.

"And you found more grief."

How could this cowboy from a different way of life so clearly pinpoint the ache?

She attempted to fill the jars with lemonade, but her hand shook at the weight of the pitcher and he took if from her. Gently, without haste or judgment, he filled a glass and gave it to her.

His kindness was what always undid her, but when he cleared his throat, the habit set her on edge. He'd already prayed, so he must have distressing news.

"I talked to Graham."

The relief was tangible. *Finally!* She schooled her features and spooned a bite of potatoes and gravy.

He chuckled. "You can't stand it, can you?"

Those blue crystals laughed at her, so she laid her fork down and pressed a napkin against her mouth. "No, I can't. Tell me before I burst with curiosity."

He downed his entire glass of lemonade in one swallow. Another heavy sigh escaped, and she began to worry.

The same urgency that had pleaded his cause yesterday evening appeared again and she felt her relief slipping away.

"Even if you have enough to make the overdue mortgage payments and clear the tax debt on your aunt and uncle's farm, Graham wants the auction to go on as planned."

The gravy soured in her stomach. "Why?"

"He wants to draw out the fella who set the fires and shot at us."

"You think it's one and the same?"

"Yes, I do. So does Graham. It was hard to accept his idea at first, but he's a lawman and suspects the scoundrel has other credits to his name. He wants to bait him into revealing that he's the arsonist and the shooter."

"Does he have any idea who it is?"

Hugh's gaze turned elsewhere and the muscle in his jaw flexed. "No. But I do."

CHAPTER TWENTY-SEVEN

Mary agreed to Hugh escorting her to town, where she opened an account at the Fremont National Bank and deposited the wired funds—every penny she had to her name—which could bring her current on the mortgage payments, she had learned, and cover the back taxes. But the ranger's plan to snare the arsonist appealed to her. Instead, she kept some of the money to repay Helen and for other necessities, though she doubted she'd return to town without Hugh riding shotgun.

He hadn't let her out of his sight all morning, and he'd worn his gun, for heaven's sake. He'd insisted she wear Helen's broad straw hat on the way, while they were at the bank, and on the return trip. He was tight as a bandbox the entire time, and they were in town only as long as it took to do her banking.

On the way home, he watched their "back trail," as he called it, as much as he watched the road ahead of them. She'd finally wheedled Oscar Thornbeck's name out of him and was thereafter appreciative of his watchful guard.

The next four weeks passed in peaceful routine, and Mary settled further into the family orchestration. The boys were away at school during the day, which resulted in a quieter, more subdued atmosphere at the ranch. But each evening they entertained the adults with their tales.

Milking one cow in the morning—which she insisted on doing—was much easier than operating a dairy. The milk was not as sweet or creamy, but what cream there was she churned and formed into blocks of butter.

The easy pace of ranch life settled her nerves, and as May warmed into a summery June, she thought less frequently of what awaited her in town on the tenth. Her quiet moments were consumed instead with what Kip had said.

Did Hugh really want her to marry him and be mother to his boys? He had made no overtures in that direction, but she nearly melted at the prospect until a completely rebellious idea sprouted out of nowhere.

It was the twentieth century. Women were more outspoken than ever. In fact, they'd been voting in Colorado for nearly twenty years.

Why couldn't she ask him?

She'd admitted to herself that she loved him, but she'd not shared that confession with anyone. Who would she tell? In her letters to Celia, she mentioned him, and no doubt her friend suspected more than Mary was telling. But holding the secret in a hidden corner of her heart had made it all the more precious.

Until Ella confronted her one morning.

"You love him, don't you."

Mary stopped kneading bread dough and regarded the young mother whose twins slept against her chest, one in each arm, as she sat at the table. "Excuse me?"

Ella had come for a visit, and a loving chuckle quietly escaped her lips. "You are smitten exactly as I was by Cale last year. It's as obvious as these babes in my arms."

So much for a treasured secret, but Mary welcomed the relief in having someone else know. "Is it that bad?"

"It's not bad—it's an answer to prayer for both myself and for Helen. She's prayed for years that God would bring Hugh a wife."

Mary's pulse pounded harder than she pounded the bread dough.

"If he hasn't asked you to marry him already, I dare say it

won't be long. He is besotted with you."

"What would you think if I asked him?"

Ella's startled reaction woke one of her babes whose sharp cry woke the other. She laughed aloud and stood, jostling the babies, and promising them they'd soon have an auntie.

~

On Monday morning, June 10, every scrap of peace Mary had cobbled together scattered like crumbs. Up well before dawn, dressed and ready, she trimmed the bedside lamp and sat with Aunt Bertie's Bible clutched hard against her chest.

"I know You hear my prayer, Lord. Please, help me today."

Turning to Psalm 37, she lifted the thin chain, fastened it around her neck, and read the now-familiar words: *Do not fret.*

The wicked would be stopped, the psalm said.

"Trust in the Lord and do good," she whispered as she fingered the locket, willing the words to sink down into her very core. "Dwell in the land, and feed on His faithfulness."

God had certainly been faithful, delivering her from violent death and ensconcing her in the generosity of the Hutton family. Continuing in silence, she read to verse 34, where she closed the Bible. The verse was imprinted on her soul, and she prayed it would apply to the ordeal she faced today at the auction.

Wait on the Lord, and keep His way, and He shall exalt you to inherit the land.

~

Breakfast was a quiet affair with the boys staying at Cale and Ella's. Oatmeal, eggs, and bacon were quickly consumed, dishes washed, and the three of them headed out the door. Hugh handed both Helen and Mary to the wagon bench.

Not a word was spoken among them until after Hugh drew up near the bank where the auction was to be held in a conference room.

"Lord, help us." Helen tugged her light shawl closer as she

stood on the sidewalk.

"He will," Hugh said, resting a hand on her shoulder.

He turned for Mary and lifted her down with both hands at her waist. She much preferred that method to the more customary assistance, but there was no room in her mind to consider his affection.

With one hand still at her waist, he cradled her face with the other, gently brushing his thumb against her cheek. "Don't worry, Mary Agan McCrae. God knows what's going on. And so does Ranger Graham."

A smile tipped his mouth on the right side.

She leaned into his hand, covering it with her own trembling fingers. Encouraged by his uncharacteristic words of faith, she offered a faint, "Yes, He is."

Others were already waiting in the conference room, standing in the back. Sheriff Payton, the bank president, the attorney from Beckman's office, and Ranger Graham. Mary and Helen took one of the few chairs arranged near the auctioneer's podium, and Hugh moved to the side of the room.

Mary regretted not standing herself, for others entered and she felt conspicuous turning around to see who they were.

It was just as well. She knew so few people in Cañon City anyway.

A side door opened. A man entered and went to the podium.

Mary's heart went to her throat.

~

Hugh exchanged a guarded look with Graham, hooked his thumbs in his pockets, and leaned against the wall. He didn't pretend very well, especially at patience and calm, but this morning both traits braced him. It probably had something to do with all the praying he'd been doin' out in the barn.

His biggest question was whether Thornbeck would show. The man could have someone else bid for him and they wouldn't even know it.

The auctioneer began by describing the property and stating the minimum bid that the bank would accept. Mary flinched when he banged his gavel on the block.

Hugh had never been a gambling man, but what he and Graham were up to certainly qualified for the vice. However, it wasn't for lucre, and greed played no part in it. He was obliged when Mary agreed to the ruse, and he didn't mind tellin' God so. The only other people who knew were the auctioneer and the bank president, who granted that Mary was the rightful heir and would receive the property. A copy of the will and her obvious likeness in the locket satisfied the judge as proof of her identity, but the bank president had nearly rubbed his hands together in glee at the prospect of catching a cheater during the auction.

Bidding was slow but climbed above the debt due on the farm. Mary's shoulders slumped.

The wall clock over the auctioneer said a quarter past the hour when Thornbeck showed.

Hugh crossed his arms and straightened, his signal for Graham.

In less time than it took the auctioneer to sing his song, Thornbeck called out, "I double the current bid."

Mary's head jerked around, and others turned to see who'd made such an outlandish offer.

Two ranchers seated farther back mumbled between themselves. One finally spoke up.

"Something on that burned-out farm we don't know about that you'd pay that much for?"

Other bidders made similar remarks.

Thornbeck's face grew red and he got twitchy.

"He wants the oil."

Hugh's jaw fell open at Mary's brash remark. What in the world was she doing?

The handful of bidders erupted with questions and accusations, and like a judge, the auctioneer banged his gavel repeatedly for order.

"I should have it!" Thornbeck stepped forward and pulled something from inside his shirt. Silence landed like a boulder. "I offered that old man twice what their land was worth, but he wouldn't sell." His voice spiked. "I found the seep, so I deserve it. And I'll do whatever it takes to get it!"

Calm as ice, Graham's words cut through the room. "Even set the place afire?"

Thornbeck raised a double-barrel derringer.

Hugh dove for the women and a gunshot roared. He spread his arms across Mary and Helen, forcing them down while chairs slid and toppled as people ran for the door.

The pinch of gun powder filled the room, and Graham's smoking Colt held steady on a slumped Thornbeck, cocked and ready for a second shot. He kicked the dropped derringer aside.

Thornbeck gripped his shoulder and swore as blood began to seep through his shirt sleeve.

Sheriff Payton and Graham escorted him out.

The auctioneer's gavel slammed on the block. "Sold. To Mary Agan McCrae."

CHAPTER TWENTY-EIGHT

"Twice now, Mr. Hutton, you have unseated me. But I thank you for it." Mary's knees were sore from where she'd slammed to the hardwood floor at the auction, and she covered them protectively with her hands while Hugh poured coffee for everyone at the table.

He sent her a sly glance as he set a plate in front of Helen, and his message tingled all the way through Mary and into her fingertips.

"I'm not so sure *thank you* is the phrase I'd use." Helen gently patted a bruised left cheek. "But I suppose hitting the floor was better than taking a bullet."

"A bullet?" Kip's eyes rounded.

"That's right," Mary said. "Your father is a hero."

All three boys turned toward Hugh, whose face turned a lovely beet red.

"Can't have people shootin' at the women folk now, can I?"

"We wanna hear what happened, Pa." Jay sat taller as the spokesman for the next generation of Huttons.

"Later. Eat your dinner."

Somewhat deflated, the boys did as their father asked, but kept one eye on him as he served a late meal of beans and cornbread around the table before taking his place at the head.

He held his hands out, one to Mary and the other to Ty, and only twice did emotion interrupt his brief prayer of thanks.

Mary's hand warmed within his strong and calloused grip,

and she offered her own silent gratitude.

Being waited on didn't set well with Helen, and after everyone took their plate to the sink, she drove them all outside with threats of chicken-picking and sock-mending for the boys.

On the porch, Hugh leaned in close to Mary's ear, and his whisper tickled the hair at her neck. "You up for an afternoon ride? I've got something I want to show you."

How could she say no? "Give me a minute to change."

~

Hugh took a trail Mary hadn't ridden that led east and north of the ranch toward a high ochre-colored ledge he called rimrock. It was fronted by a small meadow edged with shimmering cottonwood trees.

Why had she not seen this place before?

Tranquility reigned, and she breathed deeply of the pristine air, relaxing as they rode toward the rimrock. It was farther away than she had first thought, but hurry was not a matter to concern her. Upon paying off her aunt and uncle's debts before leaving the bank, she had let go of the tension that had been building since her arrival in Colorado. Though she had no home of her own, surveyors had assured her that the seep on her property would build more houses, barns, and outbuildings than she could use in a lifetime.

Her biggest issue now was where to wait out the building. She could well afford a room at the Denton Hotel in town, but was reluctant to leave the Rafter-H. She loved everything about it, one thing in particular above all the others.

As they neared the cottonwood trees, birdsong interrupted her musing. Sheltered clusters of lavender columbines bobbed beneath the cottonwoods, and off to her right, a rock outcropping raised its smooth gray head.

Hugh reined in. He'd worn his gun, and his rifle rested in the saddle boot. Surely he didn't expect more trouble.

When he stepped down and dropped Shorty's reins, Mary

joined him.

The sun shone behind them in its declining journey, angling their shadows across the meadow as they walked. Hugh watched the ground ahead, the rimrock above them, and the rock outcropping, eyes darting from one to the other. On edge, as if he expected something.

Her hands fisted on her riding skirt. Not again.

When he stopped, a heavy sigh broke from him. He laid his right hand on the butt of his gun and tipped his hat up with the other. "This is it."

She looked around them more closely. "This is what?"

"This is the place where my father saved my mother's life."

Stunned, Mary's feet rooted to the ground. Was there a seep nearby? Had someone taken shots at them? "What happened?"

Hugh tugged his hat back to its normal position and turned his attention to the gray boulders. "Evening was closing in, and my mother was out here digging up columbines to transplant by the house."

He gave Mary a smoky look and sent her pulse jumping. "The Hutton women have always had a thing about columbines."

She swallowed hard. Was he including *her* in that Hutton-women remark?

"Pa said he knew something was wrong, and he found her here not far from those rocks. When he rode up, he saw a cougar's tail whip out from the other side, but he couldn't see the cat. From the saddle, he drew his rifle and aimed between Ma and the rock."

Mary sucked in a breath, waiting for the inevitable. After a full ten seconds of anticipation, she nearly yelled, "Well, don't stop now!"

Clearly enjoying the moment, Hugh feigned dismay. "Can't you figure what happened since I'm here?"

She squeezed his upper arm, unable to wrap her fingers

completely around it. "Don't you dare tease me. Tell me what happened."

He encircled her waist and drew her into him, then brushed his lips across hers.

Already weak in the knees, she cradled his neck and held on. Maybe the rest of the story wasn't as important as she'd thought.

He tucked her head beneath his chin and protectively ran his hands up and down her back. "Ma had realized the cat was there but had frozen. She turned toward the animal. It leaped. Pa pulled the trigger."

Mary reflexively squeezed Hugh's waist as she envisioned the frightful scene.

"It landed on her, clawing the backs of her hands where she'd covered her face when it sprang. Pa told me later that it sealed his future. He'd loved her for a long time, but that was when he knew he had to make her his wife. He couldn't let her go."

Blood pounded in Mary's head as if the cougar were crouching in the rocks even now.

Hugh set her back but held one hand at her waist and cupped her face with the other. His breath was warm on her lips, with the slightest hint of beans and coffee. "I can't let *you* go."

Passion apparently ran deep in the Hutton men. Mary pressed her hands against his chest, thrumming with the beat of his heart and swimming in the blue depths that had captured her so completely. "Then marry me."

~

Shocked by her own words, Mary's mouth formed a perfect O.

Hugh seized the chance and kissed her the way he'd wanted to for a long time. At her response, he knew he'd better get them home to the ranch house before it was too late.

With his hat brim covering her, he touched his forehead to hers. "Are you proposing to me, Mary Agan McCrae?"

He felt the heat shoot through her, and he kissed her again, unwilling to miss the opportunity.

She pushed against him, blushing like a summer sunrise, but he held on. He'd meant it when he said he wasn't letting her go.

She pushed harder. "If you'll let me catch my breath, I'll answer your question."

He relaxed his hold but kept his hands at her waist.

She wouldn't look at him and set her gaze on everything around them, including the ground beneath her feet.

He squeezed until she met his eyes. "Well?"

"Yes." Her whisper lit a fire in his veins.

He swept her up and carried her to Barlow.

"Hugh Hutton, I can walk perfectly well by myself. You keep picking me up."

He set her down beside the horse and leaned in close, brushing his mouth against her neck. "The next time I carry you like this, it will be over the threshold on our wedding night."

She shivered.

The peace of their leisurely return home quickly dissipated when they rode into the yard to find a strange horse at the hitch rail. Hugh's hackles rose.

He looped their horses' reins on the top corral pole, then took Mary's hand. "Let's go see who's here."

At the back door, a familiar voice rose with a touch of drama as it recounted the auction. Hugh held the door for Mary, then followed her in. "Don't be fillin' my boys with those tall tales, Graham."

The ranger stood with a smile and offered his hand. "The truth, Hutton. The whole truth, and nothing but the truth."

Helen set two more cups of coffee on the table. "You boys go take care of Miss Mary's and your dad's horse."

Graham must have spun enough yarns to trail them out for a week, for they bounded through the door like a bunch of young bucks with nary a complaint.

Graham acknowledged Mary. "Miss McCrae. You're looking

well."

She blushed again and shot Hugh a warning glare that promised a retraction of her proposal if he mentioned it at all. He swallowed a laugh along with what he wanted to say and hung his hat on the wall.

"Mr. Graham says his father may have known one of your relations." Helen set a plate of gingersnaps in the center of the table and took her place at the end.

"Pop was a ranger too," Graham offered. "Worked with Haskell Jacobs up in Denver before Jacobs retired down here in Cañon City. He said Haskell married a gal from around here— Martha Stanton. You heard of her?"

Hugh thumbed through family history. It'd been a while since he'd thought of his pa's sister, Martha Hutton Stanton. "That's right. Martha had been widowed and later married a ranger by the name of Jacobs."

"Did she have a brother?"

"That she did. Whit Hutton, my pa." Hugh held the ranger's regard, amazed at the tight circle sometimes found in unexpected connections.

"Well, I'll be." Helen shook her head and sipped her coffee.

"You're almost family," Mary said.

Hugh took her hand and also his first risk with his bride-to-be. But if he knew her like he thought he did, she'd agree to what he was about to tell the ranger.

"Maybe you can stay for the wedding."

Helen choked on her coffee and grabbed her apron.

Graham grinned.

And Mary turned her hand over and linked her fingers with Hugh's.

"She's gonna do it!"

Every head turned for the screen door, where Kip and his brothers stood with their faces pressed against it.

"She's gonna marry us!"

CHAPTER TWENTY-NINE

Ella's skill with the sewing machine far surpassed Helen's boasting and, combined with her handwork, created the most beautiful wedding dress Mary could have imagined.

The short-sleeved, tiered-lace gown with a creamy satin cummerbund flowed over Mary's figure and gently brushed the tops of satin shoes Ella insisted she borrow. With no reason to wait and every reason in the world to continue their life together, Mary and Hugh exchanged their vows at the church in town where his family had long attended. Mary knew few of the many people who came to the wedding, but she knew those who mattered most, and was delighted that the three Hutton boys stood at their father's side during the ceremony.

With a pleased and proud expression—as if the entire affair had been his doing—Pastor Bennett pronounced the benediction.

"May the God of hope fill you both with all joy and peace in believing—in Him and in each other—that you may abound in hope through the power of the Holy Ghost. Amen."

At the reception following, Mary met Clara, the famed cook from the Denton Hotel, who made an exquisite wedding cake and served the most delicious peach punch. By late afternoon, most of the guests had left, and Mary and Hugh enjoyed an early supper in the Denton dining room, courtesy of Clara and the hotel.

Mary ate little, for her stomach was a jumble of nerves that twinged every time Hugh gave her a smoky look across their private table. But when he swept her off her feet at the door of their third-floor suite, she felt as smooth and silky as her elegant gown, cradled in his strong arms and loving gaze. He deftly unlocked the door, toed it open, and carried her across the threshold as he'd promised, pushing the door closed behind them with his boot.

~

In the last two weeks, Hugh had found himself thanking God more than he had in the last two decades. Ranching still wasn't easy. Things still broke, cattle still busted through fences, coyotes and cougars still pulled down calves. But he wasn't alone. Mary somehow made a difference in the way he thought about things. In the way he thought about God.

That's why he let her come along with him and Cale when they took the wagon to her farm to fill in the hole where the barn had been.

As if he could keep her from going.

He chuckled to himself as he flicked Barlow on. Mary rode Shorty, pacing along with them about fifty yards off the wagon road. Danged horse nearly pranced with her, as if he knew she was special cargo and not some simple-minded cowboy.

When they drove into what had been the barnyard, Hugh noticed Mary's shoulders sag. It still pained her to remember what had been lost, and he couldn't blame her. He wished he could wipe away the memories. But that sort of wish was futile, he'd learned.

She reined in next to the wagon, two wreathes of flowers looped around her arms. She'd worn one on her veil at the wedding, and Ella had worn the other. Mary had insisted on keeping them, replacing the dried flowers yesterday with Indian paint brush, sunflowers, and sprigs of pine and cedar.

"I'll be in the orchard while you two are working. I doubt

I'd be much help to you anyway."

Hugh jumped down and stepped up to his horse, where she leaned over to encourage him with a long, slow kiss. He eased back and reset his hat, motivated to make short work of the dirt-digging process.

Cale had already ground tied Doc and was waiting in the wagon with a big grin.

"Shut up," Hugh said as he climbed to the seat.

They'd found a pile of dirt north of the orchard that was likely from the pit Thornbeck had finally confessed to digging. Hugh wanted the fueler to fill the hole himself, but the law had other plans for him that lasted a whole lot longer than the day it would take to transfer the dirt.

Hugh and Cale shoveled most of the pile into the wagon bed, then drove to the rectangular patch near the yard that had been the Dodsons' barn. They'd soon be running cow-calf pairs this way, and they didn't need 'em falling in the hole.

Hugh backed up to the pit and Cale wedged a block of wood behind a wheel as Hugh climbed into the bed and grabbed a shovel.

"So this is the infamous pit," Cale said.

Hugh didn't answer but stood looking at the bottom of the hole where the sun had glinted off something. "Hold on."

He jumped down and looked again from a different angle, and sure enough, something caught light. "Grab the rope and give me a hand. There's something down there besides broken boards."

Cale tied off to the wagon axle. Hugh fed out about fifteen feet and looped it around himself, then shimmied down the dirt wall.

He could see a heck of a lot better than three months ago when he'd dropped down to a woman he feared was dead. His insides cinched tighter than the rope around him.

With a different perspective, he moved a few broken boards

aside, and felt along the bottom with his hands. *There. And there.* Picking them up, he blew dirt off the pair and rubbed them on his sleeve until they shone.

~

Doc was perfectly happy to graze beneath the apple trees as Mary took the wreaths to her aunt and uncle's markers and knelt in the grass before them.

"You brought me here, and I will be forever grateful. For because of your love for me, I found the love of my life."

She choked on the last word and leaned back on her heels, waiting for her throat to let go of her heart.

"Thank you for giving me your farm and all the years of hard work you put into it." She placed one wreath atop her uncle's cross. "Cows and their calves will roam here now—not our beloved Ayrshires, but *beeves,* as Hugh calls them."

She draped the second wreath over the cross bearing her aunt's name, adjusting the colorful circle that reflected the blooming landscape around her. "You would like him—no, you would love him. He did everything he could to keep this land in our family, including finding the locket I gave you so long ago."

Fighting tears was a hopeless endeavor, and Mary let them fall unhindered as she fingered the gold locket at her throat.

Boot steps brushed the grass behind her. Familiar steps that she had no need to verify.

Hugh knelt beside her and pulled her into him, kissing the top of her head, then settling back. In the quiet of the orchard, he squeezed her shoulder until she looked up at him. "I have something for you."

She wiped her eyes. "The last time you said that to me, it changed my life."

His throaty laugh stirred her with gratitude that God had allowed her to "inherit the land" and love this man to whom she had given every ounce of her being. But what could he give her that she didn't already have?

He reached inside his vest, and without taking his eyes from hers, slid his hand down her arm, placed something in her hand, and closed her fingers over it.

And immediately, she knew. At the familiar weight and shape, she knew he'd found what she thought she'd lost forever. "Where were they? I've walked that section of open land more times than I care to admit."

"They were in the pit. They must have come loose when you fell."

She lifted the pair of tortoise-shell combs, each edged with ornate silver scroll work, and pressed them against her breast.

"I love you, Hugh Hutton. Not only because of these, but because of you and who you are. You have given me more than I ever dreamed one person could give to another. Without limits, you continue to give yourself."

CHAPTER THIRTY

Mary sat in the sewing rocker with a cup of coffee and the loveliest card and gift from Celia. Her friend gushed with apologies for not being able to accept her invitation to the wedding and insisted she knew right from the start that the "irritating cowboy" at the ranch would work his way into Mary's affections.

Celia always had been wise when it came to love. Which was also why she hadn't made the trip west, for she was six months pregnant with baby number four.

Mary couldn't imagine where she would wear Celia's gift of a beaded, dress-collar shawl, but she knew exactly where to hang the framed color print of a prize-winning, red-and-white Aryshire cow.

Lewis had also written, and his letter arrived the same day as Celia's. Mary had invited him too, and he had also declined, citing duties at the dairy and his inability to leave.

Sadly, she was not surprised, and wondered if she would ever see her brother again. But she was completely taken aback by his closing paragraph stating what day and time she could expect her breeding stock to arrive by rail car at the Denver and Rio Grande railway station in Cañon City.

It was his wedding gift to her, courtesy of a conversation with Celia's husband, Peter.

Her relationship with Lewis was far from perfect, but he had taken a giant step forward, and Mary vowed to pray that he would soon find a companion of his own.

The only drawback to his gift was that it was arriving in six days.

Hammering broke into her thoughts—hammering that she should be entirely accustomed to by now, for Hugh was adding a bathing room to the back of the house, complete with its own hand pump and pot-bellied stove for heating water. Access was through the outside door in his father's former den, or Cale's former bedroom as Mary had known it.

After the completely extravagant purchase of a new double bed, the room was now hers and Hugh's together.

How she loved that man.

~

The following week, Helen and the boys saw Mary and Hugh off to Cañon City where he had rented a team of draft horses and a high-sided wagon waiting at the livery to haul Mary's young bull and heifers home. She would follow with the ranch wagon.

The August heat had Mary perspiring like she'd not expected in the Rocky Mountains, but the dry climate was blessedly that—dry. No sweltering humidity like Pennsylvania.

When the train whistle blew its approach, anticipation rippled through everyone waiting on the depot platform.

"What if they're not on the train?" Mary linked her arm through Hugh's, grateful to not be there by herself.

His chuckle vibrated through his chest and into her arm. "Then they'll be on the next train. Don't fret so."

Oh, would she ever let go of that dreadful habit?

Another whistle blast, and the engine came into view, crawling ever closer and slowing as it passed, passenger cars followed by freight cars.

"This way." Hugh captured her hand in his and headed toward the end of the long line of cars. "The stock cars will be down here."

At the screech of steel on steel, Mary flexed her hands and

arms as the train came to a stop. Freight crewmen slid cargo doors wide, and within minutes, horses and cattle were rushing down loading chutes and into a catacomb of corrals.

How her heifers and bull must have grown. Would she even recognize them? Were they milling in among other breeds of cattle prodded along by cowboys and pushing into open areas?

"There, Mary. Is that your stock?"

Hugh's question turned her toward the railcar as a handsome, white-on-red yearling bull walked sedately down the loading ramp, followed by five of the most beautiful Aryshire heifers Mary had the privilege of calling hers.

"Yes! Oh, Hugh—it's them!" She squeezed his arm and nearly jumped inside out. "Look at them. Aren't they the most beautiful dairy animals you've ever seen?"

He looped his arm around her waist and gave her a squeeze. "Let's sign the paperwork and get them loaded."

Mary could hardly think straight, grateful that Hugh was a stockman and knew what to do at a train station when it came to cattle. She had never transported anything other than a bucket calf to the neighboring dairy back home, and she'd done that on foot.

He soon returned, and they were off to the livery for the wagons.

"Hugh!"

He stopped dead in his tracks and looked at Mary, then around at the dispersing passengers and stockmen.

Mary looked too, but for what she had no idea. However, someone had called him. A female someone familiar enough with him to use his given name.

A woman in fancy garb caught sight of Hugh, dropped her leather bag, and came running for him. She flung herself into his arms in a most unladylike fashion, and he swung her around, laughing as if he was welcoming his long-lost love.

Mary's heart plummeted. They'd been married six weeks. What

things from his past had her groom not bothered to mention?

The woman's honey-colored hair hung in a long braid over her shoulder, and she sported fancy inlaid cowboy boots and a wide-brimmed hat with a green satin hat band.

And then without so much as a please and thank you, she kissed Hugh soundly on the cheek, and gave him another hug before stepping back. One hand on her hip, she pushed her hat up and gave him the once over. Two or three of them.

"You look good, Hugh. What happened?"

He laughed full and heartily. "You always were free with the underhanded compliments."

Mary had never met anyone quite like this woman and felt green around the gills at her familiarity with Hugh.

He reached for Mary and drew her into his side as was his habit, one she adored, but in front of a complete stranger and in public as well, Mary felt garish and out of place.

"I want you to meet someone," he said as he gave Mary a possessive squeeze that helped ease the shock of his public affection toward another woman. "Grace, this is my wife, Mary."

Grace—the name rang a dim and distant bell.

The young woman beamed and reached for Mary's hand with both of hers. "I'm so happy to meet you."

"Mary." His arm slipped to her waist and he pulled her closer. "This is my Wild-West-Show, fancy-roping, trick-shot, rough-riding sister—Grace."

~~~

Thank you for reading Hugh and Mary's story, *Hope is Built,* Book 5 of the Cañon City Chronicles series. I trust you enjoyed it and will check out the entire series chronicling the lives of the Hutton family. You can find Books 1–3 under one cover, The Cañon City Chronicles, on my website or on my Amazon author page. Book 4, *A Change of Scenery,* is the story of Hugh's twin brother, Cale, and his relationship with a lovely silent-movie seamstress,

Ella Canaday.

Follow the Hutton family through the series, which will be completed with Book 6, *Covering Grace.*

If you enjoyed this series, be sure to read my four-book Front Range Brides series and other stories, all listed on my website and Amazon author page.

As always, a brief review on book-selling sites and social media is the best thing you can give an author.

Thank you for reading inspirational Western romance.

~

Receive a free historical novella when you sign up for my Quarterly Author Update: https://bit.ly/3b4eavB

ACKNOWLEDGMENTS

Many thanks and great appreciation go out to Suzie Veatch of the Fremont County, Colorado, Assessor's Office; Lynne Schricker, life-long cowgirl and horse trainer extraordinaire; Carri Miller of Equine Digit Support System in Penrose, Colorado; Grant and Debbie Chess of Cañon City, Colorado; cover critiquers Amanda Beck and Jill Maple; amazing editor, Christy Distler of Avodah Editorial Services, and to the God of hope and my King, Jesus Christ, who fills me with all joy and peace in believing.

~

ABOUT THE AUTHOR

Bestselling author and winner of the **Will Rogers Gold Medallion** for Inspirational Western Fiction, Davalynn Spencer can't stop #lovingthecowboy. When she's not writing, teaching writer workshops, or playing on her church worship team, she's wrangling mouse detectors Annie and Oakley. Connect with her via her website at www.davalynnspencer.com.

~

Books by Davalynn Spencer

Historical

THE CAÑON CITY CHRONICLES SERIES

Loving the Horseman - Book 1
Straight to My Heart - Book 2
Romancing the Widow - Book 3
A Change of Scenery – Book 4
The Cañon City Chronicles – Collection books 1-3

THE FRONT RANGE BRIDES SERIES

Mail-Order Misfire - Series Prequel
An Improper Proposal - Book 1
An Unexpected Redemption - Book 2
An Impossible Price – Book 3

Novellas

Snow Angel
Just in Time for Christmas
A High-Country Christmas – two-novella collection
The Snowbound Bride
The Wrangler's Woman

Contemporary

The Miracle Tree

Nonfiction

Always Before Me – 90 Story-Devotions for Women

~

Sign up for my Quarterly Author Update
and receive a free historical novella!
https://bit.ly/3b4eavB

~

May all that you read be uplifting.

Made in the USA
Middletown, DE
01 November 2022